Realm of Mindweavers

Realm of Mindweavers

Marianne Ratcliffe

Matador
9 Priory Business Park,
Wistow Road, Kibworth Beauchamp,
Leicestershire. LE8 0RX
Tel: (+44) 116 279 2299
Fax: (+44) 116 279 2277
Email: books@troubador.co.uk
Web: www.troubador.co.uk/matador

ISBN 9781783061150

British Library Cataloguing in Publication Data.
A catalogue record for this book is available from the British Library.

Typeset in 11pt Bembo by Troubador Publishing Ltd, Leicester, UK
Printed and bound in the UK by TJ International, Padstow, Cornwall

Matador is an imprint of Troubador Publishing Ltd

This book is for Gubs, with love.

Chapter One

I t was the morning of her thirteenth birthday, but Zastra was not celebrating. This was the day she would be tested, the day she would be given the chance to prove to her doubting father that she was worthy to be his daughter.

A rap at the door made her jump.

'Are you ready, Zastra?' The voice, muffled by the heavy oak door, belonged to Jannal, chief of the royal household. It was time.

Zastra took a deep breath, surprised by the sudden pounding of her heart. She half wished she had accepted her mother's offer to accompany her, but it was too late to change her mind now. She steadied herself before opening the door with what she hoped was an appearance of composure. Jannal was waiting and he bobbed his head of tight grey curls.

'There you are. Come. The council of mindweavers does not like to be kept waiting.'

Zastra followed Jannal to the council chamber. A pair of huge blackwood doors opened noiselessly as they approached. Jannal nudged her, not unkindly, into the room. She turned her head to see the doors close heavily behind her.

'Come forward, child,' a sharp voice commanded. Zastra's head snapped round. A tall woman with a mass of pale ginger hair scraped back in a tight knot stared down at her. Zastra recognised her as Teona, the highmaster of mindweavers. The council room was windowless, a circle of jula-oil lamps directly above Zastra's head providing the only light. The other members of the council shuffled forwards from the shadows, enclosing Zastra in an unbroken circle. They were all wrapped in full length cloaks of red silk, their faces covered in featureless golden masks that reflected the flickering orange glow of the lamps. Teona's voice snapped out again, cold and unfriendly.

'Do you know why you are here?'

'To take the test,' whispered Zastra, fists clenched as she tried to hide her fear. Whatever happened, she must not fail.

'Very well,' said the highmaster, lowering her golden mask into position. 'We will begin.'

Zastra felt an invisible weight pressing down on her and thoughts infiltrated her mind, probing like icicle fingers.

'No – get away!' she cried.

'She… resists…' creaked Teona. 'Desist girl. Let us in.'

The pressure increased and images flashed in her head. First a raging fire and then a monstrous beast, blood dripping from pink-tinged fangs. Images and sensations were torn from her; the faces of her school friends, the feel of her sister's soft little hand, surprisingly strong as it clasped her finger.

'Get out!' Zastra screamed, and the horrible images faded, although the cold fingers continued to dig into her memories and thoughts. As darkness descended, she heard a deep voice, muffled as if wrapped in cotton.

'Enough. Let the child be. We have our answer.'

When Zastra came back into consciousness, her mother was holding her.

'Peace, dear one. You are safe now, my love.'

'Oh, Mother, it was horrible. It was, as if… they opened me…'

'I know, my love. I'm sorry I could not protect you.'

The noise of a door opening roused Zastra from the comforting depths of the embrace. It was her father, Leodra, Grand Marl of Golmeira.

'Well?' asked Zastra's mother, bitterly.

'Nothing – useless,' he said. 'No power is in her.' He looked at Zastra, unable to hide his annoyance and disappointment.

'Leodra!' Her mother's tone censured and pleaded at the same time. 'Do not blame our daughter for what she cannot help.' Zastra felt her mother's arms tighten around her.

'This is no time for useless sentiment, Anara. You know our danger. We are weak and the power you have is, well, it won't help us.' Leodra paced up and down, scowling. 'The twins are so young, it will be years before they can be tested and even then it could be too late. We needed Zastra to be a strong mindweaver.'

'We will find other ways.'

'There are no other ways,' he said, turning away and departing with a violent slam of the door.

'I'm sorry,' sobbed Zastra. 'I tried, but it was so hard.'

'Hush, dear one. Never apologise for who you are. You are my strong, precious, beautiful Zastra. You have your own strengths and gifts, and one day your father will see them.'

A soft knock at the door was followed by the entry of a tall man, still wearing the red silk ceremonial robes of the mindweavers. No longer wearing a mask, he was grey with age, yet alert and sprightly. His ugly face was weathered and a dark brown birthmark rose from his left temple and cheek like a low lying island.

'Lady Anara, please excuse my intrusion, but I was concerned about Zastra.'

'Thank you, Dobery. I know the test is important, but I do not see why you had to push so hard. Zastra is still only a child.'

'I am not,' protested Zastra, raising her head

'I fear our highmaster was somewhat overzealous. This darkness that hangs over our lands is no excuse. My dear Zastra, how are you?'

'No one told me it would hurt so much. I saw such horrible things.'

'Yet you did remarkably well. You have great resistance to the power.'

'What do you mean?' asked Anara. 'Leodra said she was without mindweaving abilities.'

'That, alas, is true. However, she was able to resist the entire council, if only for a moment. I fear that angered Teona and some of the others, so they pushed harder than they should have. I am ashamed of their thoughtlessness, my Lady.'

Dobery lowered himself on to the rug next to Zastra and laid a gentle hand on her shoulder.

'Do not despair,' he said, 'the power of mindweaving is rare. Few are chosen, and not always the most deserving. Each of us must make our own way in the world. Yours is yet to reveal itself, that is all.'

'Dobery is right, my dear,' said Anara. 'You must not be downhearted.' But Zastra could not be consoled.

Chapter Two

Zastra plucked at her soldier's blouse. The vivid red shirt was covered in dark patches of sweat. It was the height of summer and even though the sun was low in the sky, the humidity hung in the air like a heavy dew. It had been two days since the test and Zastra at last decided to act on an idea that had been forming in her mind ever since her experience with Teona and the mindweavers. It would mean returning to the southeast tower, where the council chamber was located, but that couldn't be helped.

Golmer Castle was made up of five wings, each with three levels of rooms and apartments, joined together by square towers. Within this huge structure of speckled grey stone was a large courtyard, adjacent to a covered area that enclosed the great hall. The quickest way from the royal tower, where Zastra lived, to her destination was along the inner balconies of the southern wings, past the great hall, and along the south side of the courtyard. However, these open balconies were visible from many of the interior windows of the castle and Zastra did not wish to be seen. Besides, it would be much more fun to sneak down the narrow passages that lay between the protective outer wall of the castle and the inner apartments. This dark space, continually patrolled by Leodra's soldiers, was known as the liden. It was strictly out of bounds, which only made it more attractive to Zastra and her friends, who often dared each other to try to sneak from one tower to the next without being caught. After a quick glance to check the first passage was empty, Zastra dashed across the liden, ducking under staircases and scrambling between floors to avoid more than one drowsy guard. She was highly pleased with herself when she arrived at the southeast tower, undetected, out of breath and with several cobwebs for company.

Dobery and some of the other masters had quarters on the second floor and Zastra found the old mindweaver in his chambers reading a small leather-bound book, which he set aside as she entered.

'Welcome, Zastra,' he said, removing his glasses with a warm smile. 'It is not often we have visitors.'

'I can see that,' she said, glancing around the room. Untidy piles of books and papers covered the furniture and most of the floor. The hearth rug was shabby and grey with dirt, almost as if it had aged in sympathy with its owner. Zastra, who had personal servants to clean up after her, was not used to such messiness. She rather liked the irregularity and clutter of the snug room.

'I'd like to ask you something, Dobery,' she said.

'Of course, my dear. Please, take a seat.' He cleared a chair of books, frowning as he looked around for an empty space.

'Don't worry,' she said, grabbing a cushion and placing herself firmly on the floor. 'I'll be Grand Marl before you find anywhere to put those.'

'It's a carefully ordered system,' he said, defensively. 'This pile, for instance, contains all my books on the military history of Golmeira. See here – *Concealed armies – a history of ambushes*. Not the most lighthearted book in my collection, I suppose, but at least I know where it is.'

'I reckon you could hide an army in here, if you wanted to,' said Zastra, grinning.

Dobery eased himself back into his worn leather chair. 'What is it you wanted to know, Zastra? A list of all the Grand Marls of Golmeira? Or perhaps a detailed review of the taxation system?'

'Oh, no!' she cried, her smile vanishing at the horrifying possibility of an extra history lesson. 'I just… I just wondered if there was any chance that the test was wrong?' She peered up towards him as her finger traced a nervous line on the dusty floor. 'Is there any chance I could be a mindweaver after all?'

'I'm afraid not, Zastra. The test was very thorough.'

'Oh well,' she said, feigning nonchalance. 'I guessed you would say that but I thought I'd make sure.'

'Try not to dwell on it too much. Very few have the power, and even fewer are made happy by it.'

'What is mindweaving, anyway? You and the others don't look different to anyone else to me.'

Dobery hesitated.

'I'm not sure – we are not supposed to discuss our abilities with non-mindweavers.'

'Oh,' said Zastra, unable to hide her disappointment. Dobery rubbed his knees, and then leaned forward and spoke in a low voice.

'Mindweaving is not fully understood by anyone. Where the ability comes from, and why only some have it, is a mystery. Although often it does seem to run in families, which is why your father had hopes for you.'

'Why?' whispered Zastra. 'Is he a mindweaver?'

'No, which is one reason why he was so upset when you failed the test. His father and mother were both very strong mindweavers and they say his brother has great power. I'm sure that he was hoping you would be similarly endowed.'

'But why is it so important?'

'Mindweavers have a special ability to manipulate an unseen essence, the same essence we use to think and move. With training, they can control another person's thoughts, or their ability to move.'

Zastra's eyes widened. 'When I was in the test, I saw a fire and a… a creature. I thought it was real.' She shuddered at the memory.

'We can make people believe they see things that don't exist. One of the most powerful highmasters in our history won a battle for Golmeira by fooling an entire invading army into believing that they were about to be swamped by a giant wave. They fled, the Grand Marl's army routing them completely.'

Zastra was fascinated. 'I felt something too, inside my head.'

'Ah, now *that* was interesting, Zastra. Sometimes, people without abilities can still detect when someone invades their mind. With the right training, they can resist many of the manifestations of the power. I think you are such a person, Zastra, which could be very important, whatever your father might say.'

'Can you read minds?' As she asked this, a thought struck her. 'Oh! Can you tell what I'm thinking right now?'

He sat back in his chair and chuckled. 'Well, I do have some abilities in that area if I chose to use them, but we only use mindweaving under great need. I don't see any necessity to poke around in your head right now, thank you very much. I doubt I'll learn much of interest.'

'Oh,' said Zastra, somewhat disappointed that her thoughts were not of the first importance. 'What if I had done something naughty?'

'Like coming here via the liden?'

'You're peeking!'

'Hmm – I might be, of course. Or perhaps I have observed the tangle of cobwebs and dust in your hair. Apart from the dungeons, only the liden is that dirty. You don't always need mindweaving to see things. Sometimes common sense and observation are just as good.'

Zastra scraped her fingers through her hair and attempted to flick away the sticky cobweb, wrinkling her nose in disgust.

'I don't really see what all the excitement is about,' she said, 'surely anyone can work out if they are being made to see things?'

'Not everyone has your ability to resist, Zastra. Remember, you fainted, which left you vulnerable. Many people have been sent mad by the visions a mindweaver can unleash.'

'Heldrid says mindweavers can fly and turn into fire. Is that true at least?'

Amusement flickered across Dobery's unattractive face.

'Heldrid is a stupid boy, and you shouldn't listen to his nonsense. No one can turn into fire, although I might use mindweaving to convince you that I had. I have never seen anyone fly, although – well, never mind. I've said far too much already.'

'But what about Mother? What power does she have, and why does Father say it isn't any use?'

'Your mother has the gift of sensing the fears and emotions of others. However, it is not really a power to be used in battle. Your father is much concerned with enemies of state.'

'What enemies?'

'I think we've had enough questions for one night, Zastra. It is late now. Perhaps you can ask your father himself, tomorrow?'

'He won't like me to bother him,' muttered Zastra, but not wishing to outstay her welcome she returned to her quarters. As she skipped along the south balcony, a troop of soldiers in their red and black uniforms marched into the courtyard below. How could her father be worried when he had so many men and women at his command?

Chapter Three

The twin moons of Horval and Kalin were waning and only a faint cast of silver light filtered down to the group of shadowy figures gathered in the Forest of Waldaria.

'Are you certain you were not followed?' asked a grey-clad woman, her face masked in shadow.

The other members of the group grunted their assent, but the woman probed their minds to make certain.

'Why have you called us here?' The female voice carried the strong accent of the Borders.

'You have all indicated your disapproval of our current Grand Marl,' said the grey figure.

'Disapproval!' snorted the woman from the Borders. 'Leodra is pathetic, too easily swayed by the demands of the peasants. The power and influence of the Marls would be destroyed if his new proposals to increase tenants' rights become law. Worse, these Sendoran savages try to take my land and he does nothing. Lady Migara had the right idea. She would have re-conquered Sendor. I'll never understand why Frostan passed her over in favour of his grandson.'

The grey woman held up her hand. 'We have powerful friends who share your concerns. It is they who have bid me speak with you today.'

'Who are these friends?' asked a young man in a brown leather jacket.

'You do not need to know.'

'You ask us to risk everything, without trusting us. I demand to know who is involved,' insisted the young man.

The grey woman's head snapped back.

'Get out of my mind,' she growled, grabbing the leather-jacketed man by his throat. The two figures stood locked for some moments in silent, internal battle, before the man collapsed to the ground. A blade flashed downwards, glinting in the moonlight.

'A spy of Leodra's,' remarked the grey woman, yanking the knife from the lifeless body. 'We must all be more vigilant. When we are ready to move, you will each receive a letter containing your instructions. Follow them immediately and exactly.'

'What about Leodra and his family?'

'We shall not be as weak as him.'

The grey woman turned and disappeared into the darkness.

Chapter Four

Zastra awoke to an increase in the usual bustle of the castle. On asking Elly, her maidservant, what was happening, she was informed that visitors were expected and the southwest tower was being cleaned from top to bottom for their accommodation. Zastra was intrigued and went to her morning lessons full of curiosity.

'What's happening?' she asked, as she sat down beside her friend Bedrun, a plump, fair-haired girl of her own age.

'Visitors!' said Bedrun. 'Bodel came in from Highcastle village and said that a huge procession has been seen on the main highway. Five carriages and at least a hundred horses, so they say. Don't you know who they are, oh Royal One?'

'It's probably something really dull,' Zastra said with a laugh.

'A hundred horses, dull? How can you say such a thing?'

'Depends who's riding them,' said Zastra. 'Remember last year, when those science masters visited from the Far Isles? We got all excited only for Father to cancel the weekly holiday in favour of some tedious lectures. What were they? I can't even remember.'

'Theory and practical uses of lenses,' said Bedrun, with a groan. 'I never want to see another telescope, ever.'

The two girls looked at each other in dismay.

'It couldn't be,' said Zastra, at length.

'What's the use of being Grand Marl Leodra's daughter if you don't know what's going on?' said Bedrun, prodding her friend in the arm.

'Fine,' said Zastra, 'I'll ask Mother at lunchtime.'

As soon as morning lessons finished, Zastra rushed up the three flights of stairs to her mother's quarters in the royal tower. As she barged through the door, she found Anara busy relaying instructions to the household servants.

'Oh, Zastra, good,' said Anara, 'I need to talk to you. Wait just a minute, my dear.'

Zastra fidgeted while her mother completed the dull business of household management. A few moments later, all the servants had left and they were alone.

'What's going on?' asked Zastra, bursting with impatience. 'Who's coming?'

'Your Uncle Thorlberd, Marl of Bractaris, and your cousin Rastran, shortly to be followed by the rest of the Grand Assembly. It seems that your uncle is bringing his entire personal guard and several other retainers. I have no idea how I shall fit them all in, especially when all the other Marls arrive.'

'The Grand Assembly?'

'You should know by now, Zastra, that every two years the Marls meet to discuss the laws of Golmeira. Your father has proposed some serious changes, for which we need the agreement of a majority of the assembly. However, it will be difficult – there are a lot of Marls who are resistant to anything new.'

'Sounds boring.'

'It is very important, Zastra. You need to begin to understand these things.'

Zastra looked at her mother closely. Anara seemed unusually pale and flustered.

'What's wrong?' she asked.

'Wrong? Why do you say that? Nothing is wrong. I'm just extremely busy trying to prepare everything. Now, sit down and listen to me. You must try very hard to make a good impression, particularly with your uncle. Thorlberd's support is vital to us, especially now. Your cousin Rastran will be fifteen years old now, but he was a shy young thing when I last saw him. His mother, your Aunt Jintara, has stayed at Bractaris expecting a baby, so he may feel a bit lonely. Please make him feel welcome.'

'I'll try,' said Zastra. 'How long is the assembly?'

'Usually no more than a week.'

'What about Uncle – how long is he staying?'

'As long as he wishes,' replied Anara, turning quietly away. 'Now go back to your lessons. I have much to do.'

Zastra left, a little disconcerted. Her mother was always so organised and capable; it was odd to see her so unsettled by visitors. But then all the Marls and their servants would be a lot to deal with. At least they weren't going to be subjected to any boring lectures. Zastra went down to the kitchens, where the other pupils were having lunch, and sat down next to Bedrun.

'It's my uncle, the Marl of Bractaris, and my cousin,' she whispered. 'And then all the other Marls for the Grand Assembly.'

'Oooh, how exciting!' exclaimed Bedrun. 'I wonder if there'll be a banquet. Do you think I'll be able to go?'

'Of course,' replied Zastra. 'You're friends with the Grand Marl's daughter after all. It has to count for something.'

The two girls spent the next hour discussing the joys of the potential banquet, in particular whether there would be acrobats, or maybe even fire-fountains.

The next morning, Zastra and Bedrun were delighted to be told that lessons were cancelled. They climbed to the top of the northwest tower in order to watch the guests as they arrived. From there they had a good view of the courtyard and the main gate. Golmer Castle was situated at the highest point of a gently rolling landscape and they could see the first procession as it emerged from Highcastle Forest to the east and entered the outer ramparts. A large entourage of soldiers and finely dressed courtiers escorted three gleaming ebony carriages. As the procession passed under the large archway of the main gate and entered the sunlit courtyard, the clattering of horses' hooves echoed around the balconies. One of the coaches bore a double crest on the door: a silver gecko alongside the golden hawk of Golmeira, which caught the sunlight as it opened.

'That must be my uncle,' said Zastra, as a tall man, heavyset and dressed in black, exited the carriage and strode toward the stone steps that led up to the entrance of the great hall. Zastra's mother and father stood waiting to greet him.

'And who's that handsome young man coming out of the other side of the carriage?' asked Bedrun, peering down in admiration.

'Oh, that'll be my cousin, Rastran,' replied Zastra confidently, although in truth she had never met her cousin, and had no idea what he looked like. She didn't think the pale youth was very pleasant looking, especially when he yanked a small cloak brusquely from one of the attendants.

'He looks a bit grumpy,' she muttered.

'Oh, you never seem to be bothered with boys, but I think he's gorgeous,' said her friend with a sigh.

'Let's go and meet them.' Zastra grabbed her friend by the hand and led her down the stairs. They hurried along to the large state room into which the visitors had just been ushered.

'Ah, Zastra, there you are,' said Leodra. 'Come and meet our guests. This is your Uncle Thorlberd and your cousin, Rastran.'

Zastra put forward her best bow, greeting the guests with ceremonious politeness as she had been taught. Her uncle's resemblance to her father was clear, but everything about Thorlberd was on a grander scale. He had broader shoulders, darker eyebrows and a thicker beard and he dominated the room with his powerful bulk. Rastran hovered behind his father, flicking an occasional look at his cousin from behind a long black fringe.

'Well, Zastra,' said her uncle in a deep bass voice, 'you have certainly grown since I last saw you. And where are your new brother and sister?'

'Here they are,' said Anara, just as the nurse brought the twins, one on each arm. 'Kastara and Findar, meet your uncle and cousin.' The babies remained deeply unimpressed. Findar was asleep and Kastara was distracted by the much more fascinating glow of the hanging jula-oil lamps.

'Well, Anara, they are quite as beautiful as you, my dear,' said Thorlberd, leaning over them in undisguised admiration. 'We must hope that these babes grow to be great mindweavers, given the disappointing news of Zastra's test.' He gave Zastra a hard, searching look. Was he trying to read her mind? Despite her still raw feelings, Zastra held her chin up and returned her uncle's stare. Behind him, she saw her cousin lift his top lip in what could have been a sneer, and as she shifted her gaze to him he issued a self-satisfied snort. She glared at him and he coughed behind his hand.

'Never mind cousin,' the boy said with an air of condescension. 'Not all of us can be blessed with abilities.'

There was a short, stilted silence.

'Zastra, will you and Bedrun take the twins to the nursery for me please,' said Anara, allowing a grateful Zastra to leave as a red flush of anger and shame burst across her face.

'Your cousin is dreamy!' exclaimed Bedrun, not noticing her friend's distress.

'I hate him!' snapped Zastra. 'Nasty, slimy thing. You can have him if you want – why don't you go back if you like him so much?'

Bedrun looked startled and the twins both started crying in response to Zastra's raised voice. Zastra was filled with instant remorse.

'Oh, I'm sorry!' she said to the babies. 'I'm not angry with you. Oh please, please stop crying.' The two girls were able to eventually quieten the children, Zastra forgetting her anger in the process. Once the babies were settled, Zastra and Bedrun returned to the northwest tower to watch the rest of the Marls arrive. They had never seen so many carriages before and it was late in the afternoon before the last coach had been safely stowed.

That night, as anticipated, a banquet was held in honour of the visitors. The great hall was a beautiful sight, lit with an abundance of torches. Across the western wall, a collection of jula-oil lamps with tinted glass panels had been hung, casting rainbows of coloured light across the polished wooden floor. The other walls were lined with bright silks and intricate tapestries, unfurled especially for the occasion. The hall was crowded with colourfully dressed Marls, both male and female, interspersed with soldiers, more sombrely clad in their dress uniforms. Zastra did not anticipate much pleasure in the evening, even though acrobats had been promised. She was not looking forward to facing her uncle and cousin again. She asked to be excused, but her mother insisted she attend.

'We all must try our best,' Anara said firmly, ending her protests before they had even begun.

'Well can I at least wear my trousers and my soldier's blouse?' pleaded Zastra, who never liked getting dressed up for these occasions. Alas, her mother insisted she wear her best silk gown, which Zastra hated because it made her feel itchy and uncomfortable, as well as being a pale green colour which she didn't like nearly as much as her vivid red soldier's blouse. Anara also insisted on brushing Zastra's dark chestnut hair forcefully, although, as usual, it refused to behave, unruly curls defying any attempts to arrange in a neat and tidy manner. Anara sighed in frustration.

'If you wore it longer, it might sit better, my dear.'

'But I like it short,' stated Zastra, vehemently. In the mirror, she saw her mother shake her head and smile. It was a familiar argument between them, which Zastra always won.

Bedrun came over to dress in her friend's quarters and when the gong sounded they went down to the banquet together. Zastra was highly displeased to discover that she had been seated next to Rastran, with Bedrun sent off to another table. Anara gave Zastra a significant look. With a sigh, she attempted to make conversation with her cousin.

'It must have been a long journey from Bractaris. How many days have you been travelling?' she asked politely.

'Oh, not much, only three weeks or so.'

'Don't you miss your mother? I think I would, very much.'

'I suppose I might do, if I were still a child like you. But I'm practically a grown-up now and it doesn't bother me at all.'

'Well, I've heard you'll be coming to our school lessons tomorrow, so somebody must think you still belong with us children,' said Zastra, annoyed by his haughty tone.

'Yes, well, that may be so,' responded Rastran, 'but I'm still consulted on all major plans.'

'What sort of plans?' said Zastra, with an exaggerated expression of interest. 'Like what to wear for this party? Very important plans like that, I suppose.'

The servants brought out the first course. Rastran leaned towards Zastra, smirking.

'So, cousin, it's a shame you failed the test so dismally. Mind you, it's not surprising, given that Leodra is the same way. It seems all the abilities have fallen to our side of the family. I suppose you know that I passed the test and have been practicing mindweaving for ages.' He waved his left hand in front of her face, a large silver ring on his little finger. 'See, I have my mindweaver ring.'

'Actually no one has ever mentioned you at all,' replied Zastra. 'We have much more important things to do here, you know – running the country and everything.'

'Maybe you should pay more attention to things outside this castle,' sneered her cousin.

At this moment a young servant boy came round with a large bowl of soup, which he began serving to the guests. Rastran, not noticing, raised his arm and jolted the ladle. A small spatter of soup splashed onto his sleeve.

'Clumsy idiot!' he screeched at the cowering boy. 'Look at the mess you've made of my new silk shirt. I'll have the cost out of your wages, you incompetent flekk.'

'Maybe *you* should pay more attention to things under your own nose,' said Zastra.

He turned towards her. 'Where on earth did you pick up such a fool, cousin? Such a dolt would never be employed in Bractaris. I shall have him dismissed at once.'

Zastra glared at her cousin. 'Only my mother or father can dismiss staff at Golmer Castle. I guess there are things that you don't know, even if you are a mindweaver. Thank you, Durrian,' she continued, as the boy served her, his hand shaking so much that the ladle clinked against her bowl. 'Don't worry, I shall tell my father it was an accident and you shall not be blamed.' Zastra very rarely dropped her father's name, but on this occasion she felt justified.

They ate the soup in angry silence. As the plates were cleared away and the next course was brought in, Rastran cleared his throat.

'You seem very familiar with the servants, cousin.'

'What do you mean?'

'Well, that dolt over there – you knew his name – Dirtinian, or something like that?'

'His name is Durrian. Yes, I know all the servants' names. Why shouldn't I? They are people, after all.'

'People! Oh, little cousin Zastra how stupid you are. Servants are servants. No wonder yours are such a terrible lot. I only wish we could have brought more from Bractaris, but Father said we could only bring the most essential things. I've had to do without my boot polisher for example. It's quite shocking. Makes it hard to keep up a decent appearance.'

'Yes, indeed,' said a well-dressed lady, one of the Bractarian party, who was seated just down the table from Rastran. 'My Lord Rastran always makes such a handsome figure, and so elegant.'

Zastra leant towards her cousin and nodded towards the lady. 'What's her essential function, cousin? Flatterer in Chief? I'm not sure you need her, since you have such a high opinion of yourself.'

'Don't try to be clever,' said Rastran. 'You make fun of me, but it is Golmer Castle that is the joke. To think I'll have to share lessons with children of footmen and grooms. It's not as if they need to know how to read and write. They only need to know how to obey orders. All the other Marls agree that education for everyone is a ridiculous idea.'

Zastra was shocked. She had always taken lessons with all the other children in the castle. She had no idea that this was unusual in any way.

'My mother insists everyone should go to lessons. She says everyone deserves the same chance.'

'Well, she would, wouldn't she?'

'What do you mean by that?'

'Oh, only that she's not really of noble birth, is she? Some distant poor relation, who managed to snag a Grand Marl.'

'Don't you dare talk about my mother like that,' said Zastra, slamming her spoon down on the table.

They spent the rest of the meal in mutual silence, which to Zastra's mind was preferable to further conversation with her cousin.

As the after-dinner drinks were being served, many of the guests left their seats and moved around the hall. Bedrun came over and sat next to Zastra, looking at Rastran in open admiration.

'Well, cousin, who is this pretty little thing?' he said, pleased by the attention.

'This is my friend Bedrun,' said Zastra shortly.

'Hello,' said Bedrun with a shy smile. Rastran ignored her, eyeing Zastra balefully.

'No, I mean who *is* she. Who are her parents, what is her line of descent?'

'Her mothers are Morel and Bodel. Morel is a lieutenant in the Household Guard and Bodel is a healer in Highcastle village.'

'Yes…' began Bedrun, but he had already turned away, deliberately and with calculated rudeness, and begun talking to a finely dressed lady of the Bractaris party. The slight caught the two girls completely by surprise. A red flush spread across Bedrun's plump face.

'Come on Bedrun,' said Zastra, firmly, 'he's not worth bothering with. They obviously enjoy being rude in Bractaris. Let's go and see the acrobats.'

They went to see the show, but Zastra could see her friend was very upset and she seethed at her cousin's rudeness. She could say with confidence that she had never met such a horrible person in all her life. Luckily, the show was a great spectacle and both the girls were soon revived by the athletic acrobats. Bedrun leaned over. 'I like the young fair-haired one,' she whispered. 'What a lovely face he has and such bravery.'

Zastra grinned. She was used to Bedrun switching her admiration from one object to another but this was surely a new record. 'Yes indeed,' she agreed, 'much nicer than pasty, oily-haired boys who mooch about like snooty stick insects.'

'Rastran the Rotten, he should be called!' giggled Bedrun. The girls continued to contrast the attributes of the young acrobat with the boy from Bractaris. By the end of the evening, their spirits were recovered completely. They were disappointed when Anara came over and told them it was time for them to go to bed. Zastra tried to argue that it was early and that they were nearly grown-ups, but her mother was firm.

'Say goodnight to your uncle and cousin and then go to your room. You have lessons tomorrow as usual.'

'Oh, Mother, do I have to talk to them? I don't want to talk to Rastran the Rotten ever again.'

Her mother pursed her lips in strong disapproval.

'If you mean your cousin, young lady, you are never to refer to him in that way again. You are old enough to behave with decorum. A lady is made by her own graces, not by her title.'

'You should tell that to Rastran,' replied Zastra, stung by her mother's criticism. 'He's so rude, and you should have heard—'

'Enough. I expect better of you Zastra. Do not disappoint me.' Her mother's tone allowed no argument. Zastra went and bade her uncle and cousin good night with the best grace she could muster and ran to bed.

Chapter Five

The next day, Rastran joined their classes, albeit with an air of reluctant superiority. The morning was taken up with rather dull studies of arithmetic and calligraphy. These were followed by fighting skills in the afternoon, which took place on the combat ranges outside the main castle but within the outer ramparts. Zastra always much preferred the afternoon activities, since although slender, she was tall for her age and able to compete well with boys and girls several years older than her. Since the test, she had attacked the lessons with a serious intensity, rather than her usual joy. Her father's reaction to her failure made her determined to show him her worth in different ways. She may not be a mindweaver, but at least she could do her best in the fighting skills. Martek, the master at arms who took the lessons, always watched her with a paternal gaze and a few quiet words of encouragement. The previous week he had told her that she would be a warrior of Golmeira yet, and Zastra had blushed pink with pleasure.

This particular afternoon the first lesson was crossbow. Rastran was a very poor shot and was soon red-faced with frustration. Zastra, who was especially good at this discipline, could not help feeling an extra sense joy as every shot of hers hit the centre of the target. She knew it was wrong to gloat, but she felt that Rastran deserved to feel a bit inferior for a change. Even Bedrun, who was not the best at fighting skills, scored more points than Rastran, who finished second from bottom, only beating Heldrid, who everyone knew was blind in one eye from an accident as a baby.

'Stupid crossbow,' snapped Rastran. 'I'm sure mine is broken.'

'Oh, let me look cousin,' said Zastra with extreme politeness. She took the weapon and in one quick movement nocked a bolt and, casually taking aim, fired the bolt true to the centre of the target.

'No, I think it's fine,' she said, smiling at her cousin and returning the bow. A few of the other children sniggered and Rastran stamped off, pouting and unable to hide his tears. This made them all laugh even more, since a fifteen-year-old boy crying like a toddler in a tantrum was not a sight often seen at Golmer Castle.

The next lesson was swordplay. The children took their wooden replica weapons and padded jackets and paired up. Rastran was left on his own, looking forlorn and miserable. Bedrun, always soft-hearted, took pity on him.

'I'll be your partner, Rastran, if you wish,' she said.

'Huh!' he spat. 'Surely someone of decent birth can be found to be my partner, not someone adopted from who knows where. Otherwise I'm not bothering.'

Martek stepped forward and used every inch of his seven feet to face down the boy.

'Young man, you will never treat one of my students with such rudeness again, or you will be punished, Marl's son or not.' His tone was authoritative, as if he was reprimanding one of his soldiers. 'In Golmer Castle you'll find that people are judged on their character, not who their parents are, and right now you are scoring very low indeed.'

Rastran flinched, his eyes fixed on the ground in front of his feet.

'Zastra, perhaps you and Bedrun will both practice with your cousin,' said Martek, turning away before Zastra could protest.

As the other students began to practice, Zastra and Rastran squared up to one another warily, each keen to win the contest. Rastran had greater reach and strength, being almost three years older, and he attacked with gusto, forcing Zastra backwards. However, she quickly realised that he was relatively uncoordinated and left himself open to the counter. Time after time, he found himself prodded and poked, until he was bruised and aching. His tears of frustration came again, but the angrier he got, the more his parries lacked thought and skill. Eventually Zastra put an end to the contest by disarming him and thrusting the tip of her wooden sword under his chin. He scowled and picked up his sword, swishing it viciously in annoyance.

'Your turn Bedrun,' said Zastra brightly. 'That is, if you are not too tired, cousin?'

'Shut up, little girl,' he snarled, half under his breath.

'A little girl who just beat you easily,' giggled Bedrun.

'I'll show you,' he said through gritted teeth. He narrowed his eyes, his face fixed with a look of intense concentration.

Zastra felt a familiar weight on her mind and she heard Bedrun cry out in horror. She felt a stab of fear and saw a pack of caralyx rushing towards her, teeth bared. They leapt up towards her, fangs glistening, and she felt their breath, hot and fetid against her cheek. Dimly she was aware of a terrified sobbing, then felt a sharp blow to her face. Confused and disorientated, her head felt trapped in a heavy denseness. 'It's not real,' she gasped. Somehow, she knew not how, she pushed against the weight and it left her. Like a fog cleared away by a ray of sunlight, the ferocious animals vanished and she realised she was on the ground. Bedrun was lying next to her, curled in ball and screaming in terror. Zastra became aware that Rastran was standing over her, grinning with triumph. His wooden sword was raised, ready to hit her again. She rolled away from the descending blow, which glanced painfully off her ear. She realised what was happening.

'You cheating brute!' she cried, enraged. She launched herself at him, pelting him with blows on his face and body. He tried to hit back, but was unable to deal with the ferocity of her attack and she knocked the wooden sword out of his hand. The other children gathered round, cheering and shouting, a wall of high pitched noise. Then, from nowhere, a powerful hand pulled her sharply away and she became aware of Martek glaring at her.

'Stop, this minute! What kind of behaviour is this? There's no free-for-all in this class. Both of you come with me. The rest of you carry on with your practice.'

He dragged Zastra and Rastran into the guard room at the base of the northeast tower. They made a sorry sight; Zastra caked in dirt, her left ear red and puffy from the blow of the wooden sword, and Rastran's nose bleeding after Zastra's wild, uncontrolled attack.

'Now, will someone tell me what happened?' Martek demanded.

Zastra stared at the floor and said nothing.

'She attacked me! Savage little beast – for no reason!' whined Rastran through petulant tears.

'You know the reason,' she shot back at him.

'What in the stars is going on here?' interjected a deep voice. Both children jumped in shock and Zastra felt a hollow ache in her stomach as she saw her father stride into the room. Rastran seemed no less horrified to see Thorlberd following close behind.

'They were fighting, my Lord,' reported Martek.

Leodra looked at his daughter. 'Fighting again, Zastra? Whenever I see you, you are causing trouble. It seems that you bring nothing but shame to me. You were specifically instructed to treat our visitors with utmost respect, yet you deliberately disobey.'

'That's not fair!' exclaimed Zastra, anger giving her courage. 'It wasn't deliberate, he—'

'Do *not* answer back! You shall be confined to your room for the rest of the day with no food. Maybe that will give you time to ponder your actions. Try to behave like a future Grand Marl instead of some sort of street urchin.'

Rastran sniggered, but his expression quickly changed as Thorlberd lifted a gloved hand and slapped him sharply across his face.

'And the same for you boy. You will learn to control yourself in public. Stop snivelling like a pathetic little baby.'

'See to it, Martek,' commanded Leodra. Zastra barely noticed how she ended up locked in her room. She lay on the bed and sobbed bitterly. She was torn between anger at the injustice of her punishment and deep hurt as she thought of her father, and how he was always angry with her.

Her mother came to see her. 'I hear you have been fighting your cousin, Zastra? And after I asked to you treat him with honour,' she said, saddened.

Zastra nodded dumbly.

'Well, you have been punished, and hopefully you have learnt your lesson. Now, I know that you have got off to a bad start with your cousin, but can you please try to get along? We need our family bonds now more than ever.'

'But he's so horrid, I hate him.'

'Zastra, hate is not a word I like to hear. Hate is blind and judgemental and the truth can be lost in it. Everyone has a mixture of good parts and bad parts and we must try and see those good parts, even if sometimes they are hard to find.'

'Why do we have to be so nice to them?' asked Zastra, plaintively.

Anara sighed. 'Things are not as we would wish in Golmeira. There are Kyrginite raiders in the Helgarths and rumours of strange happenings in the Forest of Waldaria. Your father fears that someone within Golmeira is plotting against him. Your uncle is our strongest ally and he has pledged his personal army and his mindweavers should we need them. But he is a proud man, quick to anger, so we must be careful not to offend him. It is our duty to treat him and his son with respect, Zastra, a duty to both your father and to Golmeira. Will you promise not to fight with Rastran again?'

'But what if he did something really bad? So that he really deserved it?'

'I don't believe violence is ever the best answer to a problem.'

'But people will think I'm a coward if I don't stand up for myself and my friends.'

'Sometimes it is braver to refuse to fight.'

Zastra did not understand and the injustice still burned within her, but responding to Anara's serious words she promised she would try and avoid fighting, resolving to make her mother proud.

Chapter Six

That night Zastra slept poorly, as her empty stomach grumbled and her mind kept replaying the events of the day. She awoke before dawn. Finding her door unlocked, she went to visit Dobery. He looked surprised to see her at such an hour, but as an early riser himself he was already awake and making himself breakfast. Seeing her eyeing his toasted currant bun longingly, he offered her half, which she wolfed down at great speed.

'Goodness, child! Be careful, or you'll choke. Have they closed the kitchens and not told me?'

'Didn't you hear?' Zastra mumbled, her mouth full of crumbs. 'I got into a fight with Rastran yesterday afternoon and was sent to my room without any food. This is lovely, thanks.'

'Fighting, eh? I thought you were old enough now to behave better than that,' he said, peering over his glasses.

'But it was so unfair!' she protested. 'He was hurting Bedrun, and you're not supposed to use mindweaving unless it's important, are you? You told me that. Especially against someone you know can't protect themselves. He's such a cowardly cheat.'

'Hold up!' exclaimed Dobery. 'Slow down and tell me what happened, while I make some chala and some more toasted buns. Would you like honey on this one?'

'Ooh, yes please!'

He made the hot, sweet chala and poured them both a large glass. Then he spread a generous helping of honey on two toasted buns and they sat by the empty fireplace to eat. Zastra gulped her food down, scattering crumbs onto her lap.

'Do try not to make a mess, Zastra,' said Dobery, 'I've only just tidied up.'

'Tidied?' She looked around in amazement. If anything, the piles of books had multiplied and the hearthrug looked ready to expire of old age. Dobery proudly pointed to a clear spot on his largest desk. The area was no larger than a slice of bread. Zastra wasn't sure that really counted as tidying up, but she decided that it was best to make no comment. Instead, she surreptitiously brushed the crumbs from her lap onto the hideous grey rug where they would surely not cause offence.

'Tell me what happened, from the beginning,' said Dobery, once they had both finished eating. Zastra told him the whole story, leaving nothing out. When she came to the part where she had made fun of her cousin for his poor shooting, she felt a little ashamed.

'I know I was mean to him, but he's such a nasty snob. And then he used his mindweaving to distract us, and hit me while I was unable to defend myself. Poor Bedrun was absolutely terrified by the visions. It wasn't right, was it?'

His untidy grey eyebrows dipped towards each other.

'You were certainly wrong to make your cousin feel embarrassed by his lack of sporting skill. It was not kind of you and if you had behaved with more thoughtfulness this whole incident could have been avoided. However, your cousin was guilty of a much more serious offence. I shall have a word with Marl Thorlberd when I next see him.'

'Oh, no, please don't,' said Zastra, recalling Anara's request. 'I don't want to cause trouble. It's all over now. I came to ask if you would teach me how to block mindweaving. I want to be able to protect myself and my friends.'

'It will not be easy,' Dobery said. 'It will take much hard work and dedication, and it must be admitted that you've not always been the most attentive student in the past.'

Zastra coloured. It was true that her mind often wandered during morning lessons as she waited impatiently for the more active afternoon sessions.

'This time I will properly concentrate, Dobery, I promise. I don't care how hard it is.'

Dobery contemplated her request for some time.

'Very well,' he said finally. 'Come to me every morning at this hour and we shall work together. But you must be prepared to put in a lot of effort.'

Zastra was not discouraged. She was determined never to be held at such a disadvantage again, even if that meant that she had to work every day for the next ten years.

In addition to requesting lessons from Dobery, Zastra paid close attention to the comings and goings of the Grand Assembly. She had never taken much notice of the serious business of running the country. It had all seemed so dull. However, both Dobery and Anara had spoken of Leodra's worries about enemies, and Zastra began to wonder if these worries might explain, at least in part, her father's attitude towards her. She desperately wished that some outside influence was responsible, rather than her own failings. She wondered if any of her father's enemies were amongst the visitors that had filled the castle to discuss laws, taxes and other matters. She often came across small groups of grown-ups engaged in whispered conversations that would stop abruptly when she passed by, and she was not above listening in at windows and doors to try and find out what was going on. However, the assembly came and went without her having overheard anything of significance. Her father's grim mood as the Marls departed for their lands suggested that things had not gone well. Thorlberd decided to stay on at Golmer Castle, along with Rastran, much to Leodra's pleasure and to Zastra's dissatisfaction.

Chapter Seven

Zastra worked hard with Dobery and within a few weeks she had learnt how to sense and block casual probes into her mind.

'It's like creating a smooth stone cover for your thoughts, so that the invading mind slides off and can gather no purchase,' explained Dobery. She learnt to push away thoughts that had broken through her barriers, getting faster and stronger as the weeks wore on. She steered clear of Rastran, not wanting a confrontation until she was prepared. Fortunately, he seemed to wish to avoid her also. Maybe he had been surprised by her unexpected resistance to his mindweaving.

One morning, as Zastra was pushing away a sequence of sharp probes from Dobery, they were interrupted by the brisk entrance of Teona, highmaster of the council of mindweavers.

'Well!' she snapped. 'What is occurring here, Dobery? It would appear that one of my masters is wasting his time teaching a talentless child.'

'She may be no mindweaver, highmaster, but she is not talentless,' Dobery replied mildly. 'I'm teaching Zastra to defend herself against those wielding the power. She is doing remarkably well.'

'Really?' said Teona, her severe blue eyes boring into Zastra. 'Well, we shall see. Defend yourself child, if you can.'

Zastra did not have time to set her block before she felt a sharp probe inside her mind, deep and painful. However, she did not panic and used what she had learnt to push back. She saw a look of surprise pulse across Teona's face.

'Party tricks!' huffed Teona. 'Do you think your father will be impressed? Last I heard he was bemoaning the shame brought on him by his daughter.'

Zastra's heart sank at this, and as she was distracted she felt another sharp probe dig into her mind. Darkness enveloped her.

She came round to find both Dobery and Teona standing over her.

'Girl, you must learn to control your emotions,' said Teona sternly. 'They make your mind weak and vulnerable. What's more, you should always have a block in place, even if you are not expecting anyone to attack you. Dobery, are you certain that this is not a waste of your time?'

'Quite certain, highmaster,' he said respectfully.

'Well, I shall allow this to continue, for now,' Teona said. She then turned abruptly and addressed Dobery as if Zastra was no longer in the room. 'I called in to talk about a problem the Grand Marl has raised, but we can discuss it after the council meeting. It's not something to be discussed in front of children.' With those words, the highmaster turned and stalked out of the room.

'Why is she so mean?' asked Zastra, rather chastened.

'Hush, Zastra,' whispered the old man, glancing down the corridor as he closed the door. 'She has long ears! And we should be grateful; she could have forbidden me to teach you. We are not supposed to teach non-mindweavers how to defend themselves against us. And she was right. You must keep your guard up at all times and you *are* too easily distracted. Shall we leave it for today?'

'No,' replied Zastra. 'I want to try again.'

That evening, Zastra was seated in her room trying to create a layer of fake thoughts outside her mental stone wall. This would allow a casual scan to be fooled into thinking her something other than she really was. It was an extremely difficult skill and she had not yet mastered it properly. As she was trying to pretend to be a common soldier, she was disturbed by a knock at the door. On opening the door she found Bedrun waiting, hopping impatiently from one foot to the other.

'Hey there,' said Bedrun, skipping into the room without waiting to be invited. 'What are you up to? There's a bit of a stir downstairs. Do you know what's happening?'

'What do you mean, a stir?' asked Zastra, intrigued.

'Well, a messenger arrived a little while ago, her horse almost dead with exhaustion. Heldrid said that he heard her say to the gatekeeper that she had to talk to the Grand Marl at once, as she had important news from Waldaria. They are in your father's offices right now. What could it mean?'

'I don't know,' said Zastra thoughtfully, 'but I've heard Waldaria mentioned before. Come on Bedrun, let's try and find out what's going on.'

'How?' asked Bedrun.

'There's a balcony above Father's outer office. Maybe we can sneak in and hear what's happening,' suggested Zastra.

'But we could get in trouble. Remember last year, when you got caught listening into the teachers' meeting?'

'Yes, well, that was Heldrid's fault. He dared me to find out who our new teacher was going to be. And I would've too – it was sheer bad luck that the vine broke just at the wrong time.'

'You were lucky you didn't break your neck,' said Bedrun, suppressing a giggle. The teachers' common room, like the schoolroom, was on the first floor of the enclosed triangular section of the castle, with windows overlooking the courtyard. This was the only side of the courtyard without a balcony, and in response to Heldrid's dare, Zastra had climbed down a large vine that hung from the upper ramparts in order to listen in at the window. The vine had snapped under her weight, causing her to crash down and ruin one of Anara's favourite flower beds. Zastra returned Bedrun's smile ruefully.

'You sound like my mother,' she protested. 'Come on, do you want to find out what's happening or not?'

'All right then,' agreed Bedrun, and so the two girls tiptoed along the second floor balcony that passed alongside the great hall and ended above her father's offices. Their bare feet made little noise on the polished wooden floor. They tried the door that led to a small alcove overlooking the outer office, but it would not open.

'I'll try and pick the lock,' whispered Zastra. 'Give me your pin.' She gestured towards the pin that held a pink silk badge on Bedrun's shirt; a reward, rather ironically, for good behaviour.

'Do you know how?' asked Bedrun.

'Well, I saw once saw one of the grooms do it, to get into a locked stable,' said Zastra confidently. 'How hard can it be?'

Unfortunately, the answer to that question appeared to be "very hard indeed" since in spite of lots of enthusiastic jiggling and thrusting with the pin, the door remained obstinately locked.

'Someone's coming!' whispered Bedrun in panic, and indeed footsteps were approaching rapidly; closer and closer with relentless inevitability.

'Quick, hide!' urged Zastra. Grabbing Bedrun by the hand she dragged her through a nearby door that, by good fortune, opened to her desperate touch. They ended up in a dark closet, filled with brooms, buckets and other cleaning apparatus. As the footsteps paused alongside them, the girls stopped breathing and froze, gripping each other's hands. Then the footsteps continued on down the corridor, and the girls let out shaky sighs of relief. Their hearts were still thrumming when they became aware of a dim echo of voices. Creeping to the back of the cupboard, they found a crack in the wall through which they could see down into the office below. Bedrun gripped Zastra's hand in excitement. The crack was narrow and only a small strip of the room below was visible. However, Zastra could see the back of a black coat, which she thought looked like her uncle's. Voices, barely audible at first, became more distinct as she pressed her ear to the crevice.

'Did anyone see what happened?' The question was asked by her father.

'No one would talk to me,' a weary female voice responded. 'Everyone was terrified. All I could ascertain was that the body had been deposited in the night, outside the blacksmith's, and that this was found next to it.'

There was a sound of metal ringing on wood. Zastra pressed her eye to the crack, but the table was out of view and she could see nothing.

'A dagger bearing the crest of Sendor, brother.' Thorlberd's booming tone was unmistakable.

'Why was I not told about this?' demanded a sharp, female voice. 'If one of my masters was in danger, as clearly he was, why was I not informed?'

Zastra could picture Teona's blue eyes glaring at their target, and was glad she didn't have to face them.

'All we had were suspicions, highmaster,' responded Thorlberd. 'We didn't wish to raise panic through the kingdom before we had evidence.'

'Well, young Xendon has died for your evidence,' exclaimed Teona, bitterly. 'I demand to know what caused you to send him to Waldaria.'

'Rumours,' replied Leodra. 'Unconfirmed tales of frightening visions and strange creatures in the Waldarian forest. We thought someone might be practicing unauthorised mindweaving and so sent Xendon to investigate.'

'In matters of mindweaving, I should be your first council. My Lord, I must protest in the strongest possible terms. I must know what concerns me and my masters.'

'Do not over-reach yourself, Teona, remember whom you address,' said Leodra. 'Perhaps we should have informed you, but these are difficult times, and we do not know who can be trusted.'

'If my loyalty is being called into question…'

'Of course not,' said Thorlberd. 'My dear highmaster, your service to this court is without question. But if a powerful mindweaver is involved, we cannot rule out the possibility that it is a member, or ex-member, of the council, however unpalatable such a view might be. We thought it best to involve as few people as possible.'

A dangerous silence followed, broken by the voice of the messenger.

'My Lord, there is one more thing. I found this hidden in Xendon's lodgings.'

Zastra strained her eyes to try and see, but her view was still obstructed by the body of her uncle and the sides of the crack.

'What's happening?' whispered Bedrun, nudging her friend.

'Shhhh,' Zastra hissed, and reapplied her ear to the crack.

'Cintara bark!' Teona exclaimed. 'I thought we had eradicated this scourge.'

'Someone has broken the law forbidding its use,' said Leodra, grimly. 'Our enemy is willing to risk all to achieve their ends.'

'Let me look into this, brother,' said Thorlberd. 'Waldaria adjoins Bractaris after all. I feel the responsibility for getting to the bottom of this.'

'Teona, what is your opinion?' asked a soft voice. Zastra was jolted by the sound. She had not realised that her mother was in the room.

'This is a matter of the utmost seriousness,' responded the highmaster. 'If cintara bark is being used in Golmeira, the dangers are deep indeed. I would suggest sending a strong contingent to Waldaria, including both mindweavers and soldiers. I shall lead the expedition myself.'

'The expedition I agree to,' said Leodra, 'but as for you going, Teona, that is out of the question. You are needed here. Let us send master Dobery; he is a man of great wisdom and resource. I will send Morel with him, along with a full company of soldiers. Our enemy has power enough to murder one of our most valued and talented mindweavers. We will find out who is behind this outrage.'

In the dark closet, Bedrun gripped Zastra's arm tightly. Morel was one of Bedrun's mothers and the proposed trip sounded very dangerous indeed.

'Very well, it is agreed,' said Thorlberd.

'And send another message to the Sendorans,' ordered Leodra. 'I have left that situation unresolved for too long. Many of our troops are in the border regions to keep the peace, stretching our resources when we can ill afford it. We must try and reach some agreement.'

'I'm not sure that is wise, brother. The Sendorans are uneducated savages, and they have no love of Golmeira or its Grand Marl. For all we know, they could be behind this trouble in Waldaria. The dagger certainly points that way.'

'Anyone can plant a dagger,' said Anara, 'and the Sendorans do not have mindweavers. We must not leap to conclusions.'

'I don't have to remind you that any submission to Sendoran demands would be seen as weakness,' said Thorlberd. 'The Sendoran War is remembered bitterly by many in this land.'

'Nevertheless, Anara and I feel we must pursue a peaceful agreement if possible,' replied Leodra. 'Of course, should Morel and Dobery find further evidence of Sendoran involvement in Waldaria, we shall take appropriate action.'

'Well, it is of course your decision to make. I suggest that the Waldaria situation be kept secret. It would be unwise to broadcast our weakness, especially with the Sendorans around. No one outside this room, excepting the leaders of the expedition, should know the reasons behind this.' At that moment, Thorlberd looked sharply upwards at the crack in the wall. Zastra gasped, jerking her head backwards. As she did so, she thought she sensed a feather of a touch in her mind. Her heart pounding, she pulled Bedrun away. They ran back to Zastra's room as quietly and as fast as they could. Gasping for breath, they closed the door behind them and sank to the floor.

'Do you think he saw us?' wailed Bedrun. 'He must have done. Oh, we shall be in so much trouble.'

'I don't think he can have known it was us,' said Zastra, although her heart was still fluttering from the shock of Thorlberd's eyes staring up at her, as well as the hectic flight back to her room. 'He may know someone was listening, but not that it was us. We mustn't tell anyone what we've heard, otherwise they'll punish us.'

'What was happening anyway?' asked Bedrun. 'I couldn't hear very well, because you were hogging the crevice. What did they say about Morel and Waldaria? I didn't catch it all.'

With a heavy heart, Zastra told her friend what she had heard.

'What was that stuff they found? Tara, or sintara bark, something like that?' asked Bedrun. Zastra shook her head

'I don't know,' she said.

Zastra called a servant and sent a message to Morel to tell her that Bedrun was staying with her and so not to worry. After talking late into the night, they finally extinguished the jula lamp. Bedrun was soon snoring gently, but Zastra could not get much rest. Too many dark thoughts swirled around inside her head.

Chapter Eight

The next day, the whole castle was alive with chattering and gossip. Word of the late night messenger had spread and a good deal of wild speculation was in the air. Zastra listened with a keen ear, but no one mentioned Waldaria, the Sendorans or any kind of bark, so she could gain no further information. At her early morning lesson, Dobery tutored her as if nothing had happened. Zastra wondered if he even knew he was to be sent away. Frustrated, she knew she could not ask any questions without giving herself away.

At morning class, she sat with Bedrun, who looked particularly glum.

'Any news?' whispered Zastra.

'Morel has to leave tomorrow. She didn't tell me why, but I could tell she was not happy about it. Of course I couldn't tell her that I knew where she was going and why. Oh Zastra, I'm scared. If someone in Waldaria can dare to kill even a member of the council of mindweavers...'

'I know,' whispered Zastra, giving her friend's hand a quick squeeze. 'But if anyone can look after herself, it's Morel. You know how amazing she is at fighting skills. No one could sneak up behind her without her catching them.'

However, Bedrun was not to be comforted and, in truth, Zastra had not much spirits herself.

'Have you found out anything about that wotsit bark?' asked Bedrun.

'No,' whispered Zastra.

'I'll ask Sestra,' said Bedrun. Zastra shook her head.

'No, you can't. They'll wonder why we are asking. If it gets back to our parents they'll know we were listening last night. Perhaps we can find out in the library. I'll go at lunchtime and have a look.'

'Good plan!' exclaimed Bedrun. 'I'll come too.'

At this point Sestra, their teacher, entered the room. Everyone quietened and the lessons began. The two girls sat through the lessons on geometry and mathematics with even more impatience than usual. The instant the lunch gong sounded, they raced away from the classroom. As they climbed the stairs to the third floor, where the library was situated, Zastra had a strange sense that they were being followed. Grabbing an uncomprehending Bedrun by the arm, she pulled her past the library and into the darkness of the outer liden. Seeing her friend's startled face, Zastra put her finger to her lips. A few seconds later, they heard footsteps proceed lightly past the opening of their passageway. They were shocked to see Rastran's thin back, bony shoulder blades protruding, as he disappeared along the balcony.

'Come out, cousin,' he called softly. 'I know you are here. I saw you and your fat little friend sneaking off.'

The two girls shrank back down one of the narrow staircases of the liden. The footsteps paused, turned back towards them, and a dark shadow blocked out the light from the balcony.

'What are you up to?' he whispered. 'Don't think I won't find out.'

The girls scurried down the staircase. Keeping to the narrow passages between the castle walls, they found their way back to the kitchens and hid within the comforting crowd of their classmates.

'Why does he have to put his nose in our business?' demanded Zastra, once she had recovered her breath.

'I really thought he would find us!' said Bedrun, her eyes wide with anxiety.

'Well, so what if he did? We weren't doing anything wrong after all.'

'Then why did you make us hide?'

'I just don't want him knowing what we are doing,' replied Zastra.

'It would be just like him to tell tales on us. We'll have to try and go up to the library tonight, when he's eating dinner with his father.'

Rastran appeared at the entrance to the kitchen and looked around until he saw them.

'Hello cousin,' called Zastra, waving at him, a bread roll in her hand. 'You are late. I think all the best stew may be gone. Did you get lost? I suppose the castle is rather confusing for some.'

He cast an evil look at her, then took some food and sat alone at the far end of the table, shooting frequent suspicious glances towards them.

'He looks annoyed,' said Bedrun, nervously.

'Oh, he'd get annoyed if an insect didn't bow as it flew by, so I don't think we should let that bother us,' exclaimed Zastra, grabbing another roll.

After afternoon lessons, Zastra and Bedrun visited the nursery and played with Kastara and Findar for a while before taking an early supper. Then, alert to anyone following them – especially Rastran – they went up to the library. It was quiet at this time of day. A couple of grown-ups were in the restricted section, but the general information area was empty. Zastra and Bedrun took up two different dictionaries, but could find nothing under "tara" or "sintara" bark.

'Maybe it's spelt "zintara",' suggested Bedrun. 'Or "sindara"? Could that have been what they said?' Despite trying all these avenues, they could not find the information they were looking for. Even the *Great Book of Knowledge*, which ran to three hundred volumes, didn't appear to have any information.

An idea struck Zastra. 'What if we look up herbs and plants?' she suggested. 'Sintara bark sounds like it might come from a tree or bush or something.'

Eventually they found it.

'Cintara – this must be it!' exclaimed Bedrun. 'It's spelt with a "C".'

'Oh, well, I always was rubbish at spelling,' said Zastra with a grin. Bedrun read the entry.

'Cintara, a rare dwarf tree, which grows in shaded mountain shale, is renowned for certain properties of its bark. When refined by a complex process of smoking and soaking, a fine red/brown power is obtained. This substance has a bitter taste and distinctive odour. When ingested by one with mindweaving ability, it heightens powers. It has also been rumoured that it can grant abilities to those who lack the power of mindweaving. The use of cintara bark has been banned in Golmeira since the fifth year of Fostran II's reign due to its addictive properties and dangerous side effects, which can include madness and death.'

Zastra sat back in her chair. 'Well!' she exclaimed. 'That's why they're all so worried. If there are mindweavers who stand against us, this cintara bark could allow them to become very powerful, and even our council may not be able to protect us.'

'Why?' asked Bedrun, who like most people was largely ignorant of the details of mindweaving. She was several months younger than Zastra and had not yet taken the test. Zastra told her what she had learnt from Dobery.

'Oh!' exclaimed Bedrun, beginning to understand. 'So, that day – the day you and Rastran fought in the combat grounds – I saw the most terrible things. I thought I'd just turned loony. That was Rastran doing his mindweaving?'

Zastra nodded. 'Yes, that's why I went for him. It's not fair to use that power like that. Dobery says—'

'Shhhh!' A short, grey-bearded man glared at them from across the room. 'Quiet in the library.'

'I didn't think we were being that loud,' whispered Bedrun.

'No, indeed,' said Zastra, glaring at the man with what she hoped was a regal glare worthy of a Grand Marl in waiting.

'What are you doing?' asked Bedrun. 'You look as if you are about to pee.'

'Nothing,' said Zastra, flushing rather red. The man continued to look at them.

'Why is he still staring?' whispered Zastra. 'You'd think a cintara tree was growing out of my head or something.'

'Shh, he's coming over.'

As the man wandered towards them, the two girls made a great show of making notes.

'Isn't it time for you little ones to go to snoozie-land?'

Zastra's eyes widened in amazement and Bedrun chuckled in response to her shocked expression.

'Snoozie-land!' exclaimed Zastra in disbelief, as Bedrun dragged her away from the library. 'Do we look like babies? He needs to go to old-men-who-need-glasses-land.' Bedrun burst out laughing. As they scurried down the stairs in high spirits, they bumped heavily into the broad chest of Thorlberd.

'Steady, young ladies,' he said, jovially. 'What's all the excitement?'

'Um, just doing some schoolwork,' said Zastra, with an unsuccessful attempt at casualness.

'Well, it's good to see young people enjoying their studies so much,' said Thorlberd. 'Tell, me, what is so interesting that it keeps you girls studying at this late hour?'

'We were, um, looking at a map of Golmeira, trying to find snoozie-land,' said Bedrun. Both girls spluttered into fits of giggles. Thorlberd shook his head in bafflement as the girls headed off towards their rooms, still laughing. It was nearly their allotted bedtime, and after a quick goodbye, Bedrun rushed away, telling Zastra she did not want to get in trouble with Morel the day before her mother left for Waldaria.

Chapter Nine

Zastra however, could not sleep. She was thinking about cintara bark. What if it could give someone like her mindweaving ability? She would be able to prove to her father that she was not useless. Could it be so? Deep into the night, she tossed and turned, but the idea refused to leave her. Eventually she gave up trying to sleep. There was only one way to find out: try it and see. It would be risky. She would be breaking the law of Golmeira and would be in serious trouble if she were caught. Yet it was worth the danger, surely, to prove herself to her father? And she would be able to show Rastran a thing or two as well. She made up her mind.

The cintara bark was certain to be locked away in her father's strong box and she knew where he kept his keys. Throwing on some clothes, she found herself tip-toeing into her parents' room, reflecting briefly that sneaking about the castle at night was becoming a bit of a habit. They were both asleep in bed. She extracted Leodra's keys from the pocket of his coat as delicately as she could, but she was unable to stop them jangling together. Her father's prone body jerked under the covers. Zastra stood frozen, clasping the cold metal keys together with both hands until Leodra settled and lay still.

The door to her father's outer office creaked alarmingly as she opened it, the sound echoing down the dark corridors of the castle. She hurried through to the inner office, where the strongbox was hidden beneath a stone trapdoor. She pulled the box out and opened it. Amongst the papers and rolls of silver tocrins, there were two small cloth bags, each containing a powder that appeared reddish-orange in the dimmed light of her jula lamp. *That must be it*, Zastra thought.

Hesitating only briefly, she licked her finger and dipped it in to the powder. She had gone too far to stop now. The bark tasted so bitter she was almost sick. A faint buzzing reverberated inside in her head. Distracted, she did not hear the creak of the door opening.

A figure dressed in a soldier's uniform loomed before her, illuminated by the lamp. Oddly, its head was that of a bear. Zastra's eyes widened in shock. The bear-soldier seemed to be trying to speak, but strange grunts came out of its mouth. Staring at it, Zastra felt an overwhelming fear and an utter conviction that it meant to kill her. She could hear a screaming noise. The giant bear split into two twin bears, one of which came towards her, claws outstretched. She fought, thrashing wildly, as the bear smothered her, realising with surprise that the screaming was her own. Another dark figure loomed behind the bear-soldier and she felt a probe enter her mind which she couldn't repel. Blackness descended.

When she came round, her head was throbbing and she was instantly sick all over the polished wooden floor. She was still in her father's office. In front of her stood Martek, Dobery and a sergeant of the castle guard. They didn't look pleased.

'Zastra!' exclaimed Dobery. She had never seen him look so angry. 'What in the stars are you doing?' Zastra hung her head. There was no point in trying to deny her purpose. The trapdoor lay open, the bags of bark clearly on display. Her guilt was obvious to all.

'I just wanted to try,' she sighed. 'It said in the book that it could give me mindweaving powers. I only wanted to help Father against his enemies.' Even as she said the words, they sounded pathetically stupid.

'I thought you had more sense, girl.' Dobery shook his head. 'Cintara bark is very dangerous. You could have killed yourself.'

'There was a giant bear,' said Zastra, defensively. 'It tried to kill me.'

'That was me,' said Martek, 'and I most certainly was not trying to kill you. I was trying to stop you hurting yourself, or anyone else.'

'Are you sure?' asked Zastra with suspicion.

'Don't you trust me?' Martek asked, looking hurt. Dobery laid a restraining hand on his shoulder.

'It's the cintara making her think that. Zastra, you know Martek would never hurt you.'

Zastra shook her head savagely, trying to clear her thoughts. She looked at the huge form of the master at arms. Of course Martek was her friend.

'I'm sorry,' she sobbed. 'I don't know what I was thinking.'

'Cintara bark reveals certain things to those without powers, but never true things,' said Dobery. 'It amplifies people's innermost fears and fools them into thinking they have uncovered some secret thoughts in the minds of others. But it is a lie.'

Martek rubbed his head. 'I guess that's why you rushed at me – look, you've torn out some of my hair. It's not as if I have much to spare these days.'

'I'm really sorry,' repeated Zastra.

'I don't know what your father will say,' said Dobery, clucking in continued disapproval.

'Oh, please don't tell anyone,' sobbed Zastra. 'Father already hates me. And everyone else would make fun of me if they knew what I'd done.' She could already picture Rastran, laughing and gloating at her disgrace. She thought she might be sick again.

Dobery and Martek exchanged looks. Martek shook his head, sighing.

'Sergeant, can we rely on your discretion?' he asked the other soldier, who had been watching everything keenly.

'Yes sir,' replied the man, an instant before sinking to the ground in a heap. Zastra gaped at the sight.

'He was lying,' said Dobery, shortly. 'I've had to take away the memory of this event and replace it with another one.' He shook his head. 'I don't like doing such things. Zastra, you see the consequences of your stupidity?'

Zastra nodded, oppressed with guilt and shame. The knowledge that her humiliation would be known only to Dobery and Martek was small consolation.

The next morning, Zastra awoke with a terribly sore head, but at least her strange black mood had lifted. After splashing some water on her face, she went to see Dobery. She was rather nervous, since he had been so angry the night before, but she couldn't bear for them to not be friends. She found him packing a small leather rucksack.

'Ah, Zastra,' he said. 'Do come in. I'm afraid I'm called away on your father's business.' He looked at her, his head cocked enquiringly. 'Perhaps that's not news to you, since you already seem to know a lot of secrets.'

Zastra stared down at her feet.

'I'm sorry about last night, Dobery,' she said. 'What I did was very wrong and stupid.'

'That we can agree on,' he said, his eyes creasing as he smiled. 'Well, well, it's in the past now, and at least you have realised the error of your behaviour.'

Zastra was relieved that he seemed back to his old self. He looked down at her with a serious expression.

'You will never be a mindweaver, Zastra. You must accept that.'

'I know,' she sighed.

Dobery turned his attention to his packing. As he folded a tunic, he continued, not looking at her directly.

'When I was young, I had a brother who was very dear to me,' he said. 'He was jealous of my mindweaving abilities so, like you, he tried cintara bark. He thought it helped him see into the minds of others, even though I tried to tell him that all it showed were falsehoods. Eventually, his belief in the visions caused him to take his own life.'

'Oh, how terrible!' said Zastra, her mouth hanging open in horror.

'Just give me your word that you'll never try it again.'

'I promise,' said Zastra, echoing his seriousness.

Dobery nodded in satisfaction and patted his bag.

'Well, looks like I've nearly finished. If only I could find my spare tobacco…'

'How long will you be gone?' Zastra asked.

'I cannot tell,' he answered, 'but I fear it will not be a short trip. You must continue your studies alone while I'm gone. In truth, there is not much more I can teach you. Practice and hard work are the main requirements now.' He looked at her with a strange look that she couldn't quite fathom and then said with great seriousness. 'My dear, you may already know something of what is happening, but let me urge you to be on your guard. There is an evil walking this land. What makes it worse is that we do not know or understand our enemy. They could be anywhere, perhaps even here in the castle. Be careful, be watchful, and above all look out for yourself. And don't go looking for danger, as you sometimes have done in the past.'

'Because danger could be anywhere!' a familiar shrill voice called from the door. Zastra spun round to see the dreaded figure of Teona. She looked a little flustered; a number of strands of hair had escaped their tight binding, framing her head in a pale orange halo. A dagger prodded into Zastra's mind, but she had instinctively raised her mental barriers and she successfully blocked the probe.

'Hah!' spat out Teona. 'Good girl.' To her immense surprise, Zastra saw the glimmer of smile break through the normally sour face of the highmaster. Zastra was momentarily speechless at the realisation that Teona was actually capable of smiling.

'Child, leave us,' ordered Teona, in a voice that did not admit argument, although it did not carry the usual sprinkling of scorn. 'I need to talk with Master Dobery before he departs.'

Zastra paused, then rushed up to Dobery and gave him the biggest hug her slight frame could muster.

'I'll miss you Dobery,' she said, suddenly realising how much she had come to rely on him, with his kind, wise words, and his constant welcoming smile. 'Be careful,' she whispered, before turning and running away with unexpected tears in her eyes.

Chapter Ten

The next morning, Zastra was halfway to Dobery's quarters before she remembered that he wouldn't be there. With a heavy heart, she changed her path and went to the nursery to see her baby brother and sister. While everyone else seemed tense and worried, the two little children were bright beacons of happy activity. Anara was already there and Zastra spent a pleasant hour with her mother and the twins. A respectful knock on the door was followed by the entry of Jannal.

'I apologise for intruding during your private time, Lady Anara,' he said. 'We have received a messenge from the Sendorans and it seems they are already on their way. They are close to Riverford and should be here within the week. With the Marl of Bractaris and his party in the main guest quarters, I need to know where I should house them.'

'The Sendorans are already in Golmeira?' asked Anara, in surprise.

'Yes, according to the Sendoran ambassador they were already on their way to seek an audience with the Grand Marl. They claim to have sent word via messenger several weeks ago, but no messenger arrived here.'

'Well,' said Anara, 'perhaps this is a good thing. The sooner we can sort out the Sendoran situation the better. I think we'd better set aside the house of Brandicant for the Sendoran party. Make sure it is fitted out in the best style. We will need to get in special supplies for the fellgryffs.'

'I've already made arrangements, my Lady. I've ordered in supplies of snellgrass and tyndalstone from Port Trestra. If you will excuse me, I must attend to the House of Brandicant. Who knows what state it will be in. I don't think it has been used for over six years.' He left with a short, well practised bow.

'What's happening?' asked Zastra.

'It seems we are to receive the Lord of Sendor and his family. You must try to treat our visitors with respect and honour. No wild behaviour please, Zastra. Promise me?'

Zastra nodded. Her ears had pricked up at the mention of the Sendorans. She had not forgotten what she and Bedrun had overheard.

'I remember learning about the Sendoran War in class,' she said, wrinkling her forehead in concentration. 'I can't remember if they are part of Golmeira or not. Why are they coming?'

'I shall have to make sure the topic is included in this week's lessons,' said Anara. 'Many years ago, before even I was born, there was a bitter war between us and the Sendorans, who wished to break away from Golmeira. Many young men and women were killed.'

'How did it end?'

'A truce. Sendor was granted independence, which included the agreement that soldiers of Sendor were no longer bound to fight for Golmeira in times of trouble. However, Sendor must pay a yearly tribute to the Grand Marl, and Golmeira retained the disputed border region, including the port of Castanton. This agreement has held thus far, but there is frequently trouble in the borders. You see, there is still a good deal of bitterness left over from the war and many of our people think we should reassert our rights, whereas many Sendorans believe the border regions belong to them. I hope that by talking with the Lord of Sendor we can try and heal some of these wounds, but it is always hard when each side holds such prejudices.'

'Why aren't they staying in the castle itself?' asked Zastra. 'That old Brandicant house is dusty and full of mice and insects. And it smells.'

Anara raised an eyebrow. 'I won't ask how you know so much about a house that is closed up and strictly out of bounds, Zastra.'

Zastra squirmed. Last summer, she and her friends had found a way into the closed up house by squeezing through a loose board. It had been a wonderful base for their secret games until the sad day that the loose board had been repaired. Anara continued.

'Since Thorlberd has the best guest apartments in the southwest tower, the Sendorans may take offence if they are given inferior accommodation. However, your uncle would not take kindly to being moved. The house of Brandicant, whilst within the castle grounds, is separate, giving the Sendorans some independence. Also they can house their fellgryffs in the stables at the back of the house.'

'Fellgryffs?' Zastra asked, eyes widening.

'The Sendorans use them as we do horses, but they are very different. They come from the mountains and are remarkably surefooted. However, they are wary of strangers, so be careful if you come across one. Especially of their horns.'

'Oh, I can't wait to see what a fellgryff looks like!' exclaimed Zastra. 'When do you think will they be here?'

'Well, we must look out for them,' replied Anara. 'Now, is it not time for school?'

Zastra hurried off just as the gong was sounding the call to lessons. She was a few minutes late and apologised to Sestra as she slid into her seat. During a lesson on botany, she told Bedrun what she had learnt about Sendor.

'Morel told me the same thing,' said Bedrun. 'Let's hope they tell us some more in the history lesson tomorrow.'

Indeed, the next day's lesson centred on the Sendoran War. Zastra hadn't realised how much control her mother had over their lessons and she briefly wondered whether this had ever happened before. She did recall a rather coincidental lesson about dangerous wood-dwelling animals the day after she and Heldrid had sneaked out of the castle and got lost in Highcastle Forest.

'Zastra, are you paying attention?' Zastra snapped out of her reverie to find Sestra looking sternly at her.

'Can you please tell the class what we've just learnt about the feeding requirements of the Sendoran fellgryff?' Sestra asked with a withering look.

Zastra racked her brains. What had Jannal said in her mother's apartments about getting in supplies for the fellgryff?

'Um, they eat sneezegrass and ticklestone?' she guessed, with a hopeful grimace. Several members of the class laughed.

'Tyndalstone, not ticklestone,' corrected the teacher, 'and snellgrass. Zastra, please try and pay attention. I shall give you extra homework after class, since you seem to have missed most of the lesson.'

Bedrun smiled sympathetically at her friend as Sestra turned her attention back to the rest of the class.

'Now, students, can anyone tell me about the Sendoran War?' she asked.

Heldrid put his hand up. 'My mother says they are vicious barbarians and we should take back the land that belongs to us,' he said.

'Quite right,' agreed Rastran. 'It is a sign of weakness that we allowed part of Golmeira to break away. They are all stupid brutes, not a mindweaver amongst them. And the tribute is a joke – barely enough tocrins to fill my hat.'

'That's only because his head is so big,' muttered Zastra to Bedrun.

'It is true there are no mindweavers in Sendor,' said Sestra, 'although some of them do have a strong resistance to the power. To use the word "barbarian" is a little unfair. They have artists and scientists as skilled as our own, although their lifestyle does tend to be more harsh and rustic than ours, due to the mountainous terrain of Sendor. The tribute is substantial and a cause of contention amongst many Sendorans.'

'Well, I think we should go there and teach them a lesson,' said Rastran, to nods of agreement around the class.

'Surely we are better to talk to them, rather than fighting?' suggested Bedrun, mildly.

'Oh, yes, let's talk,' sneered Rastran, sarcastically. 'Talking is all you girls are good at. What a stupid suggestion.'

Zastra was sorely tempted to ask Rastran whether his plan was to scowl the Sendorans into submission. Since his fighting skills were so bad, that was surely his only option. However, she swallowed the insult, remembering her promise to Anara that she would try not to fight with her cousin.

The class spent the rest of the morning learning more about the history of Golmeira and Sendor. For once, Zastra was fascinated, especially the bit about how some of the Sendorans could, like her, resist mindweaving. She awaited their visit with impatience.

Chapter Eleven

It was five long days before the Sendorans finally arrived, late in the afternoon. Zastra, watching from one of the courtyard balconies, was struck by the difference in their manner of arriving to that of her uncle and cousin. Whereas the Bractarians had arrived with great train and elegant, gleaming carriages, the Sendorans were a much smaller group; barely a dozen, and they all appeared shabby and dust-stained from the journey. Their leader was clear by his bearing and the duty paid to him, but he was dressed in similar rough clothing to the rest of the party. Two children, one about Zastra's age, the other a few years younger by the look of him, were also present. All were riding on the strangest animals she had ever set eyes on. They were the size of small horses, with unusually large hooves, and some of the grown-ups looked rather oversized for their mounts. The creatures were untidy in appearance, with matted woolly hides. Most striking of all, they had two ribbed horns, each about a foot long and pointing straight out from above their eyes. These horns ended in dangerously sharp points. The creatures were always skittering, never still, requiring a good deal of management by their riders.

Zastra was called down to meet the guests. She was introduced to Mendoraz, Lord of Sendor, a fair-haired man with several days' growth of beard across his travel-stained face. His two children were introduced as Kylen, a girl of Zastra's age, and her younger brother, Zadorax, who they called Zax. Both had inherited their father's fair hair and pale skin. They returned Zastra's greeting politely and then, at Anara's request, Zastra took them on a brief tour of the castle before taking them to their quarters in the house of Brandicant. The

Sendoran children were rather quiet and restrained as Zastra showed them the great hall and some of the more elegant rooms of state, but became more animated when she took them to the stables to see the horses.

'How large they are!' exclaimed Zax, open eyed with amazement. 'Do they bite?'

'Not usually,' smiled Zastra, and showed them how to stroke the horses' noses and feed them.

'Our fellgryffs would never allow a stranger to touch them like this,' said Kylen, patting the neck of a sturdy brown mare.

'Are they really dangerous?' asked Zastra, full of curiosity.

'Yes, if you don't treat them with proper respect,' replied Kylen. 'A fellgryff would bite your hand off, or impale you on its horns without blinking if you aren't careful. But they are the best of animals once tamed. There's no better friend you could have.'

Zax could not suppress a yawn, and with a jolt Zastra realised how tired they must be.

'I'll take you to your quarters,' she said quickly. 'It's a good old house, the house of Brandicant. Me and my friends used to sneak in and play there, until they repaired the walls. It's got the largest bath you've ever seen, with golden taps and—'

'Yes indeed!' came the unwelcome voice of Rastran from the bottom of the stables. 'Good point, cousin, our visitors could certainly do with a bath,' he said, wrinkling his nose in disgust.

'That's not what I meant!' Zastra cried, looking apologetically at the Sendoran children.

'Perhaps they'd be more comfortable here, sleeping with the animals,' Rastran continued, grinning unpleasantly.

Zax looked upset, more by the unfriendly tone than the insult, which he didn't fully understand.

'I apologise for my cousin Rastran's lack of manners,' said Zastra, embarrassed and angry in equal measure.

'Don't apologise for me, cousin.'

'Maybe you have a point,' said Kylen steadily. 'Animals are better company than some humans.' As she said this, she directed a significant look at Rastran. The Sendoran girl then turned back towards Zastra.

'We have had a long journey, so if you would show us to our quarters, we would be grateful,' she said stiffly. Zastra nodded and led the way out of the stables. Zax followed as fast as his short legs would allow.

Zastra left the Sendorans at the house of Brandicant. They had not exchanged any words with her during the short trek to the house and she was afraid that the visitors were irretrievably offended, as indeed they had every right to be.

Chapter Twelve

Lessons were suspended in honour of the Sendoran visitors. However, the warnings Dobery had impressed upon her before he left made Zastra want to concentrate even more on both her normal and her secret studies. She asked Martek for extra lessons in the fighting skills and, with a thoughtful nod, he agreed. Zastra was relieved that he seemed to have forgotten the embarrassing cintara incident. Early each morning he gave her one-to-one tuition on all aspects of fighting, including swordplay, knife throwing and hand-to-hand combat.

Towards the end of one of these lessons, they were interrupted by Kylen and Zax, who had risen early and decided to explore the castle grounds. They watched for a while and then Kylen offered to try herself against Zastra. Martek stepped back to let them fight. They had similar builds, although Kylen was slightly taller. Zastra attacked and the Sendoran weaved to one side with a rapid motion. Zastra found herself on her back, pinned to the ground and unable to move.

'Give?' asked Kylen.

'Give…' ceded Zastra, reluctantly.

'I guess it's true that Golmeirans only win battles by using their mindfogging trickery,' Kylen said, with a look of contempt.

'That's a lie!' exclaimed Zastra hotly. They faced each other again with the same result. Although she was annoyed to be beaten, Zastra insisted on trying again. She was determined to work out how Kylen was besting her. At the fifth attempt, she avoided Kylen's hold and managed to get a grip on her opponent for the first time. Kylen rolled in a manner Zastra had not expected, ending up on top of her. Zastra was forced to give way once more.

'Perhaps we should stop now?' said Kylen, not unkindly, but a fierce competitiveness had been raised in Zastra and she insisted on continuing. She was not used to being bested, especially in the fighting skills.

A good hour later, bruised and exhausted, Zastra finally succeeded in knocking her opponent off her feet. She tried to press her advantage, but Kylen was up in an instant and Zastra found herself thrown once more on her already bruised hip. She couldn't suppress a small grunt of pain and Kylen stood back.

'I'll have to stop now,' said the fair-haired girl, 'I'm exhausted.' Zastra was secretly glad, as she did not think she could have continued much longer. She suspected Kylen was being kind, but didn't really care.

'I'll have to admit defeat,' she puffed. 'You have a strange way of fighting, but it's pretty good. Do they teach you that in Sendor?'

'I've been taught different ways of fighting for as long as I can remember. Hand-to-hand and spear work are considered the most important fighting skills in our land.'

'What about archery and sword fighting?' asked Zastra, still trying to regain her breath.

'Broadsword, yes, but not until we are strong enough. We don't think much of archery. We Sendorans like to fight close, not hide in the distance.'

'I've always been taught that the archers are often the difference between winning and losing in battle. I quite like the crossbow myself. Perhaps later I can show you and Zax. Give me a chance to regain some pride.'

'Well, I suppose it's only fair,' returned Kylen. 'Is there a water barrel anywhere? I'm ready for a drink.'

Zastra led them to a nearby water store. They all drank gratefully and flopped onto the grass. All too soon, the companionable silence was broken by Rastran, who has just finished his own mindweaving lessons. He was with Mercan, a heavily built Bractarian youth.

'Well, well, consorting with the animals, cousin?' Rastran sneered.

Zastra was too tired to even bother to reply, but Zax, having merely sat and watched his sister and Zastra fighting all morning, was full of energy and faced the older boys.

'We're not animals,' he piped up boldly.

'*We're not animals*,' repeated Rastran, in a mocking, high-pitched imitation of the young boy. He and Mercan laughed unpleasantly.

'Well you smell like animals,' sniggered Mercan.

'Your mother should teach you better. You may run around unwashed in Sendor, but this is a royal court. But perhaps you don't have a mother. I didn't see one. Unless you descended from a she-fellgryff?' said Rastran.

'My mother is dead, you nasty...' cried Zax, running at the older boy. It was a complete mismatch. Rastran grabbed the young boy by the hair and dumped him unceremoniously on the ground, laughing in triumph. At this, the two girls jumped to their feet. The older boys instantly narrowed their eyes with a look that Zastra was beginning to recognise. Sure enough, she felt a touch on her mind. However, thanks to her training with Dobery, her defences were strong and she was not averted. To her surprise, she noticed Kylen was also unaffected.

'You have no power over me, cousin,' said Zastra with a warm feeling of satisfaction. Rastran blanched, clearly thrown off balance.

'Cowardly mindfoggers!' exclaimed Kylen. 'You can't trick me either.' Rastran's eyes flicked nervously from one girl to the other.

'Steady cousin,' said Rastran, backing away and licking his lips nervously. 'You know how much trouble you'll get in for fighting. Your father will probably disown you this time.'

This caused Zastra to hesitate. Rastran was right and he knew it. She could not afford to get caught fighting again. He grinned, half in relief, half in mockery. Kylen stepped forward and landed a solid punch on his nose.

'Ow!' he yelped, holding his nose, which began to bleed.

'*I*, however, won't get into trouble,' said the Sendoran girl, a fierce look on her face. 'In Sendor, it is considered a worthy thing to stand up to bullies and cowards. There'll be plenty more of that if you or your pathetic sidekick ever try and hurt my brother again.'

Her fierceness was quite intimidating and Rastran staggered backwards, pinching his bleeding nose. Mercan tugged at his arm, and they turned and headed back towards the castle. 'Y-you'll pay – you'll see!' Rastran stammered over his shoulder as they slunk away.

As the youths left, Kylen went over to her brother to see if he was hurt. As she brushed him down affectionately, he sniffled and turned away in shame for his tears.

'I'm sorry about your mother,' said Zastra, hesitantly.

'It was a few years ago now. She died of a fever. Zax was very small and he still gets upset about it,' said Kylen turning away. She stared into the distance for a while. Then she turned to Zastra.

'Why did you let him taunt you like that? Why didn't you stand up to him?'

Scorn glittered in the blue eyes of the Sendoran girl. 'I promised…' Zastra began, but stopped, unable to find the words to explain the situation in Golmeira. Indeed, she was rather confused about the whole thing herself, except for the fact that she had promised her mother she would not fight her cousin.

'You and your father are as pathetic as each other! My father says that Leodra is too weak to lead and won't make a decision.'

'How dare you talk about my father like that!' Zastra was outraged.

'Why, what are you going to do about it?' said Kylen with a look of challenge. As Zastra hesitated, Kylen spat on the ground. 'Come, Zax, we'd better go. Father will be expecting us. It seems that Golmeira is full of cowards after all.'

'I'm not a coward!' cried Zastra, stung by the accusation.

'Seems it to me,' said Kylen.

'I'm just not a Sendoran savage!' shouted Zastra, trying to find an insult to match the one Kylen had thrown at her.

'Come on, Zax,' said Kylen, contemptuously, turning her back and marching away.

Zastra watched them as they walked off. She was already regretting calling Kylen a savage, but she had never before been called a coward. Indeed, she rather prided herself on her daring. Wasn't she always willing to try anything first? Like that time in science class that the teacher asked for a volunteer to pick up the scorpion. The class had looked to Zastra, and she had not disappointed, slimy and disgusting though the insect was. She wasn't scared of Rastran, not in the least, or Kylen either, although the girl could best her in a hand fight. What was it Anara had said? "Sometimes it's braver not to fight." Zastra was starting to understand what that meant. The midday gong interrupted her thoughts and she hurried back to the castle for lunch. Her stomach was growling with hunger. She was keen to entertain Bedrun with the story of Rastran's bloody nose. She chuckled to herself as she recalled his startled expression as Kylen had hit him. She went via the castle stables, stopped briefly to make a fuss of one of her favourite horses before entering the kitchens via a back passage. Her mood was dampened by the sight of Jannal, waiting for her with a frown on his face.

'Zastra, your father wishes to see you immediately,' he said in a serious tone. Obediently, she followed Jannal to her father's offices. She was thrust in front of a row of tall figures: Leodra, Thorlberd, Mendoraz and Martek all stared down at her, not a smile among them. Also present was Rastran, holding a scrumpled bandage to his nose. She saw him peer out at her from under his dark fringe, secretly pleased about something.

'Leave us, Jannal,' her father said with barely suppressed anger. Jannal departed obediently and Zastra felt a sudden rush of concern. What could be wrong? Had her father somehow found out about the cintara incident? She shuffled nervously from one foot to the other.

'Now, Zastra,' continued Leodra. 'Rastran tells us that you assaulted him in the combat ranges and he has the wounds to prove it. I expressly told you that I do not wish to have my daughter fighting like a common peasant. It shows a lack of decorum and no respect for our honoured guests. Do you have anything to say?'

Zastra's jaw dropped in astonishment and she looked at Rastran, who avoided her gaze. His dishonesty shocked and disgusted her. She wished to defend herself from the unjust charge, but she hesitated, remembering Anara's words about the need for a peaceful agreement with Sendor. Her uncle already disliked the Sendorans – if she told the truth, Thorlberd might be so angry with Kylen that he would block any treaty. Also, despite their differences, she was beginning to like the fair-haired girl, and did not want to tell tales. She could lie, which was against all she had been taught and believed as right, or to tell the truth, which would get Kylen in trouble and probably ruin any agreement with Sendor. Neither seemed a good choice, so she said nothing.

'Well?' demanded her father, raising his voice in frustration. 'Will you not even answer me?'

Zastra swallowed, but held her silence, filled with growing dread.

Mendoraz broke in. 'It was probably just children playing about. You know how they can be. My two are always scuffling about somewhere, knocking each other on the head and whatnot. Does them good, in my opinion. Toughens them up. It might do the lad some good.' He cast a rather contemptuous look at the still snivelling Rastran.

'Do not presume to lecture the Grand Marl of Golmeira as to the appropriate behaviour for his child,' snapped Thorlberd. 'We are not savages. It does not surprise me that you do not care for such things as respect and decorum in Sendor, but here in Golmeira, I can assure you, they are prized very highly. Now, brother, how are you going to discipline this unruly child? I will not have my son and heir savagely attacked.'

'Do not worry, I shall deal with this,' said Leodra. He tugged anxiously on his beard.

'Zastra, you have disappointed me once again. This is not the first time you have been caught fighting, and it seems you do not have the courage to own up to your actions. You have run wild long enough. I regret this, but I see no other way. Martek, you have brought the rod?'

Martek nodded, grim-faced and unusually pale.

'Surely there is another way, my Lord?' he whispered quietly. 'Zastra is a good girl, and I'm sure if you let her explain…'

'She has had her chance,' snapped Leodra. 'Do your duty. Five strikes I think and don't spare her.'

'Yes, my Lord,' replied Martek, with an air of sadness. 'Perhaps we should…?' He indicated the door to the adjacent room.

'No,' said Leodra. 'She has shamed me and so she shall be shamed. She shall be punished in front of everyone.'

Zastra was distraught. Her father must hate her to treat her so. Her eye was drawn irresistibly to the thick rod of hollow wood that Martek was extracting from a black ebony case. She fought the desire to plead for mercy. At least she could show her father that she could take punishment bravely, and she was determined not to give Rastran any further satisfaction. As Martek dealt five blows to her buttocks, firmly but without malice or pleasure, she did not cry out, although tears of pain filled her eyes. When the beating was over, she looked towards her father, but he was already in close discussion with Thorlberd. That he could not bring himself to look at her hurt more than even the stinging blows of the rod. She flinched as Martek laid a hand gently on her shoulder.

'Run along now and get some lunch,' he whispered. Zastra was released. No longer hungry, she ran up to her room and threw herself down on her bed. She would not even open the door to Bedrun when her friend came looking for her.

Chapter Thirteen

The next morning, Zastra decided she couldn't stay in her room forever, and so she went down to the combat grounds. Martek was waiting for her. She was a little shy of him at first – after all, he had been the one to punish her, but he treated her with affectionate kindness and she was soon lost in the effort and concentration of swordplay exercises.

As they were finishing the lesson, Kylen and Zax came across from the house of Brandicant. Their father was deep in conference with Leodra and Thorlberd and the children had been let free for the day. Zastra eyed them hesitantly. She had not forgotten the argument of the previous day.

Kylen greeted Zastra self-consciously, as if she too was thinking of yesterday. She asked Zastra if she wanted to practice hand-to-hand fighting again. Zastra still felt sore from the previous day's punishment and had no desire to be repeatedly tossed on her aching backside. However, she didn't want to be rude and so she suggested they try archery instead, asking Martek for permission to use the crossbows and the range.

'Remember to be safe,' he said, winking at Kylen and Zax. 'You'll be in good hands. Zastra has the most natural gift with crossbow I've ever seen.'

Zax stared, open mouthed in undisguised admiration as Zastra hit the centre of the target again and again, especially when, with Zastra' s help, he had a try and realised how difficult it was. Kylen was less easily impressed, but seemed willing to try something new. She put her full effort behind the task and after a while was able to hit the biggest target with some regularity. She appeared to have forgotten her previous argument with Zastra as she concentrated on her activity.

'Not bad, for a beginner,' said Zastra.

'As long as I'm attacked by a large, circular beast, whose main strategy is to stand still, then I'll be fine,' remarked Kylen. 'Although I'm amazed at how quickly you can load these up. I'd always thought that by the time you could string the crossbow and ratchet it back, an enemy would have lopped your head off, but you can do it quick as blinking.'

'It's this lever – a special design of Martek's,' explained Zastra proudly. 'See, you can pre-load three bolts. With practice, it only takes a couple of seconds to set each of them before firing.' To demonstrate, she fired off three shots in quick succession. Kylen loaded up her bow and tried to repeat Zastra's effort. One of her bolts hit the outer rim of the intended target, but the other two sailed off to the left and embedded themselves in a nearby tree.

'Oh, that's rubbish,' she sighed.

'Don't be so hard on yourself,' said Zastra, with a grin. 'You never know when you might be attacked by evil, murderous trees. Have another try.'

However, the young Sendorans had had enough. As they were putting away the equipment, Kylen put her hand on Zastra's shoulder and said quietly, 'Father told us what happened yesterday.'

Zastra glanced up at the fair-haired girl, unsure how to respond.

'Why didn't you tell your father it was me that hit Rastran? If anyone should have been punished, it was me,' Kylen continued. 'I'm sorry you got the blame.'

'It didn't seem right to tell tales,' said Zastra. 'Anyway, I'd probably have hit him eventually if you hadn't, so don't be sorry. I'd have got into trouble sooner or later.'

'Well, thanks,' said Kylen shortly, 'although I would have taken the punishment gladly. We are taught to stand by our actions in Sendor. Why did your cousin blame you? It doesn't really make sense.'

'I think he enjoyed getting me into trouble.'

'I'd watch him, if I were you. There is something very nasty about him.'

'I'm not scared of Rastran,' said Zastra, stoutly. 'Anyway, I don't think he'll bother us again, not unless he wants another bloody nose.'

Kylen couldn't suppress a grin at this.

'Look,' she said, hesitantly. 'About what I said yesterday – the coward thing. I'm sorry, I was wrong.'

'It's all right,' Zastra replied. 'I'm sorry about what I said too – you know, about savages. I didn't mean it at all; it was a horrid thing to say. Besides, I think you Sendorans have the right idea about things. Like the way you dealt with Rastran – the look on his face was brilliant.'

They both laughed. Catching their mood, Zax sprinted around them in a tight circle, whooping and waving his arms. Kylen shook her head in disbelief as he rushed towards them and collapsed dramatically at their feet.

'We have to take our fellgryffs out for a run,' Kylen said, tilting her head to one side. 'You want to come?'

Zax sprang to his feet and laughed. 'Bad idea,' he said. 'You know what terrible riders the Golmeirans are. She'd only get hurt.'

Zastra bridled at this. 'I've been riding horses since almost before I could walk!' she exclaimed.

Kylen and Zax chuckled. 'Horses?' said Kylen. 'Those great slow lumps? A baby could ride one.'

Zastra was not to be put off. *How hard can it be*? she asked herself.

After they had taken a quick lunch, the children went to the house of Brandicant stables where the fellgryffs were housed. Up close, Zastra was even more impressed with the creatures. They were untidy and ugly looking, but an intelligence shone in their deep brown eyes. Their horns really did look deathly sharp. Kylen had a quiet word with a scruffy young groom, who came over and introduced himself as Moltas.

'Your parents know you are here?' he asked.

'No,' said Zastra, downcast. That was clearly the end of that. She couldn't see her parents allowing her to ride a fellgryff, especially her father in his current mood.

'Well,' said Moltas, looking at her disappointed expression. 'D'you accept the risks involved and agree to do as I say, without question? Your life could depend on it.'

'Yes,' said Zastra, hardly daring to believe she would be allowed to try.

'A'right then. Come outside to the paddock. Now, first of all, watch Kylen and Zax. See how they hold on with their hips and knees and use their feet to guide the fellgryff. There are no stirrups and no bridles. You must hold on to the nape of the neck, here. Balance is everything. You must *feel* the balance.'

At a nod from Moltas, the two Sendoran children sprung onto their mounts in one fluid movement. The instant the beasts felt the children land on their backs, they bucked and leapt sideways with an amazing spring, high into the air. Zastra gasped, but Kylen and Zax were not at all troubled, and the fellgryffs were quickly under control, although they still skittered around the grass paddock.

Zastra tried not to show how impressed she was. She was suddenly concerned with how her aching backside would manage the bucking gait of the fellgryff. However, it was too late to back down now without losing face. She sighed inwardly, summoning up courage as Moltas gave her instructions.

'Put this on,' said the groom, giving her a thickly-padded tunic. 'This should protect your main organs against the horns if they spear you. We are going to use one of the oldest, steadiest fellgryffs we have. Don't take it the wrong way, we always do this for beginners.'

Zastra was far from insulted. She reckoned she would need all the help she could get.

'Now, there are only a few rules, but all are important,' said Moltas with intense seriousness. 'First, you must engage the fellgryff by holding his gaze before you even try to mount. If he don't like the look o' you, then don't even bother. You must mount in one movement, not stepwise like you do on them great lumbering horses. Otherwise he'll be away afore you know it, and that'll be an end on it. Once you are on, like I say, feel the balance, hold the nape of the neck for dear life, but trust your legs, they're what'll keep you on. If he throws you, and probably he *will* throw you, try and land on your feet and get away, fast as you can. I'll have this noose round his neck. Me and Stertle here'll drag him away from you, but we can't be sure we'll be quick enough. Ready?'

Zastra swallowed, her mouth suddenly very dry. It seemed a great deal to remember all at once. Stertle, a large, strong-looking man, led a fellgryff towards them.

'Now, hold the eyes. Don't flinch,' ordered Moltas. Zastra did as he instructed. The deep brown eyes gazed back at her, fiercely, seeming to look inside her, but she returned the stare and eventually the fellgryff bobbed its head by the slightest increment. The movement was so small that Zastra thought she had imagined it. However, Moltas recognised the sign of submission.

'Good!' he exclaimed. 'Up you go!'

Zastra drew a deep breath and sprang up boldly, crashing down on the saddle. Her legs gripped the sides of the animal just in time, holding her on as the animal swung round. Then it bucked viciously, jerking her up into the air. The world spun, and as she landed the front of the saddle struck her hard in the midriff. The tunic provided some protection, but she was momentarily winded. The next twist loosened her grip, and with final flick of the animal's back legs, Zastra was thrown off, thudding to the ground. She heard a shout as she jumped to her feet and just managed to wrench her body away as the fellgryff charged at her. It passed so close that its left horn grazed her tunic.

'Run!' shrieked Zax, and she obeyed, leaping to safety over the paddock fence. She turned to see the fellgryff stamping towards her, slowed by the two men who were tugging with all their strength at the noose round its neck.

'Are you all right?' asked Kylen in concern.

'I think so,' puffed Zastra, dusting herself off. 'It all happened so fast.'

Moltas came over.

'Not too bad,' he said grudgingly. 'Most don't even get on first time, let alone hold the first leap. Do you know what you did wrong?'

Zastra thought for a moment. 'I didn't cushion the impact of the leap,' she said. 'When I came back down I hit the saddle too hard – that's what did me in.'

'That's right,' he said. 'So, do you want to try again?'

'Yes,' she said, her pride bruised. She headed towards the fellgryff, preparing to make eye contact.

'No, not that one,' said Moltas sharply. 'Once you've fallen off a fellgryff, they won't ever respect you. You'll never have a chance o' riding this one again.'

'Oh,' said Zastra, crestfallen. 'Why didn't you tell me?'

'It puts extra pressure on, so we usually don't the first time,' Moltas said. 'We do have one more old and quiet one for you to try.'

'If that was old and quiet, I don't want to know what young and frisky is,' muttered Zastra under her breath. She went over to make eye contact with the next animal as it was brought out.

This time as she leapt on the beast she felt she had a better seating and despite the violent efforts of the fellgryff to dislodge her, she managed to hang on. After what seemed like an age, the beast calmed. Zastra puffed her cheeks out with relief.

'Jump off!' commanded Moltas. Her legs buckled as she landed but she was filled with delight.

'Well done,' said the groom. Kylen came over and patted her on the back.

'Not bad for a Golmeiran,' she said.

'Yeah,' agreed Zax. 'We've had three Golmeiran ambassadors that I can remember and only one of them ever managed to ride a fellgryff. I heard she had to try about twenty before she could. They had to give her a lame one in the end.'

'Have a breather,' said Moltas, 'and then you can try and ride this one out with Kylen and Zax.'

The second mounting was almost as difficult as the first, but the fellgryff took less time to calm under Zastra's hand. The Sendorans showed her how to guide her mount. As they proceeded around the castle grounds, she had to keep all her concentration to stay seated. At irregular intervals, the fellgryff would, with no warning, buck and leap. She began to recognise the tell tale twitch that preceded these events and at last began to feel she had some control over the animal. She noted how steady her fellgryff was compared to the others, but as she dismounted at the end of the ride she was still pleased with herself, although her muscles and her aching backside were complaining bitterly.

'Could I come again, please Moltas?' she asked.

'You'd be welcome anytime,' he said, with a polite half bow, and Zastra went back to her rooms flushed with happiness.

Chapter Fourteen

Barely five hundred paces beyond the castle walls, concealed by the densely packed trees of Highcastle Forest, two men huddled over a small fire. Behind them was a tall pen, triple-lined with thick wooden posts. Inside, a large, low shadow slunk back and forth.

'It gives me the creeps,' said one of the men, glancing nervously at the enclosure. A snuffling growl made both men flinch.

'It's nothing compared to what they're breeding in Waldaria,' said the other man, rubbing his upper arms for warmth.

'Should I feed it? It sounds… hungry.'

'Here. Give it this bit o' fellgryff leg. Not too much, mind. You know our instructions.'

'Why don't they send the signal? I can't wait to be rid of it.'

'Just keep an eye on that window. Now that Mendoraz is here, it must be soon.'

They both stared towards the upper ramparts of Golmer Castle.

Chapter Fifteen

It took Zastra's sore body a few days to recover from the fellgryff riding, but then she was eager to try again. The old fellgryff became easier to manage as it learned to recognise and respect her, although the ride was never smooth and always required a good deal of concentration. Zastra enjoyed spending time with the young Sendorans. Zax was rather quiet and shy, but he had a stout heart and a playful nature. Kylen was teaching her new throws and tactics in hand-to-hand combat that she couldn't wait to try out on her friends and teachers. In return, she continued to tutor her new friends in the art of the crossbow. Kylen in particular was very quick to learn. Like Zastra, she had a natural aptitude for physical challenges. Best of all, they managed to avoid seeing Rastran the whole time.

A fortnight after the arrival of the Sendorans, Zastra went down to the combat grounds a little later than usual. At the end of a long and energetic session with Martek, Kylen and Zax had not yet appeared, so she sat in the shade of a tree and waited. The sun was rising to its zenith and it became uncomfortably hot. Bored, she began to practice her mind blocking tricks. She wasn't sure how much time had passed before she heard a snap of a small twig and sensed rather than saw a small shadow behind her. She sprung up, whirling around to find Zax tiptoeing towards her in an attempt to surprise her. Kylen was not far behind.

'You'll have to be quieter than that, Zax,' Zastra said, amused by the young boy's crestfallen expression.

'I told him he wouldn't be able to catch you out,' said Kylen. 'He insisted on trying, but a thunderstorm makes less of a racket. We can never take him hunting – he scares everything away.'

'I do not,' the boy protested stoutly.

'Well Zax,' said Zastra, 'it's a bit hot for hand-to-hand but how about some archery? I asked Martek to move the targets back ten paces since you were getting so good. We could see if you can hit the swinging target this time.'

'Oh, yes, let's!' Zax raced towards the shooting range in excitement.

Kylen and Zastra followed him and they all kitted up. Zastra went over to set the swinging target in motion. As she turned to return to the others, she heard a deep, terrifying snarl. A dark movement flickered in the corner of her eye. Swivelling her head, she made out the crouching form of a huge caralyx, creeping stealthily out of the cover of a small mess of shrubs. It headed towards Kylen and Zax, whose fair hair flashed like two golden domes in the sunlight. They too had seen the creature, and stood transfixed. For a brief instant, Zastra thought that it was a mindweaver trick, but the tell-tale pressing on her mind was absent and no one else was in sight. She realised in horror that it was all too real. Everything suddenly seemed impossibly clear and sharp. The dark-skinned caralyx, barely sixty paces away, bared its teeth. There was no cover, save a tree, a seeming infinite distance away – a cool shadow of possible sanctuary in the sun-baked grounds. Zastra's breath caught as some instinct told her the caralyx was about to launch itself towards them. She sprinted towards Kylen and Zax, yelling and gesticulating frantically at the same time.

'The tree! There! Behind you!' she yelled, and they had turned and started running in a flurry of arms and pumping legs as she overtook them. She sensed rather than saw a dark blur moving to intercept them on their left flank, keeping her focus on the the tree. Air rasped against her throat and fear gave her speed she never knew she had. She found herself up on the first branch of the tree next to Kylen without really understanding how they got there. They turned to see Zax's small white hand slip from the branch that was too high for his little hand to grasp properly. The young boy fell to the floor, the beast almost upon him.

Zastra acted instantly, instinctively jumping down in front of Zax.

Somehow her crossbow found its way from the harness on her back onto her shoulder. She pointed it forwards, flicked the lever to set the bolt with a fluid movement and fired. There was almost no need to aim, the hot, wet maw of the beast was impossible to miss as it sprang towards her throat. She thought she saw the bolt land at the back of its throat, but the caralyx did not pause, rearing up with a terrible snarl in a blur of movement. A wet, heavy impact knocked her over and pinned her to the ground. She was overcome with horror, expecting any moment to feel sharp teeth biting into her. Wriggling and writhing in panic, she struggled to release herself, backing away from the beast on quaking legs. The caralyx lay on the ground, blood foaming from its mouth. It twitched sickeningly and then was still. Zastra sank down on one knee, trembling uncontrollably, her legs unable to hold her up. She became aware that Kylen, ashen-faced, was behind her, shielding her terrified brother with her body and holding a small twig defiantly in front of her. Zastra nodded towards the pathetically thin twig.

'Fat… lot …of use… that… would be,' she puffed. A slightly hysterical laughter caught them both as the relief of their escape hit them.

They became aware of people rushing down from the guardhouse. Moltas, the Sendoran groom, was first to reach them, breathless in his haste.

'Are you all right?' he asked, his voice choked with worry. He bent over Zax who was still curled in a tight ball, checking him over with his hands for injuries as caressingly as if he were tending one of his beloved fellgryffs.

'Master Zadorax?' he implored. 'Please, say something.'

'I think we are unhurt,' Kylen said, as, to everyone's relief, Zax slowly unfurled himself. 'Thanks to Zastra.'

Moltas went over to the felled caralyx and nudged it with his foot.

'Yep, it's surely dead. Bolt straight through the neck. It must have died pretty much straight away, lucky for you. I've never seen such a large'un.'

'Yes, lucky indeed!' exclaimed one of the castle guards. 'I saw the creature slink out of the bushes there and make for the young'uns. I thought that they were lost for sure. I've never heard of a caralyx this far south of the Helgarths.'

'My Lord Mendoraz'll want to know how his children were put in such danger,' said Moltas.

'Well, there's nowhere in the castle one could live without being discovered,' retorted the guard. 'It must have been smuggled in and there's only one group of people who've recently come here from the mountains.'

'If you're saying that we'd bring a savage beast to unleash on our own, then you really should think again,' said Moltas, giving the guard a hard stare.

By this time a large group had gathered, attracted by the excitement. A lieutenant took charge.

'Everyone please get back inside the castle,' she ordered firmly. 'We need to ascertain that there are not more caralyx in the grounds.'

The thought there might be other such beasts on the loose caused a collective flutter of dread and there were few protests as the crowd was herded to the safety of the castle.

The news of the incident had spread with startling rapidity and Zastra, Kylen and Zax were greeted by their concerned parents at the north door. Zastra rushed into the warm embrace of Anara while Mendoraz grasped both his children together, one strong arm about each. They buried their heads against his chest.

'Will someone explain what happened?' demanded Mendoraz. Moltas related the tale, and Zastra felt her mother shudder as he reached the part where the caralyx had sprung towards the children.

At the end of the tale, Mendoraz turned first towards Zastra. Crouching down he took her hand in his.

'I offer you my deepest thanks, Zastra, for the lives of my children,' he said. 'Sendor and my heart owe you the highest debt of gratitude.'

Zastra could only respond with a small nod of acknowledgement.

Mendoraz then rose and pointed at Leodra. 'I hold you responsible for the safety of my family in your home and I demand to know how this can have happened,' he said, his voice shaking with passion.

'Believe me, I will have this fully investigated,' replied Leodra, his face equally thunderous. 'Someone will answer for this outrage.' He beckoned Martek and the lieutenant of the guards toward him and engaged them in earnest conversation. Zastra had never seen him so pale and grim. Anara took Zastra by the hand.

'Come, my dearest,' she said gently, 'let us get you cleaned up.' Zastra looked down at her clothes and realised in shock that they were soaked with the dark red blood of the caralyx. She shuddered and allowed herself to be led away. Her mother tended to her affectionately, bathing her and sending away callers who came to enquire after her. Zastra was grateful, since the shock of the incident was finally beginning to tell and she felt unable to face anyone other than her mother. She hoped that her father might come and see how she was, but the long afternoon passed into evening and he never came.

Chapter Sixteen

The following day, Zastra went down to the combat ranges in search of Martek. Unusually, there was no sign of the master at arms. She waited for a while, but when he still did not appear, she went to look for Kylen and Zax at the house of Brandicant. The house was deserted and when she went to the stables they too were empty. What in the stars was going on? Astounded, she rushed back to the castle to try and find out. The courtyard was full of skittering fellgryffs, mounted with Sendorans in travel dress. Zastra recognised her own mount, loaded up with baggage. She saw Zax and Kylen astride their fellgryffs and raced over to them.

'What's going on?' she cried. 'Surely you are not leaving?'

'We must,' said Kylen stonily.

Zastra was stung, both by the news and by Kylen's manner.

'Weren't you even going to say goodbye?'

Kylen relented and dismounted. 'I'm sorry, Zastra,' she whispered, looking furtively over her shoulder. 'But my father insisted we leave straight away. We've been packing all morning. We wanted to come over to the ranges to say goodbye, really we did, but—'

'Kylen!' barked Mendoraz, urging his twitching fellgryff towards them.

'Come, we must leave now,' he said, gesturing to his daughter to get back on her mount. He did not acknowledge Zastra's presence.

'Yes Father,' she replied obediently, turning to re-mount.

'Wait!' exclaimed Zastra. She pulled her crossbow from her shoulder harness, which in her hurry she had carried up from the range, and presented it to Kylen. It was her favourite bow, a real beauty, handcrafted from the finest blackwood and inlaid in gold with the eagle crest of Leodra's house.

'In case you meet any more caralyx on your journey,' she said solemnly. 'I wouldn't want to you to try and fight them off with a twig again.'

Kylen took the gift silently and then, after giving Zastra a quick hug, leapt onto her mount and followed the rest of the Sendorans. As she passed through the gate, Kylen glanced back at Zastra and raised her hand in a lonely gesture of farewell. A strange, heavy silence filled the empty courtyard.

Zastra turned away, bemused. It had all occurred so swiftly. She went in search of someone, anyone who might be able to explain what had just happened. The first person she bumped into was Jannal.

'What's going on, Jannal?' she asked. 'Why have the Sendorans gone?'

'I don't know, Zastra,' he replied, shrugging his rounded shoulders.

She decided to go to her father's offices with some trepidation. He did not like being disturbed during hours of business, but she had to know what was happening. She found his door open, the office a scene of bustling activity. Her father and uncle were at the centre of it all, soldiers and servants coming and going with extreme haste.

'What is it, Zastra?' asked Leodra, looking up with obvious impatience.

'Why have the Sendorans left?' she asked.

'I told them to leave. Be glad they are gone. Their duplicity disgusts me.'

'What do you mean?'

'We found clear, conclusive proof that they were behind yesterday's events with the caralyx. Smuggling a dangerous animal into the castle grounds and putting my family at risk. I will not stand for it.'

'I don't understand,' protested Zastra in bemusement. 'Why would they do something like that?'

'The proof was incontrovertible,' Thorlberd interjected. 'An autopsy showed that the caralyx had been fed on fellgryff flesh and we found evidence that it had been housed in the Brandicant stables. They should be thankful your father didn't throw them in the dungeons. That would have been my choice.'

'I don't believe it!' exclaimed Zastra. 'I've never seen it, and I've been in those stables loads of times. It attacked Kylen and Zax – it doesn't make sense.'

'Enough, Zastra,' said her father. 'You are too young to understand. They wished to hurt me by attacking my family, but a caralyx is not a tame animal and no doubt they lost control. Now, Thorlberd, the matter of strengthening the Sendoran border. Perhaps I could send the troops from the Helgarths? Although they were due to replace the soldiers that were sent as their relief. Without them, the castle guard would be weakened.'

'I could order a company of the Bractarian guards to come to defend Golmer,' replied Thorlberd, thoughtfully. 'They are good troops all, and loyal.'

'But would that not leave Bractaris under strength?'

'Your safety and the security of Golmer Castle is paramount at the present time. We must address the Sendor issue. To think that Mendoraz had the audacity to say he would withdraw the tribute. I worry for our citizens in the borders. None are safe in the face of such treachery.'

They seemed to have forgotten that Zastra was still present. Frustrated, she tried once more to interject.

'Father, please…'

'Zastra? What, are you still here? No more of this. Leave me in peace. I have work to do.'

Zastra returned to the courtyard. She absolutely refused to believe that the Sendorans could have hidden a caralyx in the stables. As for feeding it fellgryff, she knew enough of the close relationship between man and beast to know that they would never contemplate using their meat as feed. But it was clear her father wasn't going to listen. Her thoughts were interrupted by Bedrun, who had come looking for her.

'Zastra, are you all right? I heard about the caralyx. Did you really shoot it? I would have been so scared.'

Zastra nodded, tight lipped. Bedrun seemed to understand that Zastra did not wish to talk about the incident, and switched to another subject.

'Can you believe the Sendorans, though? What a nerve. I was outside the great hall when your father sent them away. He's quite frightening when he's angry, isn't he? But Mendoraz wasn't afraid of him and said straight out that he would not have his groom accused falsely and he certainly would not have his word questioned. But everyone could see that Moltas was lying – he had a huge scratch on his arm that could only have come from a caralyx. They refused to let the mindweavers investigate him. Mendoraz said he wouldn't allow any of his men to suffer such an indignity. That shows their guilt, doesn't it? They knew the mindweavers would see the truth. That's when your father sent them away.'

'Oh, it's all wrong!' exclaimed Zastra, unable to listen to any more. 'Moltas wouldn't do anything to hurt Kylen and Zax.'

'But everyone says he did.'

'Everyone is wrong,' protested Zastra.

'How do you know?' asked Bedrun. Zastra told her about the fellgryffs, and how the Sendorans cared too much for them to ever use their flesh as food.

'Then who did bring the caralyx in?' asked Bedrun wide-eyed. 'It can't have got in by accident.'

Zastra was glad that her friend believed her. As the day wore on, she realised that they were the only ones who did not believe that the Sendorans were behind the caralyx incident. She grew more and more frustrated, as people smiled knowingly and shook their heads whenever she tried to argue the case. Eventually Bedrun persuaded her to go and play with Kastara and Findar. They at least did not disagree with her, so long as she amused them with by swinging them up and down and pulling faces. As usual, playing with the babies brightened Zastra's mood. However, she could not stop wondering about the caralyx and where it had come from. If not the Sendorans, then who was responsible?

Chapter Seventeen

A month passed and things at the castle were almost back to normal. Much to her disappointment, Zastra had been unable to solve the mystery of the caralyx. Leodra had become ever more frustrated with her as she continued to insist that he was wrong about the Sendorans and eventually forbade her from mentioning the subject again.

Thorlberd's Bractarian troops had arrived to supplement the depleted castle guard and everyone felt safer with them patrolling the grounds. No longer would wild animals be free to attack children within the walls of Golmer Castle. Zastra's lessons had resumed and she continued working hard at all her studies. She missed the Sendorans, especially Kylen. She and Bedrun spent a good deal of time worrying about Morel and Dobery and their mission to Waldaria. Very little news made its way back to the castle. Bodel, Bedrun's other mother, had received a note from Morel a week ago, saying simply that they were well and were soon to enter the forest of Waldaria. She wrote that the soldiers were complaining about the food rations and Dobery was missing his tobacco, which unfortunately had been washed away as they had forded the Great River. Other than that, they had heard nothing.

When they weren't studying, the girls spent much of their time looking after Kastara and Findar. The twins were growing fast and developing distinctive personalities. Kastara was feisty and temperamental, whereas her brother was more mellow and placid. They were starting to recognise their big sister, reaching out to her whenever she came to the nursery. One day, Sestra having been called away on some business, Zastra and Bedrun were released from lessons a little earlier than usual. As Zastra burst through the doors to the nursery, eagerly anticipating trying to get Kastara to say her name, she was startled to find her uncle leaning into the cot. He jumped back as she entered.

'Ah, Zastra,' he said, 'thank the stars you are here. I just popped into to see my little niece and nephew, but I'm afraid I've upset them.'

Kastara was howling, and Findar was just beginning to join in. Together they made a truly awful cacophony. Thorlberd shook his head forlornly.

'Alas, I don't have the knack with the little ones. Is it my beard, do you think, that scares them?'

He looked truly embarrassed, something Zastra had never seen in all the weeks her uncle had been at the castle. He backed away with an apologetic grimace, bumping into Anara, who just at the moment was rushing into the room in response to the cries. They stepped away from each other in confusion.

'I beg forgiveness, dearest Anara,' said Thorlberd, first to recover his composure. He enclosed Anara's small hand in his large one and bowed in respectful apology. 'Not only do I appear to have frightened the little ones, now I nearly knock you off your feet.'

Anara gave a faint smile.

'No matter,' she murmured.

'I had an urge to see the twins,' Thorlberd explained. 'As you know, I'm expecting my own little one soon, and I was just thinking about him. Or her, I suppose. I won't be present when he or she is born, a thought which makes me rather sad. I thought a visit to the twins might raise my spirits. Family is so very important, Anara, is it not?'

'Yes, indeed,' said Anara. 'We are most grateful that you are part of our family, Thorlberd.'

'I have the continued success of my family very much at heart,' said Thorlberd, with a bob of his head.

'I'm glad to hear you say so,' said Anara, pulling her hand away and hurrying over to the cot. She picked up Kastara. Zastra had already taken up a screaming Findar and was smothering him in kisses.

'What happened? Why are they crying?' asked Anara anxiously.

'It was entirely my fault,' said Thorlberd. 'I came in and they started to cry and I was unable to calm them. That nurse of yours was nowhere to be seen, but what do you expect from someone who's half Sendoran?'

'Half Sendoran?' said Anara

'Didn't you know? My dear Anara, you must be more careful. I tried to comfort the little ones, but they just cried the louder.' As he spoke, the twins cried even harder.

'Just like that,' said Thorlberd with a grimace.

'Perhaps if he wasn't so loud,' whispered Bedrun to Zastra.

'I should go,' said Thorlberd. Anara did not disagree and so he bowed once more and departed.

'I'm sure he didn't mean to frighten them,' said Bedrun, 'but that booming voice of his even frightens me.'

'Hush, Findar, dearest, hush,' said Zastra.

'Where is that nurse?' said Anara. 'He should have been here.'

'I'm not sure who was more scared,' said Zastra, shaking her head as she recalled the embarrassment on Thorlberd's face, 'the twins, or Uncle once they started screaming.'

'Zastra, what is that on Findar's arm?' asked Anara, sharply.

Zastra looked down. A pink smudge was visible on her brother's pale arm.

'It's probably some pani-juice. They were throwing it around yesterday, making a terrible mess.' She licked her thumb and washed away the smudge. Findar restarted his bellowing.

'Oh, I think he's bleeding!' Zastra exclaimed. 'It's only a tiny scratch, but still… Perhaps there's a splinter in the cot?'

They checked the playpen but found nothing sharp enough to cause such an injury.

'Must have been an insect bite,' suggested Bedrun. 'That must have been what started them crying. Your poor uncle, it wasn't his fault after all.'

'Mother, are you all right?' said Zastra, looking at her mother's pale face.

'Yes, my dear,' replied Anara. 'Although I have a headache and all this noise hasn't helped. I still have so much to do, what with this party to organise. Would you girls mind staying here while I fetch the nurse?'

'What party?' asked Zastra, but Anara had already gone.

Chapter Eighteen

The party was in honor of Rastran's sixteenth birthday, a significant landmark in Golmeira. Zastra had no desire to celebrate with her cousin but consoled herself with the thought that at least there would be entertainment, music and dancing. If she was very lucky, she wouldn't actually have to talk to Rastran since he would no doubt be too busy being the centre of attention.

When the day of the party arrived, Zastra was torn between amusement and disgust as her cousin entered the room, smoothing his hair back and glancing complacently at his reflection in the window. He had clearly made a lot of effort with his appearance and was condescendingly accepting the good wishes and gifts bestowed upon him. The blatant fawning of some of the Bractarians amazed Zastra. Some were acting as though he were a Warrior of Golmeira risen from the dead. They had obviously never seen his terrible performances at the combat ranges. She went in search of Bedrun, resolving to forget about her cousin and enjoy the evening.

The great hall was filled with music and laughter. A famous orator had been hired. Zastra listened in rapt attention as he expertly declaimed the legend of Fostran the First, one of the most famous of all the Warriors of Golmeira. The tale, a favorite of Zastra's, told how Fostran, out hunting in the mountain mists, had become separated from his guards. A large group of savage Kyrginites emerged from the gloom, brandishing scythes, pitchforks and axes. Frostan was unarmed but, undaunted, used his prodigious power and strength to disarm each savage, breaking their weapons as if they were no more than twigs. The tale was greeted with enthusiastic applause. Zastra wondered if the new hand-to-hand fighting tricks she had learnt from Kylen would allow her to defeat a band of fierce Kyrgs some day. She wasn't paying attention to the beginning of the next oration and only slowly begane to realise that it was based on her adventure with the caralyx. She was more than a little embarrassed, especially since she was cast in a more heroic light than she felt was right. The verses certainly didn't reflect her terror. Also, there was no mention of Kylen, who had been willing to protect her brother practically unarmed, an act much braver than her own. Indeed, the Sendorans were cast as villains. Fortunately, the poem was short. Zastra forced a weak smile as the orator bowed in her direction. Her only consolation was Rastran's obvious annoyance at the poem. She looked around to see if her father had been listening, but saw that he was deep in conversation with Martek and Teona. Of course he was too busy to pay attention to silly stories. Zastra gave up expecting her father's notice or approval.

The food was served. To Zastra's delight, Anara allowed her and Bedrun to sit at the Grand Marl's table. All around the great hall spirits were high. Thorlberd had arranged for some special wine from his own cellars to be distributed and it was proving extremely popular. He even let Zastra and Bedrun try some of the deep red liquid, which they felt to be great honour, although both agreed it tasted horrid. Rastran smirked at them, trying to look superior as he downed a whole glass, his attempt at sophistication somewhat spoilt by the broad red-wine moustache above his mouth.

'Some decent wine at last,' he said with a burp. He attempted to refill his glass, but only a few drops dripped out of the upturned bottle, despite vigorous shaking. 'How strange. It appears to be all gone.'

'I think you've had quite enough, Rastran, dear,' said Anara gently.

'Yes, indeed,' agreed Thorlberd, frowning at his son.

'I can hold my drunk, um drink,' Rastran protested. 'And what's more, Auntie…'

'That's enough, Rastran,' snapped his father. 'Unless you want me to send you to bed.'

Zastra couldn't help grinning at the look on Rastran's face at the idea of being banished from his own party.

'Are you enjoying yourselves, young ladies?' asked Thorlberd, turning his attention to Bedrun and Zastra.

'Mm-mmm,' said Bedrun, her mouth full of fish pie. 'The food is yummy, and the orator was wunnful, 'specially the story about Zastra'nd the caralyx.'

'Yes,' said Thorlberd, banging the table with the flat of his hand. 'That was well done indeed, Zastra.'

'Humph,' grunted Rastran. 'I suspect the poet had been at the wine early to concoct such rubbish. Father, why don't you tell us about the *real* Warriors of Golmeira? Like Colinar the Courageous and the beast of the Helgarths? He wouldn't even have blinked at a little caralyx.'

'Oh, please do, Uncle,' implored Zastra. She always liked to hear stories of the warriors. Bedrun added her pleas. Thorlberd cleared his throat theatrically.

'The beast of the Helgarths was a creature so grotesque that they say even the clouds turned away in revulsion. A giant monster, with jaws strong enough to crack a man's spine, borne on two legs like a man, but with a back so hunched that its front paws scraped the ground. One brutal winter, it descended from the highest peaks of the Helgarth Mountains to attack the villages, taking the young and vulnerable and leaving death and sorrow in its wake. Those that saw it swore they had never seen such a fearful sight.'

'Except that time your best shirt was ruined the night before *your* sixteenth birthday party,' said Leodra, clapping his brother across his broad back. 'You scared the laundry boy so much that he ran away!'

'You tread dangerous ground, brother, bringing up events from our childhood, for I shall be forced to retaliate.'

'I have nothing to hide,' said Leodra with a confident grin.

'How about the time you forced the whole of the castle guard to spend three days searching for Frosty?'

'Who was Frosty?' Zastra asked.

Leodra's grin had disappeared. 'My pet mouse. I was only five and Thorlberd wasn't even old enough to remember.'

'Oh, but tales were told of the great mouse hunt of Golmer Castle for years.'

'What happened?' asked Zastra, unable to believe that her father had ever been a child, let alone one with a pet mouse.

'Alas, Frosty was never found,' replied Thorlberd. 'Your father was inconsolable.'

'Again, I'd like to remind everyone that I was only five years old,' interjected Leodra. 'Besides, I always suspected Mother had something to do with disappearance. She hated little Frosty from the beginning.'

'I'm sure the Lady Migara would have done no such thing,' said Anara.

'You didn't know my mother,' said Leodra darkly.

'Mother was not fond of pets, it's true, but you are unfair to accuse her of such things. You always thought the worst of her.'

'You were always the favourite son, weren't you?'

Anara rested her hand gently on Leodra's arm.

'Thorlberd, dear, you were telling us about the beast of the Helgarths?' she said, with an encouraging smile.

'Yes indeed,' he said, raising his glass to her. 'Colinar, Marl of Lyria, vowed not to rest until he had rid Golmeira of the beast. Day after day, week after week, he searched the length and breadth of the frozen Helgarths. Many of his guards fell to their death, unsighted by dreadful blizzards, or else succumbed to frostbite. Yet Colinar refused to give in. Alas, the beast was as cunning as it was ferocious, and they could never catch up with it.'

'He failed?' said Zastra. 'Why then is he a Warrior of Golmeira?'

'Patience,' said Anara.

Thorlberd continued. 'The next winter, Colinar vowed to continue the hunt but his guards refused to follow. Only Colinar's groom, brave Bokira, agreed to accompany him. Almost mad with frustration, Colinar strode up into the mountains and called out to the beast. To his astonishment, the beast answered the challenge, charging down towards him. It towered over the man; its paws alone were as wide as this table. Without warning it reached for Coliniar, bringing its paws together like this!'

Thorlberd clapped his hands together sharply, squashing a ripe pani-fruit between his large palms. Red juice spurted across the table and Bedrun almost choked on her pie.

'All that saved Colinar was an instinct that made him see the blow before it was thrown. He ducked out of the way and thrust his sword upwards, into the belly of the monster. As his blow struck home, Colinar felt a sharp pain in the pit of his own stomach, yet he himself was not injured. He had no time to wonder at this before he had another vision of a huge paw reaching for him. The image was instantly followed by the action, but Colinar, forewarned, was able to escape the grasping claws. They battled long into the night. Every time Colinar stabbed the monster, he felt its pain. In the end the beast bled to death from its wounds.'

'How did Colinar know what the beast was going to do?' asked Zastra.

'He had a power that no one had known existed; he could communicate with animals. Colinar not only conquered the beast of the Helgarths, but he also discovered a new mindweaving ability.'

'Mindweavers can talk to animals?' Bedrun said in amazement.

'Not all. It is quite rare and even those with the natural skill have to be thoroughly trained to be really adept,' explained Thorlberd.

'Can you do it, Uncle?'

'I'm afraid I have as little ability to communicate with animals as I do with your brother and sister, Zastra. And you know how unsuccessful that was.'

After the food was cleared away, an acrobatic show began. It was the same troupe that had performed months before to celebrate the arrival of Thorlberd and the grand assembly. Zastra and Bedrun were captivated, clapping and whooping in appreciation along with the rest of the audience.

At the end of the show Bedrun whispered to Zastra. 'I'd love to meet him – the young, good-looking one. Do you think we could?'

'Why not?' said Zastra. 'Let's go and tell them how good we thought they were.'

The two girls followed the acrobats out of the hall. It was pleasant to exchange the muggy heat of the hall for the cool air of the corridor. The troupe went to the kitchens, where they were treated to a meal as a reward for their performance. The young acrobat, whose name was Jofie, was very polite, although he seemed nervous and spoke hesitantly in endearing contrast with his confident performance. He blushed as his fellow acrobats made fun of him in a friendly manner for catching the eye of the "young princesses". Zastra asked the cooks to serve the acrobats the best food and wine, which was met with a loud cheer.

The girls made their way back towards the great hall, Bedrun blushing as Zastra teased her about Jofie. The sound of music and rhythmic clapping indicated that the dancing had started and they quickened their pace, keen to join in. At the entrance to the hall their path was blocked by Rastran and Mercan, half seated, half lying on the floor.

'Ah cousin,' said Rastran, 'where have you and your little brat of a friend been sneaking off to? It's *very* rude to leave my party. Very rude.'

'Oh, I *am* sorry,' said Zastra. 'We ran out of two-faced compliments to fill your head with, so we didn't think we were needed.'

'Oy!' said Mercan, 'Are you calling us big-headed?'

'Not you, Mercan. I don't think you have enough room in your head to hold even one intelligent idea.'

'Eh?' said Mercan, confused.

'You chil-ren should show shome respect,' Rastran slurred. 'One day, I shall be a Warrior of Golmeira. Rastran the Conqueror, I shall be called.'

'Rastran the Conked-out, you mean.' said Zastra. 'You can't even stand up.'

'Can too,' Rastran argued, levering himself upwards. However, his thin legs seemed to lack strength and he slid back down the wall like a broken puppet.

'Behold!' declaimed Zastra, with an extravagant bow. 'All hail, Rastran… the Ridiculous.'

Bedrun giggled.

'Come on, Bedrun,' said Zastra. 'Let's go and join the dancing.'

'Make the most of it,' Rastran said ominously. Something in his tone made Zastra pause.

'What do you mean?'

'Oh, you'll find out,' her cousin sniggered. He and Mercan fell about laughing. Zastra glared at them until Bedrun dragged her away to dance. They passed the rest of the evening having splendid fun, forgetting the sniggering boys and their ugly threats as they danced and sang to the music. The dancing was followed by a display of fire-fountains: impressive plumes of multi-coloured sparks leapt and glittered brightly against the night sky, bringing much applause and cheering. Eventually, although long before they wanted to, Anara came to the girls and sent them off to bed. Bedrun was to stay with Zastra, since Bodel was away, tending to her sick sister in Highcastle village. As they undressed and went to bed, they both agreed that it had been a fine party, even if it had been in Rastran's honour.

Chapter Nineteen

Zastra lay awake for some time, her head still full of the excitement of the party. She was only on the edge of sleep when something roused her. A figure loomed in the doorway of her chamber. Zastra jumped up, prepared to fend off mindweaving and all other intrusions. She was totally taken aback as a shaft of moonlight revealed the distinctive silhouette of Teona.

'Good, Zastra, you are awake,' Teona said, quietly but firmly. 'You must come now. Put on some shoes and a coat – no – just put them over your nightclothes. There's no time.'

Zastra did as she was told unthinkingly. After all, Teona was someone you obeyed without question.

'What about Bedrun?' she asked, but as they looked over they saw that the other bed was empty.

'Where is she?'

'I don't know child, and I'm afraid we haven't time to find out. Come. Quickly!'

The highmaster took her by the hand and led her out of her room and along the balcony, passing above the now empty great hall on their right.

'What's happening?' asked Zastra in a whisper.

'We are betrayed. Hush now, they must not hear us.'

As they glided towards the main stairs, Zastra became aware of noises: the clash of metal on metal, screams and shouts, the sounds growing louder as they approached the courtyard. All of a sudden a high-pitched shriek shattered the night. It was a sound like nothing Zastra had ever heard or imagined, reaching within her and wrenching at her insides. It was impossible to tell where it came from. A seething mass of dark bodies filled the entire width of the balcony ahead of them and blocked their way. One of the them carried a torch and in its glow Zastra saw that he was wearing the uniform of a Bractarian soldier. Teona hesitated.

'We must get to your father's offices,' she whispered urgently, as the group of Bractarian soldiers crept towards them. A noise behind them made them turn – another torch and more dark figures emerged from the royal tower and headed in their direction. They were trapped.

Zastra pulled at Teona's arm, leading her down a thin corridor and in to the narrow passages of the outer liden. It was dark. Thin slivers of moonlight slanting through the slitted windows provided the only light. Even in the dark, Zastra knew these passages well. She tugged at Teona's sleeve to guide her. Feeling her way against the walls, cold and rough against her fingertips, she found a familiar set of stone steps and then followed a narrow passageway. They were forced to ascend another set of steps to avoid a group of figures who marched beneath them, oblivious to their presence. Zastra brought them out of the liden on part of the second floor balcony that overlooked the courtyard.

Teona resumed the lead and guided Zastra towards the nearest flight of steps. Zastra looked around wildly. The courtyard was packed with shadowy figures, fighting. Men and women in the uniform of Bractaris swarmed over Leodra's soldiers, red shirts heavily outnumbered by black. A heavy gust of air buffeted against the top of Zastra's head. Looking up, she saw something that made her gasp in horror. A huge winged beast, a dark shadow against the stars and the twin moons, glided across the sky. It dived past them, down into the courtyard and the light of torches revealed a large, sleek face, its smoothness interrupted only by two stumpy horns above glinting eyes. The creature's mouth was wide and flat, packed with rows of jagged teeth, and its thin, sinewy body was covered in shiny brown scales and held aloft by great membranous wings. Even as Zastra watched, the mouth wrenched open to release the terrible cry that she had heard in the corridor, now much louder. It was a metallic shriek of mad fury and almost shattered her ears. There were two – no – three of the beasts, circling above the courtyard. She noticed each carried a rider on its back. As Teona pulled Zastra along, one of the creatures swooped down, shrieking with insane rage. It reached out a pair of three-fingered hands, each massive finger tipped with two claws, and picked up two guards from the turret of the northwest tower. Zastra watched in horror as the beast lifted the guards high in the air and then let them go. The soldiers fell, arms whirling frantically. Teona yanked Zastra harshly behind her to shield her from the terrible sight.

'What's happening?' Zastra cried in bewilderment.

'Thorlberd's guards turned on our own men and women, along with numerous mindweavers they had hidden in their party. They have unleashed these unnatural creatures upon us. Come, we must find your father.'

As they stumbled down the main stairs, their way was blocked by two tall figures, cloaked in black.

'Defend your mind, Zastra,' instructed Teona. Zastra felt a weight on her mind, heavier than any she had yet experienced. She struggled to repel what felt like cold, intruding fingers. Teona flicked her wrist and the two figures were lifted off their feet and thrown over the stone balustrade. The heaviness on Zastra's mind was instantly lifted. She looked at Teona in awe, but the highmaster did not pause, dragging Zastra down the stairs. They dodged their way through the melee. Most of the dark figures failed to notice them and any that tried to stop them were washed away as if by an invisible wave. Glancing up at Teona, Zastra could see the immense effort behind these events. She asked no more questions, not wanting to disturb the mindweaver's concentration. At last they reached her father's office. There they found Leodra holding the sleeping twins in his arms, his face ashen.

'Zastra, thank the stars you are safe.'

'Father!' She rushed over to try and embrace him, but with the twins in the way, she couldn't quite reach around him.

'Did you find Martek?' Leodra asked Teona, who shook her head grimly. 'My Lord, they attacked the guard room first. They didn't have a chance. Many of our guards were still recovering from the drinking – they certainly set us up nicely.'

Zastra gasped in shock. She could not believe that Martek, that indestructible tower of strength, was dead.

'Zastra,' her father looked at her with utmost solemnity, 'there is little time. You must be strong for me. Tonight, you must become a Warrior of Golmeira.'

Zastra swallowed, her mouth as dry as ashes.

'Here, take the twins. You must escape the castle immediately. There's a shoulder harness for Findar.'

He placed Findar on her back, so she carried him like a rucksack.

'You will have to take Kastara in your arms.'

'But I can't leave you. I can fight, I know how.'

'I don't doubt your courage, Zastra. But it is too late now for fighting. We are betrayed and defeated. Retreat is the only option left. Those awful creatures are unstoppable. Oh, Thorlberd, what have you done?' His anguish was painful to see. 'Zastra, what I ask of you now will take great strength and courage. Your brother and sister are your responsibility now. You must save them.'

A loud crash made Zastra jump. The door to the outer office had been broken in. Several Bractarian guards ran towards them, swords bared.

'I'll deal with this,' cried Teona, drawing her sword. She presented a daunting figure, ginger hair crackling in the firelight. Her blue eyes blazed in imperious anger. Three soldiers collapsed to the floor in agony, but more poured through the door to replace them and Teona was forced to use her sword. As she struggled to hold back the swarm of attackers, Leodra pulled Zastra through to a back chamber. He leaned deep into the fireplace and pulled on some hidden device. With a harsh grating noise, the stone at the back of the fireplace swung inward, revealing a dark space behind and stone steps leading down into the earth. Zastra gasped in astonishment.

'My grandfather showed me this passageway. It leads out to Highcastle Forest. It is the only way to escape now – the gate has been taken. Those appalling creatures won't be able to follow you underground. I just hope the way is not blocked. I don't believe it has been used in centuries. You must keep the twins safe. They are the only hope for Golmeira now.'

'I can't go alone,' Zastra protested.

'You must obey me in this. I have to find your mother. I cannot abandon her. I'm placing my trust in you, Zastra. I've not been a good father and I've not always recognised your talents. I was blinded by the fear of losing control of Golmeira and the fear that without mindweaving ability you would end up a weak leader, like me; forced to rely on others and unsure who to trust. It is a bitter irony that my fear drove me to place my trust in my brother, the one person I should have doubted. I was so proud of you, you know, when you killed the caralyx. I'm sorry I was too concerned with other things to tell you at the time. I need you to be as strong again. Make for Bodel's house in Highcastle. Once I find your mother we shall try and follow you there. If we aren't there by daybreak, you go to Lyria. Marl Orwin was always our friend and so he will surely help you. Be careful and trust no one.'

The noises from the other room grew louder and shadows started to encroach on the wall of the inner office. The outline of Teona, tall and willowy, was being pressed backward by a swathe of writhing darkness. A tall, cloaked shadow crawled up the wall, swallowing the slim outline of the highmaster.

'Strinverl, you traitor!' she cried. There was an awful, crushing sound. Teona's outline sank to the floor and was gobbled up by the shadows.

Leodra turned and pushed Zastra firmly into the passageway. He wasted no time in handing Kastara down to her. As she looked back up the steps towards him, he passed her a candle, and said, eyes reflecting the flame, 'make me proud once more, my daughter.'

The heavy stone closed, leaving Zastra and the babies alone in the dark passageway. A muffled sound of shouting and clashing metal came through the rock as if at a great distance.

Zastra hesitated, still shocked by what had happened. A quick glance at the stone in the candlelight did not reveal any lever or handle with which to open it. There was no way back. The horror of what she had seen left her nauseated and she had to breathe deeply to fend off the sickness. Kastara began to cry, a small sobbing sound at first, quickly becoming louder. Zastra turned and half staggered, half ran down the passageway, leaving the muffled clashing of swords behind her.

The journey down the tunnel was filled with a sense of unreality, as if she was not really awake but in a nightmare. The weight of the twins caused her to become breathless and her arms were soon burning from the exertion of carrying Kastara. She could feel minds reaching out, searching for her, and it took all her will to maintain her mental block. Thankfully, the horrific screams of the flying creatures did not penetrate into the tunnel. All too soon she had to rest, dropping Kastara to the floor as she caught her breath. Both babies were now awake and crying, but she had no strength to calm them. She fought against the rising panic that threatened to rob her of wit and strength. Gathering the bawling Kastara by one arm and the flickering candle in her free hand, she moved onwards, taking a small comfort in the thought that every step took her further away from the horrors of the castle. Every so often, she swapped the arm with which she carried Kastara. The tunnel grew narrower and the air became thick and stuffy. Zastra's breathing grew laboured. She dare not stop, convinced that the tunnel would swallow them up if she did not keep moving. Onwards and downwards it went, loose stones on the floor causing her to stumble. At one point, a rock fall had almost completely blocked the passage. The only way to proceed was to remove Findar from her back and pass him through the small gap, followed by Kastara. Zastra was then able to squeeze herself past the blockage, but as she wriggled through, the candle fell from her hand and extinguished itself, leaving them in utter darkness. Once more, Zastra battled against the panic. Feeling around in the dark she was able locate Findar and set him once more on her shoulders. Picking up Kastara she continued hesitantly down the passageway. A mental probe hammered against her mind, and she doubled over at the pain of it. It required all her remaining strength to ward off the probe. Her head throbbed in agony as she struggled onwards, losing all sense of time in the darkness. More than once she stumbled on some unseen object, falling and scraping skin from her hands and knees. Eventually, the babies stopped screaming, as if the thick air and the darkness had stifled them.

She had almost given up hope of ever escaping from the passage when she felt a small breath of air upon her cheek. Hastening as much as possible, she felt the tunnel widen. A hint of silver light broke up the utter blackness. She was in a cave. With eyes made sensitive by the darkness of the passageway she could make out the moonlit entrance. She staggered toward it, gulping hungrily at the fresh air as she sank down, exhausted. Her whole body ached. She had never realised how heavy babies could be.

As she sat and rested in the gloom, she began to discern the shadows of trees all around her. It must be Highcastle Forest, but she could not tell where. The nightmarish journey through the passageway had completely disorientated her. She resolved to get her bearings. She put Findar on her back and lifted Kastara into her arms and moved forwards gingerly. She held her sister close to her body to protect her against the twigs and branches that reached out to snag them in the dark. She reached a small clearing, where the canopy opened to reveal a band of stars and the twin moons. From her left, an orange glow leached into the night sky. She need to climb a tree to try and see where they were. By touch, she found one with a branch low enough for her to attempt to climb. There was no way she could scale it carrying the babies. With great reluctance she left Kastara and Findar wedged firmly between two large roots and began to climb, feeling for each branch by touch. Her head banged repeatedly against the rough of over hanging branches, but she carried on doggedly until she was high enough to look above the main canopy. By good fortune, she had climbed one of the tallest trees. The orange glow came from Golmer Castle, half a league away she reckoned. Fire leapt from two of the towers. In the light she could make out three black creatures swirling like enormous bats above the castle. Her heart sank to see her beautiful castle so ravaged, and she could think only of her mother and father, still inside. Yet another probe dug into her mind and Zastra had to battle against her emotions to block the mindweaver, whoever it was. She took another look around to gather her bearings. Thankfully, she was on the east side of the castle, which meant she was already part way to Highcastle village. She could not have faced going back towards the castle and those terrifying creatures. Further to the east, she could see a small string of lights in the distance, which according to her recollection should be the village. As long as she headed in roughly that direction, away from the large orange glow, they should make it. She climbed back down the tree, which turned out to be much more difficult than climbing up it. The branches merged with the dark ground below and she had to feel for purchase with her feet. Her heart fluttered as she slipped and slid her way down and she was overjoyed when at last she felt soft ground beneath her feet and found Findar and Kastara where she had left them. She gathered them up and made her way eastwards. The trees were quite sparse and she was able to pick her way through. The orange glow from the burning castle formed her constant guide. She made slow progress, resting frequently due to the weight of the twins. Dawn was just beginning to form a horizon by the time they reached the edge of the forest. At the bottom of a long, gentle slope, Zastra could see the outline of Highcastle village, a little further to her right than she had hoped, but less than half a league away. Wearily, she headed towards it.

As she got closer, she saw there were soldiers in the centre of the village. The sky had brightened enough for her to recognise the distinctive emblem of the gecko on the black uniforms, identifying them as Thorlberd's troops. They had already taken control. Luckily, Zastra knew the village well from her visits with Bedrun. She sneaked along the hedgerows that sat behind the houses and came at last to the garden behind Bodel's house. A light was on in the kitchen and Zastra clambered over a low wall, using the last of her strength to haul

Kastara with her. Peering through the window, she saw that Bodel was alone and, finding the door unlocked, she entered and sank to the floor in desolation.

Bodel looked up in shock.

'Zastra!' she whispered. 'Oh, my dear child, what has happened?'

Chapter Twenty

The twins woke, crying to be fed. Bodel tended to them while Zastra sat scrunched up against the wall. For some reason she had started shaking.

'What has happened?' asked Bodel. 'Is something wrong at the castle? Have you seen my Bedrun?'

Zastra couldn't find the words to answer. Bodel looked at her in concern.

'I have to go upstairs now to see to my sister,' she said. 'She has been ill with the blue fever and I must tend to her. Help yourself to some food and drink. I'll be back as soon as I can. I'll put some blankets down in the other room so you can settle the twins. But then we must talk.'

She poured a cup of water from a wooden jug, gathered up a clean sheet from the back of a chair and left. Zastra gulped some water thirstily, but her stomach was too knotted to even think of eating. She placed the twins on the blankets and lay with them as they slept. She dozed fitfully, but her dreams were filled with a dizzy kaleidoscope of the horrors of the castle and she gained no rest. She was awake when Bodel returned. Hesitatingly, in broken sentences, Zastra related the events of the night. Bodel gasped in horror.

'I knew something was wrong. We heard a lot of noise and there are Bractarian soldiers all over the village, but I had no idea... I've been tending Dalka all night. One of our friends came and said something big was happening. But what about my Bedrun? Did you see her?'

Zastra shook her head despondently. 'I'm sorry, Bodel, I don't know what happened. She wasn't there when Teona came for me. I don't know if she's all right.' The horror of the situation struck them both hard. Bodel wrung the blanket tight between her hands. She attacked Zastra with a series of questions, some of which Zastra attempted to answer, but most she could not.

'I must go to her,' Bodel said, pacing up and down the room in agitation. 'I must find my Bedrun. Morel would be devastated. Oh no – Morel! We've not heard from her for weeks. If the Marl of Bractaris is behind all this then Waldaria must have been a trap. She'll be in great danger. Oh, I must try and find out what is happening.'

Distracted, she took a shawl and ran from the house. While she was gone, Zastra kept looking out of the back window towards the edge of Highcastle Forest in the desperate hope that her father and mother would appear. Hours passed and there was no sign. Occasionally, she saw the shadows of the great beasts flying overhead, and at these times she was aware of invisible fingers prying into her mind. She was convinced that they were searching for her and the twins.

Bodel returned just before noon. She was accompanied by a thin man, with an intense, unfriendly expression. Zastra eyed him warily.

'It's all right,' said Bodel, seeing the look on Zastra's face. 'This is my friend Hedrik. We can trust him.' Bodel paused, then reached out to grasp Zastra's hand.

'I'm afraid I've got some very bad news.'

Zastra felt a hollow emptiness form within her.

'Some Bractarian guards have come down from the castle and are proclaiming that Leodra and his wife are dead and that Grand Marl Thorlberd rules in his stead. I'm so terribly sorry.'

Zastra said nothing. Strangely, she felt nothing, just a dead numbness breaking over her. Bodel was saying something else. Zastra forced herself to concentrate.

'I must go and check on my sister but we'll talk some more,' Bodel said, and then she left the room. The babies woke up. Hedrik silently fed them with milk from Bodel's larder, then washed and changed them with practised calmness. Bodel returned and nervously checked the window before she sat down on the blanket. Zastra hugged her knees and rocked back and forth.

'Zastra,' said Bodel softly, 'I know it's a difficult time, but we cannot sit here feeling sorry for ourselves. We must act. The soldiers know you've escaped and they are looking for you and the twins. They are searching the forest as we speak and I'm sure it's only a matter of time before they search all the houses. If I could hide you all here, I would, but it's too dangerous. I've had an idea. The soldiers are looking for a young girl with two babies. I think we could pass you off as a boy if we cut your hair and find you some clothes. You'd have to pretend to be a villager though. How does that sound?'

Zastra nodded dumbly.

Bodel continued. 'I had a thought about the twins. It's risky, but the more I think of it, it seems like the best solution. Even dressed as a boy, you are bound to raise suspicions if you are carrying two young babies. Now, poor Dalka, ill upstairs with the blue fever, lost her baby girl to the same disease not two days since. I buried the little one myself. No one knows but me, not even Dalka, who has been too sick to notice. If we substitute Kastara for little Joril, she could be hidden safely here. Hedrik lives about twelve leagues away and he has agreed to take you and Findar as far as his village.' Hedrik said nothing, standing with his arms folded and staring out of the window.

'I can't leave Kastara!' cried Zastra. 'Father said I must look after them.'

'You can't take them both, child,' muttered Hedrik.

'She'd be safer here, Zastra. I know it's hard, but I think fate has sent us this opportunity.'

'But you're so close to the castle. They are sure to find her. The mindweavers will make you tell.'

'They won't suspect a child with a proven family history. Only I will know, and I have the power to resist mindweavers. Oh yes,' she nodded, as Zastra looked at her, 'soldiers are trained to resist mindweavers and Morel always shares everything with me. It turns out I have a real knack for it. As do you, apparently, which is fortunate, for all our sakes.'

'I don't know…' Zastra protested.

'I'll not take the three of you,' said Hedrik, harshly. 'It'll be too obvious. A young lad and a littlun – we might just get away with it, as long as you do exactly as I say. This is my only offer. And it's only as a favour to you Bodel, for what you've done for my littluns. I'll be setting off in a few hours, so you best be getting her ready. I'll rustle up some likely clothes for the girl and be back within the hour. You best bury all them fancy clothes – you'll have something for the babies, no doubt?'

Bodel nodded and Hedrik departed. Bodel set about making preparations. First, she cut Zastra's hair; an untidy, close cut that removed her wavy curls and disguised its natural chestnut colour. As Zastra sat wrapped in a blanket, Bodel buried her clothes and everything else she had brought, even the baby harness which had the crest of Leodra on it.

'You must take nothing that marks you out as having come from the castle,' she explained. 'Here is a bag with some provisions – not much, but all I can spare. I've put in some fruit for Findar and he should manage some bread if you soften it with water first.'

Bodel dressed Kastara in the clothes worn by poor little deceased Joril and held her up in satisfaction. 'They look similar enough. No one will know the difference except Dalka, and I'll deal with her when the time comes.'

She was finishing packing when Hedrik returned with a bundle under one arm.

'We must leave now,' he said tersely. 'They are starting to search every house in the village. Quick child, put these on. And make yourself look dirty – remember you're a farm boy now, not royalty.'

Zastra put on the trousers and shirt and some rather ill-fitting boots, one of which had a hole in the toe.

'Right, you take the bag, I'll take the boy,' ordered Hedrik, and with practised movements he made a sling for Findar so he could carry him across his chest. 'That's it, we must go.'

As Zastra went over to Kastara, he snapped, 'There's no time for goodbyes.'

'I'll come back for you, I promise,' whispered Zastra to her little sister. Casting a forlorn look back at Bodel, she followed Hedrik through the kitchen door.

Keeping a wary eye out for soldiers, they skirted the hedgerows at the back of the village and made for the nearest cover, an extension of Highcastle Forest. Zastra waited for a shout to tell them they had been seen, but none came, and they finally reached the outskirts of the forest, breathing heavily. They paused to look back, but no one had followed them.

'Come then, lad,' said Hedrik, brusquely. 'Try not to talk if we meet anyone. I'll tell them you're dumb if I have to.'

They strode along in awkward silence. Zastra felt misgivings at every step which took her further away from Kastara and further into the unknown.

Chapter
Twenty-One

They travelled through the forest for several hours. Fortunately, they met no one. Only once did they hear the distant beating of wings that signalled the passage of a flying creature. They ducked off the path and hid under cover of the trees until it had gone.

Hedrik spat as it headed off into the distance. 'Unnatural beast,' he muttered.

Evening closed in and they set up camp. Hedrik lit the fire by scraping his knife along a metallic fire-ring, generating a shower of sparks. In spite of herself, Zastra was fascinated. 'The ring contains a portion of firedust and that gives the sparks,' explained Hedrik briefly. Bodel had packed some bread and cured meats, and Hedrik cut some and offered some to Zastra.

'I'm not hungry,' she muttered.

'Eat,' he ordered, holding the bread under her chin until she took it. Zastra was not used to being spoken to in this way, but she was too weary to argue. As she forced the food down, she realised how hungry she was. She hadn't eaten since the party, the previous evening. She fed Findar some of the fruit. He burbled quietly and went to sleep.

'Get some sleep now, we'll be up at dawn,' said Hedrik, wrapping himself in a thin blanket and turning away. Zastra lay staring at the stars until extreme weariness overtook her and she fell asleep.

She was awoken the next day by the sound of Findar bawling. It was only half light.

'Make the porridge while I change the boy,' ordered Hedrik, taking

Findar down to the nearby stream. Zastra was still sitting wrapped in her blanket when they returned.

'What? Are you too prissy and proud to light a fire and make porridge?' asked Hedrik.

'I don't know how,' muttered Zastra, sulkily. He shook his head, but showed her how to clear some ground, set the twigs and make shavings for kindling, and then how to use the fire-ring to make sparks. Soon they had a decent little fire. Next, he showed her how to mix the oats and water and heat them until soft.

'Porridge is good food for trekking. Oats is light to carry but fill the stomach. All you need is water and a fire. The littlun'll eat it too – here, add a bit of sugar, he'll be fine. Just let it cool a bit first.'

They ate the porridge in silence. Hedrik cleaned the pots and packed up camp, stamping out the fire. 'Never leave a fire alight, especially in a forest,' he said.

Zastra hoisted the bag onto her back and they set off. She was sore and had blisters on the soles of her feet from yesterday's trek in the ill-fitting boots but her pride kept her from complaining and she limped along as well as she could. Even carrying Findar, Hedrik easily outstripped Zastra, and every so often he waited impatiently for her to catch up. In this manner they continued, throughout the day, stopping only occasionally to rest. The woods were strangely quiet and they met no one throughout the whole day. To Zastra, the hours become lost in a blur of trees and pain, as her blisters became increasingly sore. Eventually, as the sun was setting, Hedrik found a thin stream and set up camp. With relief, Zastra removed her boots and bathed her feet in the cool water of the stream.

'Don't just sit there, your brother needs changing,' said Hedrik. With a sigh, Zastra obeyed, changing Findar's undergarments and then washing the dirtied linen in the stream. Even then, she needed Hedrik to show her what to do, as she had never had to change the babies herself. At the castle there had been nurses and servants to do all that. She felt Hedrik's scorn. He lit a fire and heated some sugared water for the baby, while he and Zastra ate a little bread and meat.

Findar was awake now, and Zastra watched as he investigated various twigs and seed cones with profound fascination. It brought back memories of playing with the twins in the castle and she had to push back on her emotions to hold them in check. Hedrik stared silently at the sky and she had no intention of making conversation with him. The fire died down and they slept.

Again Zastra awoke, cold and stiff, to the sound of Findar crying for food. It was still dark and she tried to comfort him until it become light enough for her to see. She set the fire as she had been shown, and had started the pot boiling as Hedrik awoke. He busied himself with something while she made a passable attempt at porridge, only intervening to whip the pan away from the fire when it threatened to burn. They ate in silence, Findar happily slurping down the porridge. Zastra took the pots and washed them in the cold stream and returned to get ready. Sighing, she took up the dreaded boots, ready to put them on even though her blisters were still raw.

'Wait,' said Hedrik, handing her some bits of material that he had been working on. 'Line the boots with these, they may be more comfortable.' Zastra did as he suggested. She could still feel the blisters but they no longer grated with severe pain as she walked and she made better progress. She sensed Hedrik had slowed his pace slightly and no longer roamed ahead, for which she was grateful. Around noon, they came to the edge of the forest. A lush green landscape of rolling hills lay before them. They stopped for a brief rest and something to eat.

'Now we're out the forest, we're bound to meet people. Just keep your head down and say nothing,' said Hedrik tersely. 'We must try and go faster if we are to make it to Trindhome by tomorrow evening. Are you ready?'

Zastra nodded, quickly finishing her hunk of bread and they set off. It was hot now that they were out of the shade of the forest. Hedrik kept Findar covered in his sling and the boy slept. They met a few people on the way, mainly farmers and goatherds, but attracted little attention. Everyone seemed preoccupied with their own business. Late afternoon they arrived, hot and sweaty, on the brow of a small hill. It overlooked a hamlet which straddled a fast-flowing river.

'Wrylford,' observed Hedrik. 'We'll have to go down, as it's the only river crossing within five leagues. I can see some soldiers, there on the bridge – do you see?' He pointed and Zastra made out four figures in dark uniforms on the approach to the bridge. She shrank back. Hedrik looked at her.

'Come, we must go. Follow my lead. Remember, you're a farm boy. It's my neck as well as yours if they suspect anything.'

Zastra paused, unsure, a knot of fear binding her to the spot. Hedrik sighed, but waited for her to speak.

'The last time I saw those uniforms...' she whispered, trying to explain, but even her voice gave way as her throat dried out. She was shaking.

'It'll be fine,' said Hedrik, patting her shoulder in encouragement. 'Come, the sooner we go, the sooner it's over.'

He strode off down the hill. Zastra hovered, undecided for a moment, but Findar's cry wafted up to her and that made up her mind. She ran down after them. They entered the town and made their way towards the bridge. Her heart was fluttering, but she forced herself to move one foot in front of the other. There were several groups of soldiers around the village, searching the homes and manhandling the villagers. Some of the soldiers were strange looking men indeed: short and stocky, with coarse, straggly hair, their beardless faces lacked noses, having simply a pair of flattened nostrils embedded in red, peeling skin. Zastra shrank back, trying hard not to stare.

'Kyrg savages,' muttered Hedrik under his breath. Zastra's eyes widened. So these were the Kyrginites of legend. What were they doing wearing Thorlberd's Bractarian uniforms? As they reached the bridge, they were halted by two of the Kyrginites.

'State your name and business,' the taller Kyrginite said in a gruff, rasping voice.

'Hedrik of Trindhome, with my cousin's boy and my son. I'm returning home.'

'Where have you been and why?'

'To Frestfall,' replied Hedrik evenly, naming a town twelve leagues south of Highcastle village. 'I went to see the healer there, who has an ointment to treat the scar-rash. My wife is ill and needs this medicine.'

The other Kyrginite pawed at the sling containing Findar and Zastra bridled. Hedrik laid a warning hand on her shoulder.

'Let's look at the baby. Open your packs.'

'What reason do you have to search us?' asked Hedrik mildly.

'We have orders to search everyone. Now do as I say, unless you want to feel my metal.'

'We've nothing to hide,' said Hedrik, shrugging his shoulders. He held out Findar to be examined.

'You, boy – open the bag.'

Zastra unslung the bag and opened it. The soldier rummaged around, taking the cured meat and setting it aside.

'That'll make a nice meal,' he said, smacking his dry lips together.

'Hey!' protested Zastra, and then stopped her voice as the guard looked sharply at her.

'Let's look at you boy,' he said, reaching out to lift her chin. Just then a loud cry came from a nearby dwelling. They all turned to see three soldiers dragging a young girl out of the house. Another soldier came out, holding two howling babies. They were followed by an older woman, who was screaming and hitting out at the guards.

The two Kyrginites guards from the bridge went over to join the affray, pulling the woman off the other soldiers and throwing her roughly to the ground.

'Let's look at them all. Especially the babies,' ordered the tall Kyrginite guard. 'If they are who we seek, we shall soon know.'

Hedrik grabbed Zastra by the hand and led her over the bridge away from the fracas. She wanted to run away as fast as possible. As if sensing her mood, Hedrik gripped her hand tighter.

'Walk,' he commanded, softly yet firmly. She forced herself to obey. Behind her the woman was still screaming. Every second she expected them to be called back. It took an age for them to reach the end of the village. A number of Bractarian soldiers ran past them, attracted by the fuss, and they were able to leave the village unmolested. As they passed over the brow of the hill and out of view of the bridge, Hedrik quickened his pace. Zastra needed no urging to keep up. As soon as the village was out of sight completely, he cut off the road. They climbed up a dried out culvert until they reached the top of a long ridge. In spite of Zastra's now laboured breathing, Hedrik forced them along the ridge at a fast pace until they had left the valley and Wrylford far behind them. It was dark before they stopped.

'We'll make no fire tonight,' he said, 'there are too many soldiers around and not enough cover to hide the fire. There are no streams in this area – we'll have to make do with the water in our flasks.'

Zastra was hot and thirsty, but following Hedrik's lead drank only sparingly from her water carrier. She wetted some bread for Findar, who twisted his head away in disgust, but eventually was persuaded to eat a few mouthfuls.

'We were lucky,' stated Hedrik. 'I told you to say nothing.'

Zastra lowered her head. 'I'm sorry,' she said. Hedrik scratched his chin.

'You must swallow your pride and try to become invisible,' he explained. 'Practice saying a few words in the way of a country boy. Your accent gives you away. Never, ever, answer them back – you see what happens.'

Zastra nodded, and she resolved to practice mimicking Hedrik's dialect.

'Were those really Kyrginites?' she asked.

'Aye,' spat Hedrik. 'For years upon years they have come down into the Helgarth Mountains, taking all the food and leaving whole villages to starve. They're savage and deadly fighters, so I've heard, and there are rumours that their hunger is not always satisfied by stealing alone. Thorlberd must have paid them to join his army. He'd best be careful, allying himself with such savages. I wouldn't trust them.'

Zastra recalled the tale of Fostran's fight with Kyrgs. Now she had seen them, she was even more in awe of the famous warrior.

110

'They said they would know if they found who they were looking for. How could they know?' she asked, more to herself than Hedrik.

'Perhaps you or the babies have a birthmark?' he suggested. 'Your uncle would know of it maybe?'

'No, I don't think so,' mused Zastra. 'Oh, but wait, I do have a scar on my thigh from when I fell off my horse. I was only small at the time. It kicked me and left a mark. But my uncle wouldn't know – he wasn't there.'

'By now your uncle probably knows everything that anyone at Golmer Castle knew,' stated Hedrik.

'How could he?' Zastra began to ask, but stopped, as she recalled that her uncle was a mindweaver. He could rip the thoughts out of anyone if he chose to.

'You must avoid attracting their attention,' Hedrik said. 'It's lucky we didn't have the other baby, else it would've gone badly for us. As long as they've no reason to suspect you, you'll be safe. But if you give them a reason to look more closely, then we are in trouble.'

Zastra was only half listening. Her mind was back at the castle, visions rising unwanted in her mind and she turned away, wrapped in her own thoughts. Hedrik said no more.

The next morning they again rose early, making a small breakfast of their remaining bread before they set off.

'We should reach Trindhome by nightfall,' said Hedrik. 'That's if you can stay out of trouble and we keep up a good pace.'

'Aye,' said Zastra, in her best attempt at a country voice. The barest twitch of a smile flicked the corner of Hedrik's mouth. They left the ridge by mid-morning and entered another area of woodland. Every now and then Hedrik stopped to show her some nuts which were edible and instructed her how to shell them. He warned her off eating the berries as he said they were mostly poisonous. As they neared Trindhome they met people with greater frequency. Hedrik nodded politely while Zastra looked at the ground and practiced making herself invisible. Just before dusk, the path led them into the large village of Trindhome, which sprawled out on either side of a main highway. Zastra was relieved to see there were no soldiers. Hedrik led them to his house, a small, well-tended dwelling on the outer edge of the village. Zastra guessed that the entire house would have fitted into her bedchamber in the castle. A light was on, and as they entered two young boys cried out in excitement and rushed to grab their father by the legs. Zastra followed him, feeling awkward and out of place. The warmth of Hedrik's greeting to his boys made her throat catch with emotion. A pale woman was seated on a cushioned chair, wrapped in a blanket despite the warm mugginess of the evening. Hedrik went to her and kissed her gently. The woman looked inquiringly at Zastra and then at Findar, asleep in the sling on her husband's chest.

'I'm doing a favour for Bodel. The boys needed my help and I promised to deliver them safely here.'

Turning to Zastra, he nodded towards a door and said, 'The kitchen is through there, lad. Sort yourselves out with something to eat. I need to talk to my family.'

Zastra went through to the kitchen, which was neat and tidy like the rest of the house. She could hear a murmuring of voices from the other room, interspersed with the high pitched cries of the little boys. The woman had a pleading tone which was periodically interrupted by the quiet voice of Hedrik. When Zastra had fed Findar with some milk and bread and found some bread and cheese for herself, Hedrik came into the kitchen carrying a threadbare blanket and a pillow.

'You can sleep in here tonight,' he said. 'There's a corner here that's quite snug. We'll make plans in the morning.'

Zastra nodded her thanks and soon she and Findar had settled down together. Thankfully, for once her sleep was dreamless.

Chapter Twenty-Two

edrik was gone the next morning, leaving Zastra to spend an uncomfortable morning in the sullen presence of his wife, who clearly wished them gone. The woman didn't even want to be in the same room with them and Zastra and Findar were left alone in the kitchen for most of the morning. The two boys had been sent out to play with friends and the silence was broken only by Findar's occasional gurgling. He was astonishingly placid, given what they had been through over the last few days. Every time Zastra looked at him she thought of Kastara. Their experience in Wrylford revealed the wisdom of Bodel's suggestion, but Zastra could not acquit herself of blame for leaving her sister behind. True, Kastara – or Joril, as she was now – was almost certainly safer hidden in the heart of a caring family, not chased and harried as she and Findar were, but still she wished her sister was with them.

Hedrik finally returned around lunchtime and he and his wife were soon engaged in a heated exchange, albeit spoken in undertones. From the few words and phrases that she could overhear, Zastra could tell that she and Findar were the source of the disagreement. When Hedrik left his wife to come and sit with her in the kitchen, Zastra began to gather her belongings.

'Don't let us trouble you further. We shall be getting on our way,' she said tremulously.

Hedrik looked at her thoughtfully and rubbed his stubbled chin.

'Aye,' he muttered, 'I'm afraid it must be so. We cannot take you in here. It's too dangerous, both for you and for my family. Two soldiers rode through the village this morning. They proclaim the new rule of Thorlberd, the new Grand Marl of Golmeira, and their search for a thirteen year old girl with chestnut hair and twin babies. Anyone caught harbouring them will face death.'

Zastra stopped what she was doing, ashamed of her prideful outburst. She looked at the thin man, who appeared suddenly worn and tired. He rose to his feet, agitated, unable to meet her gaze.

'My grandda served in the army under Leodra's grandfather and always spoke well of him. Said he was a good man who cared about his men, not just glory. So it saddens me, what has happened. I don't like to see so many soldiers in our villages, and those Kyrgs – the way they treated that woman and her family in Wrylford. It's not right.' He shook his head.

'Bodel told me you were headed east – no, don't tell me where, I don't wish to know. It's probably wise to get as far away from Golmer Castle as you can. I've been to our village schoolmaster and asked him to copy me a map of Golmeira that runs from here to the border regions. Here – it's yours. Keep it well hidden. If anyone asks who you are, always say you are from a local town, using the map. You will be less likely to stand out that way. You remember what I told you about navigating by the sun and the eastern tri-star?'

Zastra nodded. Hedrik had taught her many things as they had journeyed. He left the room and came back with a small, weatherbeaten rucksack.

'Take this. I've put in my grandda's fire-ring. I think he would've wanted you to have it. Also a knife, your blanket and some food that we can easily spare. Do you have any money?'

Zastra shook her head. 'There wasn't time,' she said.

'Well, here's a few tocrins,' he said gruffly. 'It's not much, but should help you buy a loaf or two of bread on the way. And this is an old cap of mine, it might disguise you a bit. It's amazing how different people can look in a cap.' He set a frayed and faded brown hat on her head. It was slightly too large, especially with her shorn head, and flopped low over her eyes. Hedrik grunted in satisfaction.

'One more thing. Hilfrik, a good friend of mine, has been ordered to drive a wagon load of jula oil into Riverford. You'll have to cross the Great River there as it's the only bridge for many leagues. He's agreed to hide you in his wagon and let you out once you are over the river. I haven't told him who you are, just that you need to escape the soldiers. He's a good man and don't like Kyrgs any more than I do. The wagon arrived just a few minutes ago, but it'll take him an hour or so to load up and hitch up his horses. I said we'd meet him just south of the village.'

Zastra was amazed by the sudden flow of words, more than Hedrik had mustered in all of their previous three days together. He spent the next hour checking and repacking her bag. Zastra filled the time by examining the map. She found Trindhome and Riverford, but beyond that was a blur of unknown names. Finally she found Lyria Castle, where, if she were to obey her father's last instructions, she must head. Beyond Lyria lay only the borders and Sendor. She folded away the map and hid it in the lining of her jacket, a shapeless, coarse thing that Hedrik had found and deemed suitable for her guise as a country farm boy.

The time soon came to leave. Hedrik took her out of the back of the house and round to the south end of the village. They waited round the first bend in the highway, out of sight of the southernmost dwelling. Soon enough, a deep rumble announced the arrival of a large covered wagon, drawn by four large horses. A plump man with a red face acknowledged them and drew the horses to halt. He jumped down and pulled aside a triangle of the wagon cover.

'In here lad,' he called out jovially. 'I've cleared a space just behind me. That way, no one'll see you and I can warn you if any soldiers are coming. If you've got a blanket, I'd put it down now – it'll be long old ride.'

He helped Zastra into the wagon and Hedrik slung her bag in afterwards. She barely had time to whisper a quick word of thanks to Hedrik, who nodded back at her, before the wagon drew off. She glimpsed Hedrik's thin back through a tear in the cover as he walked slowly back to the village. She regretted there had not been time to say goodbye properly. True, he had been a grim and surly companion, sometimes even rude. But he had risked his life to keep them safe and she wished she had been able to better express her gratitude.

The wagon rumbled along at steady rate. Hilfrik was a cheerful, chatty fellow, always either whistling, singing or talking. Fortunately, he did not appear to require much in the way of response from Zastra, who was able to practice 'Aye' 'No' and 'Oh' in her best country accent. Such occasional acknowledgement was all that was needed as Hilfrik told tales of trips he had made, moaned about his wife who nagged him mercilessly, and recounted the varied adventures, large and small, of his son, now grown up and moved away. She was happy to listen to him chattering away. It saved her from her own reflections and she buried away snippets of his country dialect for future use. Only once did he pause for breath. The road was cutting through a steep valley when they overtook a troop of soldiers. A couple of the soldiers questioned Hilfrik while Zastra crouched in the back of the wagon and held her breath, willing Findar, who was sleeping, not to wake and make a noise. Hilfrik explained his business and they were allowed to continue on their way. Zastra sank back in relief. Barely ten minutes later, Findar was awake and crying, but there was no one but Hilfrik to hear him.

Late in the afternoon, Hilfrik stopped to feed and water the horses. As he let Zastra out, he explained that after this short break they would be travelling through the night.

'We should make it to Riverford by tomorrow lunchtime.'

Zastra enjoyed the chance to stretch her legs and tend to Findar's needs, but she was continually aware of the closeness of the road and the chance that soldiers may come by at any time. It was not long before the horses had been watered and re-harnessed and they were on their way again. The steady rhythm of the wagon lulled both Zastra and Findar to sleep.

A sharp tapping awoke Zastra and she was quickly alert. A whisper from Hilfrik told her they were approaching the Great River.

'It would be handy if the littlun were quiet for a bit,' he said. Unfortunately, Findar chose that moment to wake and make some tentative cries, which Zastra was beginning to recognise as the precursor to the ear-deafening bawl of a hungry baby. There was just enough early morning light filtering through the wooden slats that formed the base of the wagon for her to change Findar's undergarments. This however, did not make the crying cease. Hilfrik's voice came again, this time more urgently.

'If he don't quiet in the next few minutes, we're done for lad!'

Zastra tried feeding Findar some moistened bread, but he spat it out and bawled even louder. In desperation, Zastra dipped her finger in the small bag of sugar that Hedrik had provided and inserted it into her little brother's mouth. He suckled contentedly and at last was silent.

'About time!' exclaimed Hilfrik with undisguised relief. A short moment later he gave a hearty hail, which was returned by gruff orders to halt. Zastra fed some more sugar to Findar, who seemed happy to suck at the sweetness. Hilfrik explained his business, as well as half his life story, to the guards. Zastra detected a shaft of light from the back of the wagon. One of the guards had lifted the covering and was peering inside. She sat rigidly, hardly daring to breathe.

'Have you seen any children on your travels?' queried a clipped, female voice. 'In particular an older girl with two young babies?'

'No, indeed not,' said Hilfrik. 'If I ever saw such a thing, I'd be sure to send them on home. Children should be kept indoors at present. You don't know what dangers might be lurking about. I don't know any parent'd let their littluns wander off on their own, especially with all things turned upside and about as they are now.'

'Order will return very soon,' the voice responded. 'Just as soon as we catch those malcontents who refuse to acknowledge the benefits of having Grand Marl Thorlberd in charge. All right, move along. The Prefect of Riverford will be happy to receive this shipment.'

By the altered sound and rhythm of the wagon, Zastra guessed they had moved from the dirt track onto paved road. She could hear the rush of flowing water. They must be crossing the Great River. She looked down anxiously at Findar. Her brother stared back at her, still happily suckling on her finger.

'Stay quiet,' whispered Hilfrik, 'there are more guards the other side.'

A short while later the changing rhythm told Zastra they had reached the other side of the bridge. The covering at the back of the wagon had been left loose and flapped with the motion of the cart. Through it, Zastra could see that they were leaving behind a whole troop of soldiers.

'It's less than half a league to the Westgate of Riverford,' said Hilfrik out of the corner of his mouth. 'I'll let you out in just a moment. What the…? There's some kind of large bird hovering over the city. Why, it must be huge, for me to see it from here – maybe a giant eagle, or – hmm, it looks a bit frightening, brings a shiver to your heart. Come and look lad, it's quite something.'

Zastra's heart sank. She did not need to look to know what the creature was. For the first time in several days, she felt a touch on her mind. Fortunately, she had kept her mental walls in place and the probing touch hovered only briefly before moving on. Her thoughts raced. Their original plan had been for her and Findar to leave the wagon before it entered the gated city so that they could skirt round it, but that was impossible now. The creature and its rider would surely see them. They would have to stay with the wagon and try and escape some other way. As Hilfrik halted the horses and made to dismount, she whispered to him to carry on and take them into the city.

'The soldiers can't see you from this far away boy,' he chuckled. But Zastra knew that she couldn't take the risk. For all she knew the creature could have eyes sharper than an eagle. They must take their chances in Riverford.

'Please, Hilfrik,' she pleaded.

'Oh well, it's no concern to me what you do. Although once we are past the gatehouse guards, you'd better slip to the back of the wagon and sneak out before I make my delivery to the Prefect, or they'll be sure to find you when they unload.'

They set off again. They were questioned briefly by the guards at the city gate, but were quickly waved through. The bustle and smell of the city hit Zastra even through the covered sides of the wagon. She whispered a word of thanks to Hilfrik then, folding the sling around the now sleeping Findar, she moved to the back of the wagon and peered out. She waited until they had turned a corner, then leapt out of the moving wagon and dashed to a nearby alleyway. No one shouted or reached out to stop them. She sank with relief onto a set of stone steps. Footsteps approached, and she lowered her cap to cover as much of her face as possible. The footsteps passed by without pausing. Other people, often in groups, passed by without taking any notice of them. It seemed as if, in this large city, they could become invisible.

Chapter Twenty-Three

Their good fortune was not to last. A servant came out of the house on whose front steps they were seated and shooed them away. Zastra did not protest, moving off and wandering aimlessly through the city. She was overwhelmed by the size and noise of the place. The paved streets, wet with recent rain, glimmered dimly in the shafts of sunlight that filtered down from the thin strips of sky overhead. The buildings appeared tall to Zastra, almost as tall as the high towers of the castle, but because they were built so close to each other they seemed to lean over her, closing her in. The narrow alleyways were full of people, densely packed. Zastra was used to large numbers of people in the castle, but not herded together as they were in Riverford. In spite of the crowds, there was a strange air of despondency upon the place. Troops of Bractarian and Kyrginite soldiers appeared frequently, marching up and down the main streets; the crowds parting silently and obediently before them. The beating wings of the terrible creature contributed to the dark, fearful mood. Zastra's were not the only eyes that peered up in concern whenever it passed over the city.

Zastra ducked into the smaller alleyways to try and avoid both the troops and the airborne beast. Riverford was set on a steep hill and Zastra found herself heading sideways across the base of the hill into increasingly narrow streets and alleyways. The imposing grey stone houses gave way to smaller, more ramshackle dwellings, patched with wood and dirty pieces of cloth. The city seemed to age, morphing from tall, upright strength to tired, weatherbeaten facades that looked as if they might fall over at the slightest touch. There were fewer people in these streets. Here and there, a figure would trudge along, head bent, uninterested in their surroundings. This was a poorer part of town, and Zastra was shocked by the appearance of some scrawny children, only partly dressed, some with running sores on their faces. A few beggars, one with opaque, sightless eyes, called out to her, but she hurried past, head bowed. Even the rats looked emaciated and Zastra saw several of them lying dead in the streets. A pungent odour of decay hung in the damp air and foul streams of brown sewage ran down the ever narrowing passageways. A motionless bundle lay in one gutter, covered in gray cloth. Zastra did not dare imagine what horror lay beneath. Doors slammed shut as she passed. The stench grew worse, the heavy atmosphere causing Zastra to cough and she turned to head up the hill, desperate to rise above the foul miasma. A woman peered out of a window directly above them, stopping herself just as she was about to empty a bucket onto the open street. A splash of reddish liquid landed just in front of Zastra's boot.

'Sorry love,' the woman muttered and then, looking around her, she whispered cryptically, 'get out while you can, my dear – this is no place for littluns, or anyone else for that matter. Get out of the city…' With no further explanation, the woman leaned back into the house and closed the window. Startled and increasingly worried, Zastra continued upwards. She was relieved as the atmosphere began to clear and the streets widened and began to fill up with other people. Even though the chances of meeting soldiers was greatly increased, Zastra felt they were safer here than in the stifling confines of the lower edges of the city.

Riverford was much larger than it had appeared from the outside, and it was a good while before they found themselves in a large paved square at the top of the hill. A crowd had gathered by a tall gateway set at the north side of the square, behind which sat a large, square building, two stories high with tall, shuttered windows. Zastra thought it looked like two sets of stables placed one above the other, and half expected the tall shutters to open to reveal a row of horses. She joined the crowd, figuring she would be less conspicuous. She was also anxious to hear any news. The crowd continued to build until the gates opened with a fanfare and a wooden platform was wheeled forward. A plump man stepped up onto the platform. He was ordinary-looking, with pale brown hair and a pink, clean shaven face. However, his wardrobe was far from ordinary, dressed as he was in bright red and yellow silks and a sumptuous black velvet coat. He was accompanied by several guards, including a powerful looking Kyrginite warrior, whose face was half covered in an elaborate green tattoo. The plump man raised his hand for silence.

'Citizens of Riverford. It has been six days since Grand Marl Thorlberd, in alliance with our Kyrginite friends, took command of Golmeira in order to restore order and glory to our lands. I, Finton, have been appointed Prefect of this city until a new Marl of Riverford is appointed.'

At the mention of the Kyrginites, there was a general murmur of discontent around the crowd.

'You see the power which is ours to command,' Finton proclaimed, gesturing upwards towards the circling beast. 'The mighty migaradons are invincible, commanded by the strength of mindweavers. Resistance to their will is useless.'

The noise of the crowd was reduced, although not completely quieted. Finton continued, shaking his head in a theatrical expression of disappointment.

'Sadly there are some among you who fail to understand the huge benefit that the new order will bring, and instead seek to wreak disruption and chaos. This will not be tolerated. During this period of transition, order must be kept. The evening curfew will continue for the foreseeable future. As of now, all people entering and leaving the city must report to the gatehouse guards and present themselves for mindweaver scans. Anyone defying these instructions will be arrested. Supporters of the old, disgraced regime will be tried for treason. Anyone assisting these traitors will be put in jail.'

'It's your tailor what should be sent to jail, matey,' muttered a woman who was standing just behind Zastra. There were a few muted chuckles.

Finton extended his arms outwards in an expansive gesture.

'Come, let us work together. If you help us, you will be well rewarded. We have the opportunity to build a new era of glory and prosperity for the land of Golmeira. Join us in our quest.'

'Work together, he says,' snorted the woman behind Zastra. 'Somehow I don't reckon all this glory and prosperity will be for us working people. We'll have to suffer for it, but it'll still be the rich ones as'll get the benefit.'

A general rumble of discontent spread through the crowd as if in agreement with these sentiments.

'Traitorous flekk!' cried another voice from somewhere within the crowd.

'Who said that?' shouted Finton, looking around nervously. 'Whoever said that will be caught and punished.'

The Prefect gestured a pair of large Kyrgs into the crowd to seek out the trouble-maker. The murmurings of the crowd increased, the body of people seething and gathering, as if a storm was beginning to break over a choppy sea. The Kyrgs re-appeared, dragging a teenage lad.

'It weren't me!' the boy protested, shaking in fear. 'Honest, it weren't me!'

'That's right,' an anonymous voice shouted from the crowd. 'The lad said nothing.'

'Quiet!' shouted Finton tremulously. 'We do not make mistakes. Take him to the dungeons.'

The rumble of the crowd increased and it pushed towards the brightly dressed Prefect. He turned quickly and scurried back into the safety of the City Hall. Sustained jeers were aimed at his receding back, but the appearance of archers at the windows of the square building quietened the crowd and it began to disperse. A number of people peeled off the back and headed away from the square. Zastra joined them, pondering what she had heard. She and Findar would have to leave Riverford as soon as possible. It was not safe for them, now that they were considered traitors. Her reverie was broken by the familiar sound of her father's name.

'I'd no particular liking of Leodra, or any of them Grand Marls,' a short, stubby man was saying to a couple of friends, 'but I don't agree with this business. Bringing those Kyrg savages to do their dirty work. You know old Yoland, the baker? All he did was break curfew to get his wife some medicine and refused to stop for those Kyrginite thugs. Now he's been locked up as a traitor.'

'And that flekk Finton,' piped up another man, 'last week, he was just a secretary, hated by everyone for being a real stickler for protocol. Now some idiot has made him Prefect.'

'Aye. I heard it were him as ordered Lord Miraval's guards to open the Westgate and let in the Kyrgs. What with that migaradon, the guards had no chance. Some good men and women amongst them too, as well as Miraval himself. To think we have a lousy backstabber ruling the roost like a cock hen.'

'Hush,' whispered the third man, casting Zastra a suspicious look. 'We could all be locked up for saying such things. Think of your wife and littluns.' The three men disappeared into the maze of alleyways.

Chapter Twenty-Four

It had not been a good day for Grindarl, newly promoted Lieutenant of the Bractarian guards. Not only had they had trouble with one of the migaradons which had, for no good reason, flown into the northwest tower and caused considerable damage as well as nearly throwing its rider, but worse, there was still no news of Leodra's children. It was more than a week since they had slipped out, in spite of the gatehouse guards and mindweavers who had been ordered to apprehend them, and he was due to report to the Grand Marl within the hour. Thorlberd would not be happy with the lack of progress. Grindarl had earned his promotion in the fight for Golmer Castle, where his cunning plan to lace the drinks of Leodra's guards during Rastran's birthday party had considerably weakened resistance to the coup. He had no intention of losing out now; he would have to find those children. Surely then a further promotion would be forthcoming. A chiming bell interrupted his thoughts, indicating that the time had come for him to make his report. He went to the Grand Marl's offices with some trepidation.

Thorlberd was in deep conversation with a group of ministers. A grey figure was seated in the far corner of the room, half obscured in shadow. Grindarl squinted, but could not make out who the seated figure was. Thorlberd dismissed his attendants and turned his intense gaze upon the lieutenant.

'Well, Grindarl?'

'No word as yet, my Lord. We've searched everywhere within ten leagues of Golmer Castle, with no luck. The huge reward has not helped. Indeed lots of people have been wasting our time by turning in their own families and friends. We have investigated hundreds of children, but all have been accounted for.'

'Not good enough,' bellowed the new Grand Marl. 'We must find those children. I made this clear to you – I will not tolerate failure. It seems that you are not up to the task.'

He glanced towards the seated figure. A woman, strongly built, with cropped hair speckled in various shades of grey, moved towards the light with the menace and constrained grace of a she-caralyx. Grindarl gasped involuntarily. A fearful scar ran across the woman's face, from the right ear to the mouth, an icy white track against an already pale backdrop. The woman grinned at Grindarl's response. She was well used to such reactions. The mouth and scar melded together, giving the appearance of a lopsided grin across the face, but the mirthless smile did not reach the pale grey eyes, which were cold and amphibious. Too late, Grindarl became aware of a flash of metal swiftly followed by a searing pain in his chest. The shock barely had time to register in his eyes before his life was extinguished. The grey woman stepped back, cleaning her knife, taking great care to avoid staining her hands, which were protected by gloves of soft grey leather.

'Good, Brutila,' said Thorlberd, looking with disgust at the heap in front of him. 'I've allowed this to slip for too long. Findar and Kastara must be found. They will be key to our success. The blood tests revealed that both twins will have great power.'

'Blood tests?'

'One of my scientists recently developed a test that can determine whether a child will be a mindweaver, even before they reach the age at which abilities are manifest. It requires a small sample of blood, which I was able to obtain from the twins, although Zastra and her friend nearly caught me in the act, the babies screamed so much from the pin prick.'

'What will you do with them?'

'When we find them, we will keep them close and supervise their education. As they grow up, they will think it natural to join us. They will become our strongest allies. However we must get them now, before others can teach them to hate us.'

'And what about the girl, Zastra?' asked the woman in a husky tone.

'She must be eliminated to maintain order,' said Thorlberd. 'She could act as a rallying point for resistance. I take no pleasure in it, but unfortunately it is necessary. All my resources are at your disposal. You shall carry the title of master at arms and I shall give you my personal seal.'

Brutila smirked. 'You should have asked me in the first place, rather than this imbecile,' she said, nudging the body of Grindarl with her foot. 'I hope you don't doubt me, Thorlberd.'

'Your loyalty and efficiency I have no concerns about. However, I thought your personal hatred of my brother might cloud your judgement. Remember, I want the twins alive.'

'You should not have denied me my request to dispose of Leodra personally. I would have taken much pleasure in it.'

'I owed it to my brother to allow him a dignified death,' said Thorlberd.

'Sentimentality is weakness, my Lord. We've always agreed on that.'

'Do not mistake my words for weakness, Brutila. I did what had to be done.'

'And that pathetic little Anara too?'

Thorlberd gave her a dark look.

'Yes,' he said bluntly. 'I suggest you leave before I lose patience and arrange for you to share Grindarl's fate. You have your orders.'

Dismissed, the grey haired woman left to stalk her prey. She found Strinverl, the new highmaster of mindweavers, entering his rooms without ceremony. The gaunt man jumped up as she entered, but the sight of her scarred face stopped any protest at the intrusion before he could utter it.

'Any news of the brats?' asked Brutila, not bothering with the niceties of introductions. Strinverl shook his head nervously.

'Not a whisper in the essence has been detected since Thorlberd's victory.'

'How can it be that the entire body of mindweavers cannot find two babies and a child no taller than my chest?'

'I thought Grindarl was in charge of this operation,' protested Strinverl.

'Not any more,' Brutila said with a smile of satisfaction.

Strinverl's eyes opened wide at the sight of the terrible, lopsided grimace.

'As you know, the power only works over short distances,' he stammered, 'half a league at most. It's not simply a case of closing my eyes and picking them out. We have mindweavers stationed all over Golmeira. I'm sure they will find them soon.'

'Not good enough,' barked Brutila. 'I begin to wonder where your loyalties lie. You were a member of Leodra's council for many years after all.'

'Do not presume to question me,' retorted Strinverl. 'It was me who disabled half the mindweavers on the council, me who was Thorlberd's inside man and me who disposed of Teona, our over-promoted highmaster.' His eyes glinted with pleasure at the memory.

'Once a traitor, always a traitor, the saying goes,' remarked Brutila dryly. 'Perhaps I'd better check?'

Ignoring his cry of protest, she dug into his mind. His defences were weak and his thoughts were easy to steal. Like many people with great mindweaving abilities, Strinverl had relatively little resistance to the entry of others. Arrogant and complacent, never imagining that anyone would dare to challenge them. It was no wonder the council had fallen so easily.

Brutila continued to rummage long after she had confirmed his loyalty to Thorlberd – or at least loyalty for as long as Strinverl gained by the arrangement. Then she released him. 'Just what I expected,' she snorted.

Strinverl staggered back as if he had been punched.

'I have never…' he began, but Brutila raised a grey-gloved hand. His protest died in his mouth.

'Now, what explanation do you have for your current lack of success?' she drawled, as if they were at a polite tea party, with no hint of the violence she had just visited upon him.

He smoothed back his few remaining strands of hair in a feeble attempt to regain his dignity.

'Of course the babies are too young to have conscious thoughts and so cannot be detected,' he said. 'Zastra was always a resourceful child and when she took the test she demonstrated some ability to resist mindweaving. Not enough to protect her against even the weakest of us, unless…'

'Unless what?'

'Unless someone taught her. If one of the council took it upon themselves to train her, she might have developed the skills to evade us. But it would take a great deal of study to achieve such a feat. I can hardly imagine that any offspring of Leodra, that weak and insignificant man, could manage such a thing. Especially a mere talentless child.'

'Your lack of imagination may have already cost us,' said Brutila. 'We still have some members of Leodra's council imprisoned in the dungeon – those who were not killed. I shall enjoy paying them a visit.'

Chapter
Twenty-Five

Zastra hurried along the streets of Riverford, plucking up courage to ask a passer-by for directions to the Eastgate. She was anxious to leave this dark, forbidding city whose tall buildings seemed to be closing over her head like a fist of stone fingers. With nowhere to spend the night, she did not want to be caught out by the curfew. She travelled down a steep cobbled street, hesitating as she reached a fork. A gang of Kyrgs was heading towards them on the left-hand route, so she took the other. She had gone barely thirty paces, when, without warning, she was clattered by a young lad, dark skinned, with a head of tight curls, who had rushed headlong out of one of the houses lining the street. They crashed to the ground in a heap.

'Sorry,' muttered the boy. He scrambled up and ran off down the hill, then darting to his left and into a narrow alleyway.

Findar had been woken by the bump and began to bawl with some vigour. Two angry looking Kyrgs emerged from the same house as the boy. One of them grabbed Zastra roughly.

'Got you!' he exclaimed.

'Wait, Tholgar, that's not the one,' said the other Kyrg, looking closely at Zastra. 'Where did he go, boy?'

When Zastra did not respond, she found herself shoved roughly against the wall of the house behind her.

'Tell us now and we'll let you go. Otherwise, it's to the dungeons,' the one called Tholgar said menacingly. Findar wailed at an even higher pitch. Zastra looked around her, thinking quickly.

'That way,' she said, pointing up the hill in the opposite direction to where the boy had gone.

'If you're lying, you'll be sorry,' snarled Tholgar, gripping her hard by the shoulder and grinding her bones together. 'Show me where they went.'

As he pulled her along, Zastra faked a limp, slowing him down.

'I can't go any faster,' she cried plaintively, refusing to speed up. Findar was crying with the violence only babies can muster. Zastra did not try and calm him. If they could be really irritating, perhaps the Kyrgs would just let them go. Zastra dragged even more, faking a coughing fit.

'I can't... go... on. Must... stop,' she whined.

'Show me where he went,' insisted Tholgar.

Zastra pointed up towards a narrow passage about forty paces away.

'There,' she cried. 'I saw him go that way.' She sank to the ground in a dead weight.

Tholgar snarled with frustration

'Oh, let's just leave it,' said the other Kyrg.

'No – the boy insulted us. I cannot let that pass. Come on, leave these two, they'll just get in the way.'

The Kyrgs released Zastra and headed for the passageway. She turned and hurried back down the hill. Hearing a cry, she glanced over her shoulder. Tholgar was running towards her. He did not look pleased. Zastra broke into a run, skidding on the greasy cobbles as she turned and ducked down the same dark alley that the dark skinned boy had disappeared into. She ran as fast as she could, but carrying Findar slowed her down and her pursuers were gaining. A wooden door opened in the side of the alley and a skinny brown arm reached out and grabbed her.

'Quick. Hide here!' a voice whispered urgently, and they were pulled inside in a heartbeat, the door closing behind them just in time. Two pairs of heavy boots thundered past, the door shaking in their wake. Zastra turned, making out the outline of the curly-haired boy in the gloom. He held his finger to his lips and beckoned them to the back of what appeared to be a large cellar. A small barred window looked out onto a small courtyard. The two Kyrgs, having lost their quarry, were pacing in frustration.

'They must be hiding in one of the houses,' said Tholgar, eyes searching every nook and crevice. 'Fetch the rest of the troop, while I stand guard.' Zastra shrank back behind a large barrel. Findar, who had temporarily quietened in surprise at their hectic flight, filled his lungs as if to begin wailing again. Hastily, Zastra reached in her bag for the sugar. She and the boy both heaved sighs of relief when Findar chose to suckle quietly on her finger.

'What do we have here?' a well-mannered voice drawled from the street outside the cellar.

Zastra and her new companion peered once more out of the cellar window. A handsome young man was seated in languid pose on the sill of a first floor window of the house opposite. He was well groomed, but dressed in ill matched, poorly fitting clothes. He peered down at the Kyrgs and then glanced across at their barred window and winked. Zastra shrank back. The man knew they were there. A second man, as ugly as the other was handsome, popped his head out of the same window.

'Looks like we have snared some Kyrgs,' the handsome man said gaily. 'Bullying children as usual.'

Tholgar snarled up at them. Without hesitation, both men sprang down into the courtyard, swords appearing in their hands as if from nowhere. The Kyrgs adopted an aggressive crouch, each pulling two short, serrated blades from pouches on the sides of their hips. A rattle of pure aggression poured forth from each Kyrginite throat.

'Looks like a spot of fun to be had, eh, Marik?' said the ugly man.

'There's only two though,' replied Marik. 'Hardly worth bothering with, if you ask me. Still, children in distress, it behoves us to do something Godral, don't you think?'

'Absolutely,' replied his comrade. The two men sprang upon the Kyrgs in a flurry of blades. The children watched the battle in awe, the quick flashing blades of the young men contrasting with the short, savage thrusts of the Kyrginites. The battle did not last long. The Kyrgs were both slain, although the handsome man had been caught by one the serrated blades and had a deep cut on his upper arm.

'Blasted scythals,' he said, plucking his sleeve in mild annoyance. 'A blade of savages, if ever there was one. Dratted animals, these Kyrgs.'

'Brave though,' said his companion. 'That big one fought to the end, even after you had disarmed him.'

'Too brainless to think of surrendering,' remarked Marik, cleaning his own blade and replacing it in a scabbard strapped to his back. Crouching down, he peered through the window and into the cellar.

'It's safe now children.' At that moment, Findar began to cry, no longer placated by the sugar. There was no point in hiding anymore, so the two children reluctantly exited their refuge.

'I like your style,' said Marik, grinning. 'If you are going to pick a house to hide in, pick one belonging to one of Finton's mistresses. You've got some nerve.'

'I didn't know who it belongs to,' muttered the young boy, appearing shy in front of the two men. Zastra's eyes were drawn to the bodies of the dead Kyrginites, and she shivered. As if sensing her thoughts, the ugly man got down on one knee in front of them, masking their view of the bodies.

'I'm Godral and this is Marik. We won't harm you,' he said gently. His handsome companion bowed with a grin and a flourish.

'Erstwhile humble soldiers in the Marl of Riverford's guard at your service,' he said.

'Humble, my backside,' remarked Godral.

'Shush comrade,' said Marik, waving him away. 'We are loyal soldiers of Grand Marl Leodra, sadly fallen upon hard times. Resigned to be soldiers of fortune, flitting about in the shadows, rescuing innocent children, such as your good selves, as well as maidens in distress, at any opportunity.'

Godral snorted. 'Maidens in distress? What rubbish you talk.'

'Tush tush, dear Godral. Did not we aid a fair maiden in distress only yesterday?'

'As I recall, she was not so much fair maiden as a weather beaten old shopkeeper with several warts and at least three chins.'

'Beauty is beneath the skin, comrade, and she was as fair a personage as I have ever met. Did not she supply us with a feast fit for a Grand Marl?'

'A bit of mouldy cheese and some stale bread a dog might think twice about. Mind you, I was ready. I'd not eaten for two days. It's hard being on the run.'

'And the wine Godral, the dear creature supplied us with the wine of the grand master vintners themselves.'

Godral raised an eyebrow at Zastra.

'Some old hogwash that she had been unable to sell. Tasted like a mixture of medicine and mould.'

'Are there many soldiers still loyal to Leodra?' asked Zastra hesitantly.

Godral sighed. 'It was a terrible day, the day the traitor Thorlberd's ruffians took over. Finton betrayed us, opening the gates to the Kyrginite hoard. We tried to muster a defence, but Lord Miraval was already dead, murdered in his sleep. And that evil beast, the migaradon, must have killed a hundred of us. We tried to fight it but any spears and arrows that reached it just bounced off its hide. I've never seen anything like it. We even tried using the large catapults, but it dodged our shots easily. They say the riders are mindweavers and I can believe it. Every time the beast swooped, my sight seemed to blur and my head was filled with unnatural fear and strange, confusing visions. We didn't stand a chance.'

'How did you escape?' asked the boy, wide-eyed.

'Marik and I became separated from our troop. I'm ashamed to say we all scattered, desperately trying to escape the migaradon. Since then we have hidden in the shadows, trying to disrupt Finton's plans where we can. There are a few others who escaped with us, but we are few and there is little we can do.'

'Oh, how you complain, Godral,' exclaimed Marik. 'Always looking on the gloomy side, and dimming the mood. There's such fun to be had, chasing Kyrgs and meeting such companions. Might I have the honor of your names, noble Sirs?'

Zastra was half tempted to tell them the truth, to see what reaction she might get, but she remembered Hedrik's warning about pride and she kept quiet. It would be a foolish risk. *Trust no one*, her father had said.

'Hedrik of Trindhome,' she muttered, trying for her best country boy accent.

'They call me Boltan,' said the curly-haired boy.

'Well met, dear comrades,' said Marik, bowing low with a flourish and a wink. Boltan laughed at his strange foolishness, but they were soon disturbed by the sound of marching boots. A large troop by the sound of it, heading in their direction.

Marik bowed again. 'Sadly, our short acquaintance must be curtailed, to my deepest regret. We continue to fight for a free and just Golmeira. Let the tyranny of Thorlberd be overthrown!' The two men reeled round the corner and were gone.

Chapter
Twenty-Six

The boy Boltan eyed Zastra with curiosity.

'Thanks for not telling them ugly brutes where I was,' he said. 'What you doing with a littlun on your own? Where's yer Ma?'

Zastra found herself unable to say anything. She had tried not to think of her parents, since the feelings that came with such thoughts were crippling. Boltan seemed to understand.

'Me Ma and Da are dead too,' he said.

Two chimes rang out.

'The curfew,' said Boltan. 'It's early today.'

'It can't be the curfew already!' cried Zastra. 'It isn't close to sunset and we need to leave the city today.'

'Too late now,' remarked Boltan. 'No one leaves the city once the curfew bells've rung.' He looked at Zastra's crestfallen face. 'Got anywhere to stay the night?' he asked. She shook her head, rocking Findar as he began to fidget.

'Come with me,' the boy commanded. Zastra saw no reason to argue. She followed him as he flitted across the maze of streets and alleyways. At length they arrived at a row of shops, where Boltan made for the door of a shop. Its windows were filled with hundreds of candles of different shapes and colours. Seeing Zastra hesitate, he gently tugged on her arm.

''Salright,' he said. 'Nula won't mind – a few more ain't gonna make no difference.'

They made their way past rows of heavily scented candles to the back of the shop and up a set of narrow wooden stairs set against the wall. Zastra began to hear voices and as Boltan pushed open the door, a discordant clamour overwhelmed her.

They were in a large, rectangular room, with a fire already lit, although the evening was not particularly cold. On the fire, a pot full of a bubbling concoction was set upon a tripod, giving off a delicious array of aromas. But the most striking image was that of a flock of children, dashing around in circles, laughing and screaming as they played.

'Boltan, where in the stars have you been?' A full-throated female voice yelled out of the chaos. 'I've been worried ever since the curfew rang out.'

The cry came from a large, tousle-haired woman, who was seated by the fire, alternating stirring the pot with nursing a baby.

'I was chased by some Kyrgs and they nearly caught me. Hedrik here helped me escape. They need somewhere to stay tonight and I said it'd be alright to stay with us, Nula. It is, ain't it?'

Nula squinted across the room and beckoned to Zastra. As Zastra shuffled towards the woman, she became enveloped in a heady scent of herbs and smoke and caramel.

'Let me look at you. Hmm, looks like you could do with a bit of feeding up. And you've a littlun, have you?'

Findar took that moment to pop his little head out of the sling, his blue eyes gazing in rapt attention at the broad face of the over-sized woman.

'Well,' said Nula, smiling kindly. 'There's always room for another one, if you don't mind sharing a blanket. Although by the smell of it, this one needs a bath. Phew! I've just done my own youngest. Boltan, would you please take the baby's linen downstairs and wash it. And little…what's his name, duckie?'

'Er, Hilfrik,' said Zastra, saying the first name that came to mind.

'Right, Boltan, you can do Hilfrik's too.'

'Aw, Nula,' protested Boltan, 'I only did the washing last night. Ain't it someone else's turn?'

'That's what you get for staying out late and worrying me so much,' said Nula, sternly enough to end the argument, although there was a hint of a smile behind her eyes. 'When you come back, you can tell me all about your adventures.'

So it was settled. The new arrivals were welcomed into the heart of the riotous and friendly family, as if it were the most usual thing in the world for two strays to be taken in. Two of the young girls came and took care of Findar, playing with him as delicately as if he were a precious doll. Once the baby linens had been seen to, Boltan regaled the company with the tale of his adventures. He spoke with spirit, aping the actions of the Kyrgs so that the younger children gasped in terror. He'd seen a troop of them manhandling a young girl, so he'd thrown a lump of mud and shouted insults. Two of them had chased him and he'd tried to shake them by running through a house whose back door had been open. As he had burst out the front he had bumped into Hedrik and little Hilfrik. He related how he had turned down the alley and slipped into the cellar. Then, by peering through a grating he had seen Hedrik send the Kyrgs the wrong way. He'd been glad to have an opportunity to help when Hedrik ended up rushing down the same alley.

When he came to the part where the soldiers had appeared, he mimicked Marik's exaggerated mannerisms so well that the other children were crying with laughter. Zastra said nothing; she was not yet ready for laughter. Nula let Boltan tell his tale, offering only a few remarks on the foolishness of baiting Kyrgs and the likelihood of him getting himself killed well before he ever reached manhood. When he was finished, they were joined by another woman. She was of average size, but the family resemblance to Nula was strong.

'Merle, we've picked up another couple of strays, it seems,' said Nula brightly. 'I hope you don't mind – I'm sure they'll be no trouble.' Nula's sister rolled her eyes, but seemed unsurprised, and the large family sat down to a lively supper. The meat stew was the best meal Zastra had eaten in days, and she ate hungrily, mopping up the tasty sauce with a large piece of freshly baked bread. Bolton raised his cup of water in Zastra's direction, a wide grin stretched across his face.

'Wine from the grand master vittler himself,' he said.

'What's a vittler?' asked one of the younger children.

'Vintner,' said Zastra absently. 'Someone who buys and sells wine.'

'Well, I think vittler sounds better,' protested Boltan, who proceeded to exchange extravagant toasts with everyone in turn. As she was eating, Zastra couldn't help notice that Nula kept looking at her. She lowered her head but felt the eyes of the large woman still on her. After they had eaten and the younger children had been settled down for the night, Zastra tried to hide in the darkest corner of the room but Nula beckoned her over to two chairs in front of the fire. Zastra had no choice but to obey.

'Sit by me, duckie,' Nula said, easing her body into one of the chairs. Sturdy though it was, it creaked in protest, seeming destined to break under her weight.

'I wanted to thank you, for helping our Boltan. It must have taken some guts. Them Kyrgs can be quite scary.'

Zastra tried to mutter something appropriate, but Nula did not pause for breath.

'I'd hate for anything to happen to our Boltan. People told me he'd be a bundle of trouble, but that ain't so, he's a good little soul.' She looked fondly over at the boy, who was wrestling with Yusa, one of the other children. As they tussled, they knocked over the iron cooking tripod with a huge clatter. Nula raised an eyebrow as she looked at Zastra and shook her head, smiling.

'Like I said, no trouble at all.'

Zastra couldn't help returning the smile.

'Boltan, that's enough,' called Nula. 'Time for bed now.'

'All right, Nula,' he said, setting the tripod back on its feet. Nula shifted in her chair. It let out a volley of creaks and groans but by some miracle held firm.

'So Hedrik, how do you come to be at Riverford, all alone?'

'I'm not alone,' said Zastra, 'I've got Hilfrik.'

'Boltan tells me your parents have passed away?'

Zastra nodded.

'Do you have anywhere to go? Anyone who can take care of you?'

Zastra shook her head, hoping that Nula would stop asking questions.

'I don't like to see littluns on their own,' said Nula, with a frown. 'But I don't like deceitfulness, neither.'

Zastra stared at the floor, unable to look at the woman. Nula bent closer to her, her wild hair blocking out the candlelight.

'They are stopping anyone with children and it ain't pretty, I can tell you. Some of the soldiers are a bit overzealous. I worry for you and little Hilfrik. You look a bit conspicuous, just the pair of you. I'm not saying you've anything to hide, but you're no country lad, however you might try to appear like one. I think you'd better tell me the truth, don't you?'

Chapter
Twenty-Seven

Zastra flinched back, wide-eyed. Nula placed a calming hand on her arm.

'S'alright, my dear. You'll fool most people but I'm more observant than most. Nosey, some would call it,' she chuckled. 'But I say there ain't nothing wrong in taking an interest in people.'

'How did you know?' asked Zastra.

Nula snorted. 'Vintner, indeed! No county boy would know how to pronounce that word, let alone know what it meant.'

Zastra was mortified to have made such a mistake.

'And you aren't quite smelly enough,' remarked Nula.

'Who's smelly?' cried Boltan.

'Boltan here is a good example,' said Nula. 'He always manages to sit or roll in something disgusting.'

'What's disgusting?' said Boltan.

'Bed!' cried Nula. 'Unless you want a flannel bath. And remember we only have cold water.'

Boltan screwed up his eyes and shook his head comically, before ducking under the nearest blanket and pulling it tight over his head.

Zastra hesitated. She had not forgotten her father's words but all her instincts were to trust Nula.

'You are right,' she said at last, 'but I can't tell you the truth. It could put you in danger. I'm sorry.'

Nula patted her lap with both hands.

'It's me as should be sorry. Always poking my nose in other folks' business. It's a terrible habit of mine. You helped our Boltan, that's enough for me.'

'Thank you,' said Zastra.

'Now,' said Nula, 'We plan to stay in Riverford a few more days and then we'll be returning to our home in Borsha. It lays a few days journey east of here. My husband is due back anytime now. He's a sailor on board a trading ship and I'd like to be sure that he's safe, in these strange times. Would you like to come with us?'

They were interrupted by a heavy pounding on the door of the shop. Zastra sprang up in alarm.

'What's that?' she cried. Merle took a candle and went to investigate. After a few moments, she returned, accompanied by a young woman with a sharp nose and thin lips.

'This is Kep, who helps us in the shop,' explained Merle.

'Blue fever!' cried Kep. 'Blue fever in the southwest quarter!'

'Ssh,' hissed Nula. 'Kep, keep your voice down. Now, what's this about the fever?'

'I overheard a healer telling a friend to leave the city,' said Kep, still breathing heavily. 'He said to keep it quiet so he can leave the city before the alarm is raised.'

Nula nodded. 'Quite right. If Finton finds out they'll close the gates and quarantine the city.'

'We'll be trapped,' exclaimed Kep with a shudder.

'I don't believe it,' said Merle. 'It's scaremongering, is all.'

'I'm not so sure,' said Nula thoughtfully. 'Me and Boltan were down in the southwest quarter this morning and we saw a little baby dying in her mother's arms. She was in the street, homeless, poor dear, but there was nothing we could do to help them. I thought the baby's lips looked blue, so I came right away. That's the tell-tale sign, you know. Blue lips, that's why they call it the blue fever.'

'Is it very dangerous?' asked Zastra.

'Oh, yes duckie. A terrible, terrible thing. Not many people survive once the fever is fully upon them. The disease sits in the brain and even them that live through it can have problems for years afterwards.

Visions, loss of memory, things like that. It's awful contagious too.'

'There was a woman,' said Zastra, frowning, 'She told us to get out of Riverford. I didn't understand her at the time, but maybe that's what she meant.'

'Where did you meet this woman?' asked Nula.

'I'm not sure where we were. Not far from the Westgate. There were beggars on the street and the houses looked about to fall down.'

'The southwest quarter,' Nula said, glancing at her sister. 'What exactly did this woman say?'

'Not much,' replied Zastra. 'Just to get out of the city, it wasn't a place for littluns. Something like that.'

'We must get out, now!' said Kep, pacing nervously first to the door and then to a cupboard. She flung open the door and began to rummage around furiously.

'Stop floundering about, Kep,' said Nula firmly. 'We can't leave until they open the gates in the morning. But I suggest we try to leave first thing. You too, Merle.'

'I will not. I won't leave the shop for looters and beggars to fight over.'

'You always were a stubborn one,' sighed Nula. She turned to Zastra. 'You'll come with us, won't you? You'll be less noticeable hidden amongst my brood.'

'But what about the mindweavers at the gate?' Zastra asked. 'They'll read your mind and then they will know we aren't your children.'

'We'll think of something,' said Nula. 'Anyway, not all these littluns are mine. I take care of them of course. Look at Boltan, his Ma died in childbirth and then his Da drowned in the floods five years ago. No one else would take him in, so now he lives with me. I like a noisy household as you can see. Only three of these are mine, the other three are strays I've picked up along the way. Another two won't look so odd. Let's just hope they don't close the city.'

The next morning, they were awake early. However, much as Nula tried to chivvy her family along, it took a good deal of time to round everyone up. The little ones in particular did not understand the urgency of the situation. Four-year-old Yusa thought all this running around was great fun. Deciding that hide and seek would be even better, he hid himself in the wash basket and Nula and Zastra wasted valuable time searching for him. When Yusa had at last been found, Zastra got Findar ready and packed her bag, looking in dismay at the disarray around her. When the bell rang to lift the curfew, Nula and her family were still not ready.

'Where's Boltan?' asked Nula, her hair even more wild than usual. She had a baby on one arm and a toddler clutching her other hand. Zastra helped load the bags and the other children into the back of a rickety cart, grabbing hold of the miscreant Yusa before he could disappear again. An ancient plough horse was fetched from the stable, backing with infuriating slowness into its harness. It then refused to accept its bridle until Nula bribed it with a large pani-fruit. At long last, everything was stowed and Nula heaved herself onto the front seat. The cart tilted alarmingly to one side. Zastra looked over the side of the cart in concern. The front axle was bowing under the weight.

'Don't worry,' cried Nula, 'this dear old cart has never failed me.' She shook the reins and the horse inched forward at a painfully slow plod. Zastra chewed her lower lip in frustration. The streets were already filled with an assortment of carts and barrows. The gaps between were crammed with pedestrians, walking or running towards the gate. The rumors of blue fever had spread fast.

'Wait!' cried Zastra in dismay. 'We still don't have Boltan.'

Nula pulled the horse to a stop. 'Where is that boy?' she sighed. 'I told him…'

The cart jolted and they turned to see a grinning Boltan crash down on top of little Yusa, who screamed in protest. Boltan was carrying half a pie and his mouth smeared with something that looked suspiciously like gravy.

Nula glared at him.

'Where did you get that?' she said.

'Stole it,' he said, taking another bite.

'That's so naughty,' cried Nula. 'How many times have I told you?'

'S'alright, I stole it from Kyrgs.'

'Then it's both naughty and stupid,' said Nula. 'If we don't make it to the gate in time because of your stomach I'll...'

'Why?' asked Boltan, mouth full of pie. 'Wos'matter?'

Zastra and Nula exchanged looks and Nula chivvied the reluctant horse onwards.

The tide of people thickened as they approached the Eastgate. Zastra sighed. There were so many people already waiting that it would be ages before they made it to the front of the queue. Finton could order the gates to be shut at any moment. Somehow Nula nudged the cart forward, finding gaps where none seemed to exist, until, with a mixture of oaths and apologies, she had guided them to within twenty paces of the Eastgate, far sooner than Zastra had expected. Bractarian guards were attempting to bring order to the chaos, lining up the people in front of a plump, black robed woman, who was seated on a raised chair. Zastra stiffened. The robes were familiar; the same as she had seen on that terrible night on the courtyard stairs of Golmer Castle as Teona had dragged her towards her father's offices. Was it really only seven days ago?

Mindweaver, she thought to herself, nudging Nula to draw her attention. The large woman nodded.

'Mindmeddler,' she said. 'Try not to worry. They can sense fear, so I'm told.'

'I can hide my thoughts. At least, I think I can – I've been shown,' said Zastra.

Nula's eyes widened.

'Oh aye,' she exclaimed. 'You're full of secrets, aren't you? Well, that'll help. I use plainer methods myself.' Zastra was intrigued, wondering what Nula's methods might be. Taking advantage of a gap in the crowd, Nula had again manoeuvered them forward and all of a sudden they were in front of the gate. A lieutenant gestured for Nula to dismount.

'State your name and your reason for leaving the city,' he said.

'Nula, weaver of Borsha. Returning home from this stinking pit,' she said, hands on hips. The plump woman's eyes narrowed. Whereas others had blanched, or even fainted under the mental probing, Nula stood defiantly, a red hue across her face the only outward sign that she was at all affected.

'Your thoughts are coarse, woman,' said the mindweaver, throwing back her head in disgust.

'Mebbee,' replied Nula, 'as yours might be if you had to find a way to feed all these littluns.'

As if on command, the younger children all started wailing and rawping.

'I remember this lot,' the lieutenant said, 'they came through a few days ago. Local villagers, we don't have to worry about them.'

The mindweaver nodded almost imperceptibly and the lieutenant waved them through.

'Move along, move along,' he shouted, and the cart with the still bawling children rolled forward. Zastra exhaled, releasing the tight grip she had taken of the side of the cart. They were nearly free. Just in front of the gate they were stopped by another bank of guards demanding taxes.

'I will not!' Nula exclaimed. 'I've earned that money and you can keep your grubby little hands off.'

'Ten percent tax on all monies and goods entering or leaving the city. Orders of the Prefect. Quiet yourself woman.'

Nula continued to protest and the babies redoubled their wailing.

Zastra wondered why Nula didn't just pay up, and eventually the large woman handed over a few coins from a pitifully small store and they were released.

'Did she read your mind?' she asked Nula in a low voice, once the gate was far enough behind them. 'How did you get away with it?'

'A little trick I've discovered. Concentrate on a big, juicy thought, preferably something a little on the raunchy side – a little buttoned up prude like that, that's all they'll see, and they'll not want to probe any deeper.' Nula chuckled. 'I've certainly given her something to think about. Ha!' She remained in a state of high amusement for quite some time. Zastra didn't fully understand how Nula had fooled the mindweaver, but she didn't care, as long as they were free of Riverford. She glanced back at the receding walls of the city with a shudder. Nula caught her look.

'S'alright my dear. If they'd suspected anything they'd have come after us already. I reckon we'll be safe, at least for now.'

'It's a horrid place,' said Zastra, shivering. 'I hope I never have to go back.'

'Oh, it ain't so bad,' said Nula. 'Not that I'd choose to live there, mind. I much prefer the open country and village life, but my sister likes all the bustle and variety. Of course at the moment, everything is upside and about, but it'll soon sort itself out. These things always do. I just hope they're wrong about the blue fever. I do worry for Merle.'

Zastra turned to her large companion.

'Nula, how come there are so many poor people? Why aren't there enough homes for everyone? Surely people will rise up against the evil of Thorlberd, to stop such things.'

'Thorlberd is not responsible for the poor and homeless of Riverford. They've been there as long as I can remember. It's a terrible shame, but nothing has ever been done about it. It's not an uncommon sight in other big towns either. You've a good deal to learn young Hedrik, I reckon.'

Zastra was stung and upset equally, although Nula's words were not spoken unkindly. To think there had been such suffering and poverty under her father's rule. And even worse, that nothing had been done about it.

'Surely Leodra did not know. He would have done something,' she protested.

'Mebbee, mebbee not,' replied Nula. 'There's a good many poor people scattered about these lands with no chance to make a living because their leases were given away after one poor harvest. The laws of the land favor the rich and don't give the poor much chance. And the Marls and Grand Marls and such like have always taken the best horses and the best food for themselves. Sometimes it makes me so angry. There's other things, too – take firedust, for instance; that's precious to someone like me. A fire-ring and a sack of firedust are a big help in the cold winters to light fires and keep them hot. But the rich buy up most of it, pushing the prices so high that us poor folk can't afford it. And what do they do with it? Make it into fire-fountains for entertainment. Imagine – fire-fountains, what a waste. Meanwhile some poor family can't afford to keep their house warm of a winter.'

Nula's bitter diatribe was halted by the wailing of her youngest child. By the time she had attended to the baby, her thread of thought had been lost. Zastra was relieved. Although Nula's anger had not been directed towards her, she felt a strange feeling of shame. She had always taken great delight in fire-fountain displays. She had no idea that they caused so much resentment.

As they left Riverford increasingly far behind them, Zastra began to breathe more easily. The children in the back of the cart began to balk against the enforced inactivity. A few of them jumped off to run and play by the side of the slowly moving vehicle. Every so often, Nula would call to them to make sure they didn't stray too far away. Zastra remained seated by Nula, listening closely to the accents and expressions of the children. Findar's safety could depend on how well she disguised herself and it seemed that she was not doing very well. In spite of her worries, the day passed pleasantly. Only the occasional sally of the Riverford migaradon intruded on the happy mood, but the huge winged creature flew high in the sky and did not appear to be concerned with their little group. Night was drawing in as Nula directed the cart off the road, stopping by the side of a small stream.

'We'll stay here tonight,' she announced. 'You are welcome to join us. We've some halsa nut paste and a nice selection of root veg for a stew.' Stepping off the cart, she pulled Boltan down with her.

'Not you,' she snapped. 'Thieves do not deserve honest food.' While Boltan protested, Zastra helped some of the older children gather firewood. After a hot supper of tasty vegetable stew for everyone except a very sulky Boltan, they all huddled together in the cart and slept.

The next day, they continued on, passing through several villages. Nula directed affable nods and greetings to many of the folk as she passed. She seemed to be on friendly terms with a great many people. However, at present there was little cheer in the faces of the villagers. Thorlberd's soldiers had taken command of all the larger houses and Nula muttered a few oaths under her breath as they rumbled by.

'The nerve. Turfing good people out of their own homes and setting themselves up. They better not try it in Borsha, that's for sure.'

A few leagues further on, Nula looked sideways at Zastra, who was bouncing Findar on her lap, much to the little boy's delight.

'We'll reach Borsha late this afternoon. If you want, you and the littlun can rest with us tonight. There's not much room, but you are welcome to snuggle down if you can find a spot.'

Zastra sighed.

'You are very kind,' she said, 'but you've already done more than enough. I don't want to get you into trouble. Perhaps you could drop us off a few miles short of Borsha? We'll make our own way from there.' Nula nodded, and they continued along in the hot sun, the cart horse flicking away insects with his tail. Zastra was happy to be putting further distance between herself and Riverford. It was another long, lazy day, mercifully uneventful. Even the children became tired at last and tumbled into the back of the cart and slept.

As the sun began to sink toward the horizon, Nula nudged Zastra, who was dozing beside her.

'Here's a good spot. We can't be overlooked by anyone. North lies the Evergreen Forest and the way to the sea lies to the south. I'll let you off here if that is still your wish, although again I say you are welcome to stay the night with us.'

Zastra was not to be dissuaded from her resolution. She had not forgotten the punishment offered by the Prefect of Riverford for those harbouring fugitives. She lugged her backpack over her shoulder. Adjusting the sling for Findar, she waved goodbye to Nula and her family, waiting until they were out of sight before heading north. The Evergreen Forest was on her map, extending far into the east. She felt they would be safer there under the cover of the trees. At least then they would be hidden from the prying eyes of the migaradons. She had no desire to stay on the exposed main road, especially with Thorlberd's soldiers in every village. As she reached the summit of a small hill, she looked back to the road. She could just make out Nula's cart, creeping slowly into the distance. She gazed at it wistfully for a moment and then turned and headed in the direction of the thin smudge of green that lay against the horizon. She walked as fast as she could, but it was night by the time she reached the edge of the forest. The tiny glimmer of remaining light was quickly extinguished as the trees gathered over them, blanketing them in black night. Zastra felt blindly outwards, until her hand reached rough bark and she sank down at the foot of a tree.

A deep despair fell over her. For the first time she felt truly alone. The thoughts and emotions she had been pushing down since the night of their escape from Golmer Castle would not now be stilled. The darkness gave them strength. Her parents cruelly murdered, Kastara left behind, abandoned, and herself, lost and friendless, blundering around just waiting to be discovered. There was no hope, no reason to go on. Guilt, fear and loss took their turn to assail her and she had no strength to resist. It was as if her blood was draining out of her, drop by drop, and she didn't care. Her mental block, hitherto constantly maintained, shivered and died. She was defenceless. Dimly, she was half aware of Findar, crying, but she could not rouse herself to attend to him. It was the longest, darkest night of her life.

Chapter
Twenty-Eight

Brutila smiled coldly at her reflection as she put on a fresh pair of soft grey gloves. The dungeons had been dirty and foul but her visit had been worth it. There had even been some pleasure to be had. Some of the old council members held a ridiculous loyalty to Leodra and his offspring. She'd had to take an extra dose of cintara bark to increase her powers and now she had the answers she needed.

She made her way to Thorlberd's offices, where she found him seated with his son. The new Grand Marl looked up as she entered.

'Well?' he demanded.

'It appears that Zastra received training from Master Dobery in the art of resisting mindweaving. This may explain how she was able to escape without being detected.'

'How did you find this out?' asked Thorlberd. Brutila curled her lip slightly.

'The remaining members of the council were most helpful.'

'I hope you have not been resorting to cintara bark,' said Thorlberd. 'I know the power it gives you, even over other mindweavers, but remember the dangers. We agreed it should only be used during our uprising and sparingly at that, in order to give us a tactical advantage.'

'I need no lectures,' retorted the woman. 'I am fully in control.'

Rastran piped up.

'That's right,' he said. 'Zastra was able to resist me when I tried to teach her a lesson with my mindweaving, the vicious little…'

Thorlberd turned on him.

'Why did you not say something sooner, boy?'

'I…I… you said I wasn't to use mindweaving before the day we took our rightful place as rulers, Father,' he stammered. 'I didn't want to get in trouble.'

'This knowledge could help us find them,' said Thorlberd angrily. 'You need to start thinking bigger, Rastran. Thinking strategically. How many times do I need to tell you this?'

Thorlberd shook his head in disgust and turned his attention back to Brutila.

'It still does not explain how Zastra and the twins got past the gatehouse guards.'

'I've questioned all the guards personally and do not believe Zastra could have sneaked out via the gate. There must be some other exit from the castle that we don't know about. One of the older members of Leodra's council was aware of rumours of some underground tunnel, but knew nothing specific.'

'What is your plan?'

'We need to try and think like Zastra. Where would she go? What would she do? For instance, does she have any friends outside the castle she might go to?'

'I know!' cried Rastran excitedly. 'Her friend Bedrun has also disappeared. I know because I was going to teach her a lesson. Her and my cousin, daring to laugh at me. One of Bedrun's mothers lives in Highcastle village. I bet that's where they went.'

'I'll follow this up at once,' said Brutila, her scar twitching with annoyance.

Thorlberd turned to his son and clouted him round the ear.

'If you'd told us this sooner boy we might have them by now. I should not have to tell you how important this is.'

Rastran folded his arms and dropped his shoulders in a sulky, defensive pose. He gave a loud sniff.

'What?' asked Brutila with a sardonic grin. 'Ruling Golmeira not as much fun as you thought?'

Brutila rode into Highcastle village unaccompanied. She had no fear for her personal safety. Upright and taut in the saddle, she exuded menace. The villagers shied away from her instinctively as she rode past. The captain of the troop that controlled the village took her to Bodel's house. Finding it locked, Brutila ordered the guards to batter down the door. They burst into the house but found it empty.

'Find out if anyone knows where they've gone,' snapped Brutila. She prowled around the house, looking for any clue, anything that might tell her were Zastra was. A thin layer of dust spoke of several days of emptiness. Brutila shook her head in disgust at the incompetent flekks that she had to work with. No one should have been allowed to move during the current period of transition and yet clearly the house had been abandoned. The captain had a lot to answer for. She opened up the back door and scanned the garden. Her eyes narrowed and she sprang forward. A small patch of earth had a slightly darker shade than that which surrounded it. Brutila began to dig with her gloved hands, yelling for a guard to help her. Scrabbling furiously, she uncovered the tip of a garment, and with a yell of triumph she pulled it out. It was a finely embroidered nightgown, caked in mud. The dirt could not disguise the golden seal of Leodra's eagle alongside the hawk of Golmeira.

'Fit for a princess,' exulted the woman in bitter triumph. Rooting around further, she uncovered two small baby blankets, bearing the same seal.

The captain came round the corner of the house, accompanied by a slovenly young woman.

'Look!' shouted Brutila, thrusting the garments in his face. 'They were here, and you let them slip past you.'

The captain swallowed nervously. 'This girl says she has some information,' he muttered, shoving her forward. The woman turned her glacial stare on the girl. She could tell at once what sort of peasant she was. A brazen, dirty little slut.

'Well?'

'I know something, but it'll cost you,' said the girl boldly, although her eyes flicked nervously around the garden.

'Tell me.'

'Not 'til I get those three tocrins he promised me,' insisted the girl, glancing toward the captain.

Brutila smiled her icy smile. Three tocrins was a small amount to pay if the information was useful. But that was not her way. A quick scan of the slut's mind yielded the information without any difficulty.

'You saw a young boy and a man, a stranger to the village, sneak out of this house with two large bundles. You thought you heard a baby crying. Most interesting. And this just after the new regime took over.'

The girl gawped in shock.

'How d'you know that?'

'Oh, don't you worry your pathetic little mind about it. Leave now. People like you disgust me.'

'I still want me money,' insisted the girl.

'If you go now, you'll escape with your life,' said Brutila calmly. The village girl looked at the damp, emotionless eyes. Her courage failed her and she fled.

'But we are looking for a girl, not a boy,' mused the captain.

Brutila exhaled in annoyance. 'Look.' She brandished the soiled clothes. 'They disguised themselves. Find out about this man was – this stranger. Who was he, and where did he come from? The idiot girl didn't know his name but he was scraggy looking, not too young, but not too old either.'

She turned her back as the soldiers hurried away, once again bemoaning the fools she had to work with. Once she had succeeded in this mission she would surely be repaid with better things. Although this was a task she would have performed for no reward. Her reverie was broken by one of the guards returning, panting in his haste and eagerness to please.

'A man – Hedrik – visited the healer Bodel around the time of our victory. From the description, he sounds like the man we are after. No one has seen him since that day. Trindhome, they say he's from. It's nearly sixteen leagues east of here.'

'Excellent,' said Brutila. 'Ready my horse and find me a guide to Trindhome. We've lost enough time as it is.'

'What about the healer?' the guard asked. 'No one knows where she has gone.'

'She is of no importance,' snapped Brutila. She stared over the hills that rose gently to the east. 'I have your trail now, Zastra,' she whispered. 'You'll pay for what your father did to me.'

Chapter Twenty-Nine

For Zastra, the weeks passed with aching slowness. That first night in the forest, Findar's crying had eventually broken through the thick shell of despair that threatened to crush her and she roused herself enough to feed and change him. It took all her effort. The smallest glimmer of determination told her that she must save her brother. She must not give in, for his sake if not her own. She managed to reset her mental block although somehow it took more effort than previously.

Eastwards they journeyed through the forest, using the shadows cast by the sun to guide them. Occasionally there were paths to follow, but more often they made their way through the spongy undergrowth, away from prying eyes. Within the first hour of every day the weight of Findar and the bag caused a deep ache in her back and shoulders. She had to rest frequently, her muscles shaking with fatigue.

Findar, mercifully, had been well-behaved and placid, but one morning he staged a protest. He did not reach up to his sister as she prepared to put him in his sling. Instead, he wriggled and writhed, screaming and wailing, until she was forced to set him down upon the ground again. He sat and fixed his blue eyes questioningly upon her, as if to ask the meaning of all these wanderings. Where was the castle? And where was his twin? Or at least that was what Zastra imagined he was thinking. Not sure what to do, she waited until Findar had cried himself quiet. Yet still he looked at her in unspoken protest.

'I'm sorry Findar,' she said. 'I wish things were different too, but we can't just stay here. We must go on.' Findar cocked his head as if trying to comprehend. He must have understood something in the tone of her voice, since he did not protest as she gently lifted him into the sling and headed off. He did not repeat the performance again.

In the evenings, when she could walk no further, Zastra set camp. She had not dared to set a fire for the first few nights in case the Riverford migaradon should spot them. As they moved deeper into the forest she gained more courage. She was soon well practised in using the fire-ring. Hedrik had packed her a large supply of oats and she made the porridge as she had been taught. It took her a few attempts to master the art, and neither undercook nor burn it, but eventually she learnt to rustle up a bowl with some degree of confidence. It was not up to the standard of the castle kitchens, but it was warm and edible and that was enough. Every morning, stiff and sore, she was roused by the sound of Findar crying. Her feet collected more and more blisters, and each footstep had to be willed.

She struggled on, each day merging into the next, as interminable as the forest that stretched out ahead of her. However, the days, painful as they were, were no match for the nights. Zastra found sleep hard to come by. Any that did was filled with nightmare visions of flying beasts, falling bodies and floating faces of the dead. She would shudder herself awake, briefly thinking she had woken up in her room in Golmer Castle, ready for a morning of school, only to find herself still inside the nightmare. Her baby sister also haunted her. The guilt of leaving Kastara was almost constant, this pain much worse than the mere physical pain of blistered feet and sore limbs. Perhaps Hedrik and Bodel had been right – a thirteen year old girl carrying two babies together would have been like waving a flag in the air. She reviewed the terrible choice, unable to decide if it had been the right one. Not knowing whether Kastara was safe, or captured, or worse, was a constant torture.

To make matters worse, their food supply was running low. Water was plentiful, as there were many streams. This was fortunate, since the air in the forest grew hot and sticky during the day, and Zastra was always thirsty. However, the bread and meat had long gone. Although she looked out for nuts and fruit as Hedrik had taught her, she saw none that she recognised. She began to ration the oats, gnawing hunger adding itself to her other aches and pains.

One afternoon, they came across a large bush laden with greenish nuts. In desperation she wolfed them down despite their bitter taste. She regretted it later, as her stomach cramped and she was sick, leaving her weak and lightheaded. That night, after she had settled Findar down, she fingered the few coins Hedrik had given her, hidden in the lining of the jacket. Tomorrow, they must find a town or village where they could beg or buy food. It was a risk, but a necessary one. The next morning she used their last handful of oats. There was only enough porridge for Findar, but at least it kept him quiet. By consulting the map, she reckoned that if they left the forest to the south they should come across a main road, upon which they must surely find a village.

It was almost noon before the trees began to thin out and she found herself looking down onto an open valley. Shielding her eyes from the harsh midday sun, bright after the shade of the trees, she scanned the sky and to her relief saw no sign of migaradons. On the floor of the valley below a track ran alongside a large stream. Several distant wagons crawled along it. They were moving toward a large village, and Zastra decided to head in the same direction. Her heart began to race. It seemed an age since she had last had contact with people. As she got closer, she made out the glint of metal and the uniforms of soldiers, but there was nothing for it; they must have food or starve. Anyway, she had fooled the soldiers before. She only hoped she could do it again.

In a happy coincidence, they had stumbled upon market day. Zastra sneaked into the village via an unguarded side path. The soldiers, mainly Kyrgs, were preoccupied in stopping and searching the wagons as they came in along the main road. The nearness and bustle of the crowds was strange at first, after so many days of lone travelling and for a while Zastra contented herself with observing and listening. Lost in the crowd, no one paid any attention to a dishevelled, scrawny-looking youth.

'What kind of price is that for a loaf of bread?' a woman was protesting. The stall keeper shrugged.

'Ten percent of all my goods taken,' he complained. 'That's before I've even sold anything. And my carthorses have been impounded by the royal guards, so I've had to pay to borrow some.' He looked surreptitiously around before spitting on the ground. 'I'm sorry, but that's the way it is these days.'

'Well, I've got four mouths to feed. At your prices we'll have nothing by the end of the week. Come, I'll give you a quarter tocrin for two loaves.'

'Sorry, but I've littluns of my own. The price stands.'

'Gouging flekk. I'll go elsewhere,' said the woman as she stomped off.

'Good luck,' muttered the stall keeper turning his head towards the watching Zastra.

'Well? Are you going to buy, or just gawp, lad?'

Zastra purchased a loaf of bread and a couple of fresh rolls, stuffing the rolls hungrily into her mouth as she continued down the market. Everyone was complaining about the price of food. Soldiers were constantly patrolling and Zastra could feel the touch on her mind that indicated a mindweaver was in the area. She looked around anxiously, but found it was impossible to see past the wall of taller people who surrounded her. Suddenly, a gap opened in the crowd and she spotted a tall, black robed figure only a few yards away. The mindweaver. It was a man, judging by his build. Fortunately, he had his back turned to her and she ducked through the crowd, away from the figure, not daring to glance back. She wasted no time in making their other purchases. Not for the first time, she whispered silent thanks to Hedrik. Seeing the haggling and half empty baskets of the country people made her realise what a generous gift his few tocrins had been. She was able to replenish their supplies and even purchase some milk as a treat for Findar. Her brother drank it greedily. She looked hungrily at a stall filled with cakes and sweets, but they were expensive. Reluctantly, she decided they could not afford to use their precious funds for such things. Her backpack full, she headed towards the eastern exit of the village, eager to escape the crowds and return to the relative safety of the forest. She was twenty paces from the edge of the village when she felt a strange creeping feeling, as if she was was being watched. She whirled round. There, not ten paces away, two men sat perched in a smart two-horse trap. Closest to her was a man with a thin, neat beard, elegantly dressed in a bright yellow tunic. He was watching her closely. Somehow, she knew he was laughing at her, although his face was inscrutable. Stunned, she realised he must be in her head and as the realisation came, she identified the tell-tale touch in her mind. She didn't know how she could have missed it. The touch was somehow different, more delicate than any she had felt before. Battling the desperate urge to panic, she nudged her cap lower over her head, the echo of silent laughter roiling in her mind. Had he been able to get through her defences? Did he know who she was? All she knew was they had to leave, and quickly.

'Oy, lad, watch where you're going!' a harsh voice shouted, as she clattered into a burly frame. The jolt loosened the sling and Findar began to wail.

'Sorry,' Zastra mumbled, without stopping. A pair of grimy hands reached out at her, seeking to tear Findar from her grasp.

'My own dear boy!' a wild-eyed woman was yelling. She was emaciated, dirt ingrained in her skin and fingernails. 'You've stolen my boy. Give 'im back. Give 'im back now.'

'No!' protested Zastra with instant vehemence. 'You crazy woman, leave us alone.'

But the wild woman continued to paw at them and Zastra could not shake her off.

A man stepped in. 'What's going on?' he said.

'My boy, my baby boy. They've stolen my baby boy,' wailed the woman.

'He's not hers,' protested Zastra. 'He's my brother – she's mad.'

Drawn by the noise, a pair of Kyrginites bustled over, the crowd parting to let them through. As they arrived, an older woman came over and gently drew the wild woman away from Zastra.

'There, my dear, he's not your boy. Your boy is dead – they killed him, remember? Let this poor lad be.'

The woman stared blankly up at the old lady, the wildness leaking out of her eyes and replaced by emptiness. She allowed herself to be led away.

'I'm sorry,' whispered the old lady. 'The soldiers came to examine her baby and when she wouldn't let go of him, they killed him. It weren't more than two days ago. She's been distraught ever since, keeps thinking she sees her littlun.'

Zastra's relief in their deliverance was short-lived.

'You there, boy. Take your cap off. Let's have a look at you. And let me see that baby.' A Kyrginite glowered down at them and Zastra reluctantly scraped the cap off her head. The Kyrg reached out a hand and lifted her chin, tilting his head as he made close examination of her face, particularly her eyes. Without removing his gaze, he called over his shoulder to those behind him.

'I think we've got something here. Come and see.'

A sinkhole plunged through Zastra's stomach, removing air from her lungs, and strength from her limbs. It was over. That stupid crazy woman had ruined it for them.

A gasp came from the crowd, a collective inhalation as if it had been dealt a firm body blow. To her astonishment, the Kyrg in front of Zastra crumpled to the floor. One by one, the other Kyrgs collapsed in a similar manner.

'Here!' called a voice. The man in the yellow tunic was looking down at her from the trap, arm extended, his companion barely holding the skittering pair of horses at bay.

'Come, I've made them sleep, but not for long. Hurry, girl!'

Zastra hesitated for only a fraction of a second. She clambered into the back of the trap, which was half filled with boxes and chests, and was sent sprawling to the hard floor as the energetic horses were released, the trap almost overturning in the haste of their departure. Behind her the crowd were gathering around the fallen Kyrgs. A tall, hooded figure burst from the crowd. It was the black cloaked mindweaver. The hood obscured his face, but she felt his shaded eyes glaring at her.

Zastra... a voice echoed in her head. The mindweaver knew her name. She shuddered, crying out in fear as the black figure began to chase after them. She felt another strong probe attack her mind before they rounded a corner and left the village and the mindweaver behind them. She clung tightly to the side of the trap, expecting another attack on her defences at any moment, but none came. They had escaped.

Chapter Thirty

Zastra tried to adjust herself to the motion of the trap, but the constant pitching and jolting knocked her off her feet and sent boxes skidding into her shins. There seemed to be sharp corners everywhere and she received a succession of painful blows as she protected Findar with her body. At last, to her relief, the horses slowed to a rapid trot and the man in yellow turned to address her.

'Even these lovelies can't keep up that pace for long, but they'll trot on at a good pace now. I doubt those Kyrgs will catch us. I'm Gildarn and this delightful chap is my husband Draygal, but you can call us Gil and Dray, everyone else does.'

Zastra nodded mutely.

'And might I have the honor of your introduction?'

'Don't you already know who I am?'

Gildarn raised an eyebrow. 'Interesting. So you knew I was in your head. But you are no mindweaver, I'd venture?'

'No, I'm not.'

'He's always nosing about in people's minds,' said Draygal apologetically. 'It's a terrible habit of his, and I do keep trying to make him stop, but he's just too interested in other people's business.'

'Nonsense,' protested Gil. 'It was you who made me. "What an interesting young boy," you said and so I took a small peek. Who knew it would be a girl?'

He turned back to Zastra.

'My dear child, I apologise for invading your privacy. It is simply that, things being as they are at the moment, I like to know who is who. I couldn't read much. You have been well taught by someone but your mind is still a girl's mind. I can tell these things, although it is a subtlety lost on most mindweavers. And I caught a glimpse of Golmer Castle. Given that the Kyrgs seemed to have found what they were looking for, I'd guess that would make you Zastra, Leodra's daughter. This bundle of screaming joy – would that be one of the twins?'

Zastra didn't see any point in denying it.

'This is Findar,' she admitted.

'Well Zastra, you are welcome to travel with us as long as you wish. We are heading out of Golmeira, before these terrible Kyrgs overrun us all. Dray has some masterful plan of stealing a boat and heading for the Far Isles.

'Oh, you do exaggerate,' the smaller man said, rolling his eyes. 'I never said steal. I said we'd buy passage. Seacastle still holds out against Thorlberd's troops, so the port might be open.'

'Why are you running away?' Zastra asked.

'Not running away, my dear,' said Gildarn, 'a sensible retreat that's all. I don't see that there will be much demand for quality clothing in the new Golmeira, what with the Kyrgs and their furs and Thorlberd's terrible drab uniforms. So I suspect there won't be much call for our trade. Besides, I have always hankered after a return to the Far Isles. I'm from there, you see.'

'In any case, Golmeira is not now a good place for a delicate soul such as Gil,' remarked Dray. 'Too much unpleasantness around.'

'Delicate? Me?' protested Gil, eyes glittering. 'You were the one in tears when you heard the news of Lady An…' He glanced at Zastra and left the sentence unfinished.

'Won't you come with us?' asked Dray to cover the awkward silence. 'We go to Gorst Town, where we will change horses, and then south towards the coast.'

As Zastra hesitated, Gil looked at her closely.

'Be careful what you tell us, my dear. Dray here has a very loud and uncontrolled mind – you don't have to poke at all, he broadcasts his thoughts aloud to any mindweaver in the area. Not that they are usually worth listening to.'

'Loud and uncontrolled!' exclaimed Dray. 'This from the man wearing yellow.'

'Yellow is very fashionable at present, Dray. Besides, you swore this morning that you liked it.'

'I was lying. Couldn't you tell, oh marvellous mindweaver that you are?'

'Lying? Why in the stars did you lie to me, dearest?'

Dray sighed. 'We'd never have made it out of the inn otherwise.'

They were interrupted by Findar being sick, no doubt due to the combination of the rich milk and the juddery ride. Some of the vomit splattered onto the shoulder of Gil's bright yellow tunic. He looked down at the mess in shock.

'Sorry,' mumbled Zastra, reaching inside her bag for a rag to clean up the mess.

'No need to apologise,' said Dray. 'The boy's response is a perfectly reasonable one to such a garish tunic.'

There was a moment or two of awkward silence while Zastra cleaned Findar's face. He protested vigorously. Gil cleared his throat.

'I only meant to say that I would not wish us give any secrets away should Dray and I come across one of Thorlberd's black ravens.'

'Black ravens?'

'That's what they are calling the mindweavers, due to those floppy black cloaks that they all wear. Terrible cut, very unflattering, but what can you expect? Now, child, what do you say? Will you flee with us?'

'I'm not sure,' said Zastra, kissing Findar in an attempt to soothe him. 'How long before we reach Gorst Town?'

'A good while yet, my dear,' said Gil. 'Now, will that boy ever be quiet? I've never understood why people have babies. Just a lot of unnecessary noise and mess in my opinion.'

'He's usually pretty quiet. I think he doesn't like the bumpiness.'

'We'd slow down, only I don't know how long my sleep suggestion will keep those blasted Kyrgs quiet. Indeed, I'm quite astounded that they are not already chasing us down. We cannot afford to tarry.'

'How come you don't have a mindweaver ring?' Zastra asked. 'I thought all mindweavers were supposed to wear one.'

'If they know you are a mindweaver you get dragged into service to one of the Marls or the Grand Marl. I don't care to take orders from anybody,' replied Gil. 'Luckily, my parents were living in the Far Isles when I reached the age they make you take the test and so they missed me. I didn't see any need to point out their mistake. You won't tell anyone will you?'

Zastra shook her head.

'How did you get into my mind without me knowing?' she asked. 'I've always felt something before.'

'Ah, well, those official mindweavers don't do subtlety. They just like to take and so they try to break down the door, so to speak. But there is often a back entrance if you know where to look.'

'And where was my back entrance?'

'Well, the surface of your mind didn't fit with your appearance, that was all. I dug a little deeper into those thoughts that didn't fit. As I say, I couldn't read much, but I could tell you weren't who you were pretending to be.'

'Then how will we ever escape my uncle and those black ravens of his?' cried Zastra in despair. 'I'm just not strong enough. Dobery was teaching me but he had to leave. He always said I had to learn to control my emotions more, but it's so hard.'

'Control your emotions, eh? Yes, I supposed that often helps, when you need to maintain focus. But here's a little tip for you – sometimes a strong emotion is the best way to defeat a mindweaver.'

'Really?' asked Zastra. 'How?'

Gil smiled knowingly. 'Once a mindweaver is in your head he or she can see what you think and feel what you feel. I have learnt that if you catch them unawares with a strong emotion, like pain, or sorrow, then it can throw them right out. If you can learn to harness that emotion and let it out in one burst just at the right time, it's very powerful.' Gil paused, before continuing with great tenderness. 'I suspect that you have a good store of sorrow my dear.'

It was dusk when they clattered onto the streets of Gorst Town and they only just beat the curfew. Zastra was relieved when the soldiers waved them through without stopping them. Seeing the look on her face, Gil winked at her, tapping his head with a smug look.

'Don't worry,' he said, 'I can take care of the soldiers. We'll stay at an inn tonight and in the morning you can decide what to do.'

That night, Zastra slept deeply on a mattress that, although thin and coarse by the standards she had been used to at Golmer Castle, felt to her like the softest featherbed ever to have existed. The next morning, Gil and Dray treated her to a large breakfast of toast and honeyed porridge. Once her belly was full, Zastra consulted her map. Despite the kindess of the two men, she felt bound to stick to the plan her father had outlined. It was his last command to her and she must not fail him this time. The main road skirted the Evergreen Forest, heading southeast out of Gorst Town. About twenty leagues from Gorst Town, the main road divided, one fork heading south towards Seacastle, the other due north up the valley to Lyria. However, following the road until it split would take them a long way out of their way, before they could head north. Zastra reckoned if they left the main road and headed northeast on foot, they could cut across a large spur of forest and find a more direct route to Lyria.

She rode with Gil and Dray in the trap until Gorst Town was well behind them. She then asked Gil to stop the cart long enough for her to dismount and say her goodbyes. As she tried to express her heartfelt thanks to the two cloth merchants, Dray turned away, burying his face in a large white cloth.

'He doesn't mean to be rude,' said Gil, 'he just hates goodbyes.'

He handed down her bag.

'Be careful my dear,' he said. 'If you ever need a friend in the Far Isles, just come and find us.'

She nodded and waved at the trap as it disappeared down the road. She found a small track that seemed to head in the right direction and set off. She made good progress. The food and rest had done her good and her body was beginning to adjust to the physical demands placed on it. She had become used to carrying Findar and even her blisters had begun to heal. Nevertheless, they travelled all day without reaching the forest. In the gathering gloom she came across a large barn, where she found a pile of straw and she and Findar bedded down for the night. They were rudely awakened next morning by a savage looking woman with a pitchfork.

'Get out!' she yelled. 'I'll not have beggars and brats hanging around my barn. Go on.'

Findar began screaming and Zastra scrambled to collect their belongings. Keeping Findar well away from the sharp prongs, she skirted the woman warily and then hurried away.

'Don't come back!' yelled the woman.

'Don't worry, we won't,' muttered Zastra, heading as quickly as she could for the welcome cover of the forest. The ground began to rise steeply as the terrain changed from rolling hillside to steeper mountain ranges. Before long, they were back under the deep green blanket of the Evergreen Forest and heading towards Lyria.

Chapter Thirty-One

Brutila paced up and down Riverford's great hall, cursing with impatience. They had already wasted far too many precious days in this stinking city and were no closer to the truth. Yet they had been within five days of catching Zastra and the twins. Of course that flekk Finton hadn't helped, with his lies and deceptions.

A hard ride and relay of horses had taken Brutila to Trindhome within two days of leaving Highcastle village. They had found Hedrik's hovel easily, and she hadn't even needed to use mindweaving to get answers. Hedrik's wife had been most helpful. Brutila curled her lip in disdain.

'I told him there'd be trouble,' the peasant woman had said, bitterly. 'He came back from Highcastle with those brats, wanting us to hide them here. Stupid soft-hearted fool. I made them leave. He sent them off to Riverford with Hilfrik on his wagon.'

'When did they leave?' asked Brutila.

'Must be, what, four, mebbee five days ago,' said the woman.

'And where is this Hilfrik?'

'I don't know. He came back here but then left again yesterday, heading west with a big load.'

Brutila hardly needed to scan the woman's mind to know she was telling the truth, although she made sure all the same. It never paid to take chances. A decision had to be made quickly. Should they go on towards Riverford, or backtrack to try and find this man Hilfrik? In the end the choice was simple – they most go on. Speed was of the essence if they were to catch the children. Too much time had already been wasted by Grindarl's ineffectual efforts. She would leave instructions for the guards to stop and question Hilfrik when he returned. She sent back another soldier to carry the news of her progress to Thorlberd and then, wasting no time, she called for a fresh horse and was on her way to Riverford.

That had been six days ago. The first delay had been at the Westgate, where they had failed to recognise her authority. Brutila shook her head. They would learn. Soon her name would be feared throughout Golmeira. Thorlberd was right; you had to gain both fear and respect from the people in order to rule effectively. The beardless youth who had dared to try and scan her mind had paid the price. He was even now writhing in the agony of the perpetual nightmares that she had planted in his head. Brutila smiled inwardly. She had enjoyed making the soft-bellied fool pay for his presumption. Since she had begun her routine of taking cintara bark every morning with her chala, she felt invincible. Thorlberd might counsel caution but it had been his genius to revive the old custom so as to gain the advantage over Leodra's council. Of course, weak willed fools had succumbed to its madness, but they deserved their fate. She herself had the strength to control the cintara. One dose a day only, despite the continuous desire for more. It was only those who broke this rule that risked losing themselves.

After an inexcusable delay, she had been granted an audience with Finton, self-styled Prefect of Riverford. Brutila had noted with disdain the large personal guard of Kyrginites that Finton felt he needed. Clearly he was unpopular and even more clearly he was a coward.

'My dear Master Brutila,' he had gushed. 'It is a pleasure to welcome you to Riverford. Let me assure you that we shall extend you any possible courtesy you may require. Tonight I shall lay on the best banquet that Riverford can offer, and I—'

'That will not be necessary,' she snapped, cutting him short. 'I have an important job to do and no time to waste. We are searching for the foul offspring of Leodra, disgraced former Grand Marl. They must be caught and dealt with. Nothing must interfere with the succession of Thorlberd and his line.'

'Of course, of course,' agreed Finton, bowing and plucking nervously at his ridiculous outfit of gold-embroidered trousers and a clashing yellow tunic. 'Tell me what you require, Master Brutila and I shall order it done immediately.'

A close examination of the Westgate log indicated that Hilfrik and his wagon had entered Riverford five days earlier. But there was no record of a young boy or girl with two little babies leaving via either gate, suggesting that they were still within the city walls. Brutila ordered that the gates of the city be closed and a thorough search be carried out. Finton acceded to this request, although rather reluctantly, in Brutila's opinion. A three day search had failed to uncover the fugitives, although a good many people had been added to the already overcrowded dungeons.

'They must have gone,' said Finton. 'We must re-open the gates at once.'

'But there are no records of them leaving. Is that not right?' said Brutila. 'Are you certain that you have searched everywhere?' Finton swallowed nervously, wilting under the gaze of her pale grey eyes. Her eyes narrowed. What was he not telling her? She probed deeper into his mind and saw something which worried her.

'You are having trouble with blue fever?' she asked.

'Who told you that?' She merely fixed her wet-eyed glare more firmly upon him and at last his eyes widened in understanding.

'Of course, of course,' he smiled, attempting to cover his fear with nervous joviality. 'Just a small problem. There have been some fatalities in the poorer areas and we have had to seal off the southwest quarter to prevent the fever from spreading. It's only beggars and vagrants at present and we wish it to remain so. We don't want to spread panic across the city, so we are trying to keep it quiet. Rumours of blue fever are bad for trade.'

'This is no time for worrying about your tax revenues,' snapped Brutila. 'You should have told me this as soon as I arrived. We must search the quarantine areas immediately.'

'Yes of course, Master Brutila. I shall see to it at once,' stammered Finton. He scuttled out of the room in search of the Captain of the Guards. Brutila shuddered inwardly. She had no fear of soldiers or mindweavers. But contagion, foul and indiscriminate, that was different. She would have to be careful. The door opened and Finton came slinking back in.

'Well?' she snapped.

'I'm afraid the Kyrgs are refusing to enter the southwest quarter,' Finton said, apologetically. 'They are afraid of catching the fever.'

'They shall fear me more,' said Brutila. 'Send me your mindweavers.'

The two remaining mindweavers of Riverford were brought to Brutila and she explained her plan. Both were eager to help. They had no wish to share the fate of their young compatriot from the Westgate. Together they forced the Kyrginite soldiers into the fever zone. Any children were hauled to the edge of the temporary boundary erected to quarantine the area. The barrier had been doused in jula oil and set on fire to ward off the infection. Brutila stationed herself on the safe side of the barrier. Wave upon wave of children were brought forth, several with the tell-tale blue lips of the fever. Using her mindweaving skills Brutila determined that none were the ones she was after. It was an exhausting and disgusting task. When they had finished, the Kyrgs attempted to leave the fever zone. That could not be allowed. Brutila and other mindweavers tried to force them into obedience but there were many Kyrgs and fear threatened to give them strength to shake off the mental hold. Finton instructed his archers to shoot any who tried to cross the barrier, but the Kyrgs looked as if they feared the fever more than arrows. Brutila, sensing their danger, turned her attention to Finton's large tattooed Kyrg and took control of his mind. She forced the large Kyrg to bark out a set of orders and his compatriots within the quarantine zone obeyed instantly and made no further attempt to leave.

Brutila might have saved Riverford from being overrun by the fever, but she was still no closer to her aim. Perhaps Leodra's brats had caught the fever and died. It would explain why no one had seen them. If the bodies had been burnt, as many had been, there would be no way to identify them. It seemed as if they were at a dead end. However, Brutila refused to deal in possibilities. She required facts. Just that morning, she had ordered the gate records be re-examined for any discrepancies and steeled herself for a round of deeper probes into the minds of the guards. If she could get into their memories, she might be able to spot the children herself. Such an exercise would be extremely challenging, since memories were changeable and not always accurate. Even with an extra evening dose of cintara bark, she would struggle to retrieve what she needed. Her reverie was broken when Finton dashed into the room carrying a large, leather bound ledger.

'I think we may have got something,' he cried, as eager as a small child trying to please its mother.

'Well, what is it?'

'Here, an entry the day after we believe the chil… the traitors… entered Riverford. A woman, Nula of Borsha, is recorded leaving with a large family. Nothing unusual there, you might say. But see here, her entry three days prior lists her with six children but on the way out she had eight.'

'Eight?' enquired Brutila. 'Not nine?'

'Ah, but listen,' said Finton. 'The mindweaver Ilursa remembered this woman, and said that she was certain that the woman had at least two young babies.'

'Bring Ilursa to me,' ordered Brutila. The plump Mindweaver was brought before her, pale-faced and trembling.

'I'm sorry Master Brutila,' she stammered anxiously. 'I had no idea that these might be the ones. The weaver is well known around these parts for her unruly brood. We had no reason to suspect them.'

'But you scanned all of them?' It was a statement rather than a question. Ilursa shrank before the amphibious gaze.

'Of course. I recall she had foul and dirty thoughts.'

'I don't care about the woman. What about the children?'

'I don't remember,' stammered Ilursa, 'but I am sure I would have spotted anything unusual.'

'I will need to look into your memories,' commanded Brutila, moving closer to the mindweaver. 'Do not resist me.'

Ilursa closed her eyes and nodded once.

Brutila accessed the memories without much trouble. The image of the large, strident woman and the sound of crying children were strong, but the children were faceless and blurred. It was no good. Brutila snarled with frustration.

'Useless. You are not observant enough. All we can do is try to find this woman. You are fortunate that I have not the time or energy to punish you.'

Turning to Finton, she demanded a guide to Borsha and two of the best horses to be found in Riverford. The Prefect was most happy to oblige and sent her on her way with a fawning bow.

Chapter Thirty-Two

Brutila looked around Borsha in disgust. It was a dirty village, full of stupid, dirty peasants. However, she was satisfied to note the fear in the villagers' eyes as they looked at her. No one dared to hold her gaze and most slunk away as she rode past. It didn't take them long to find Nula's wooden shack. 'My, my Leodra,' she said to herself with an unpleasant grin. 'Your children really have been brought down to live in the dirt.'

Only two soldiers had been stationed at Borsha as the village was not considered of any strategic importance. They seemed reluctant to be roused from their present happy idleness, until Brutila's guide explained things to them, at which point they sprang to attention. At her command, they emptied Nula's house of its occupants, flinging them onto the street as if they were mere sacks of rubbish. Nula herself refused to move, and the soldiers' ears stung from the various insults she hurled at them. They would have had difficulty removing her considerable frame, but the children were lighter and Nula was drawn out of the house by their cries. Eyeing up the situation, she quickly determined who was in command and confronted the grey woman defiantly, hands planted on her ample hips. Brutila did not deign to dismount her horse, casually leaning down to flick away an insect from her boot before speaking with dangerous mildness.

'You assisted a boy with two young babies leaving Riverford. Where are they?'

'I don't know what you mean,' responded Nula belligerently. 'Now, I demand an expla—'

Brutila held up her hand, shaking her head in a pale mimicry of sorrow. Nula caught sight of something in the damp, emotionless eyes that silenced her.

'Come now. There is no point in resisting. It's not you we want. Tell me what you know and I'll spare your children.'

The woman wavered, looking anxiously at her children. This was the moment Brutila enjoyed; the moment they gave in.

'So what if we did?' Nula's voice retained some of the bravado, but worry clouded her eyes.

'They are traitors and must be apprehended.'

'They were just children. How can children be traitors?'

'That is none of your concern, woman.'

Brutila narrowed her eyes, delving into the peasant woman's thoughts. She had to swim through a swamp of crude thoughts and images, but eventually she found what she was looking for. She backed out in surprise.

'There was only one baby? What about the baby girl?'

'There was no baby girl,' Nula admitted reluctantly. Brutila delved deeper, harder, causing Nula to cry out in pain, her knees buckling. A dark skinned boy with curly hair rushed towards Brutila and pounded at her leg.

'Boltan, no!' Nula cried.

Brutila swatted at the boy, but he would not be shaken off and he grabbled hold of her left leg and tried to drag her from her horse. Brutila kicked him away and drew her sword. A crowd of villagers closed around them, muttering and glaring.

Brutila was perplexed. She was certain the woman was hiding nothing. Nula had a good memory for faces and Brutila detected some of the hated features of Leodra in the "boy" Hedrik. Indeed, the choice of the name Hedrik was enough to give the game away. But then what had become of Kastara? She turned to the impetuous boy and pried deep into his mind. He had not the wit to assemble distractions in the way of his mother and Brutila was able to extract several images before the boy fainted under the probing. Two of these images had significance; the sadness in the eyes of the pretend Hedrik, which spoke of recent loss and the image of a small baby with blue lips, dying or dead on the streets of Riverford.

That must be it. Kastara must have perished in the blue fever in Riverford. Brutila didn't know whether to smile in triumph, or be upset that one of Leodra's children had escaped her. She turned her gaze on the younger children. They cowered in terror before this ghostly apparition that had withered their invincible Ma with a mere glance. Brutila looked them over, prepared to dig into their minds. They may have more information to confirm her suspicions.

The murmurings of the villagers grew louder as they closed threateningly around the group. Brutila noticed that several carried makeshift weapons. She realised with shock that here were more than thirty men and women. Where had they come from? She could take many of them, but she only had three guards and the villagers looked very angry.

Discretion was called for. They had the information they needed, there was no point risking more. Brutila extricated herself from the restive crowd and left the village with the guards. She elected to return to Riverford for reinforcements, guiding her horse back along the main road.

Zastra, Zastra… Where are you going? Brutila tried to anticipate the thoughts of her quarry. There was nothing to the direct north save the Helgarth Mountains. Zastra would be extremely foolish to head that way. The main road headed east past Gorst Town and then the options were to head north to Lyria or south down to the coast and the fortified port of Seacastle. Brutila had been informed that Seacastle was still holding out against Thorlberd's forces. Perhaps Zastra planned to head that way and seek passage on a ship to the Far Isles, well beyond the edge of Golmeirian territory. It was a sensible strategy and should not be discounted. But Brutila's thoughts were drawn to Lyria. The scene of Leodra's infamy and Brutila's humiliation so long ago. The grey haired woman shivered, pulling her grey fur lined coat tight against her body, even as the evening sun shone down upon her.

Yes, he may well have sent you to Lyria.

An image of snow and the bitter sensation of cold rushed and swirled in her mind, almost solid, almost real. She fought the rising panic, knowing the image to be a memory, no more. With an effort of will she was able to quell the vision. Nevertheless, the strength of the vision and the apparent reality of it concerned her. A side effect of the cintara? Possibly. But it must be borne, there was much work to do. Her iron grip was closing around the two remaining children of her enemy. Soon they would know terrors they had never dreamed of…

Chapter Thirty-Three

ot, hungry and tired, Zastra shaded her eyes with her hand and looked down onto the sunlit valley below. Embedded in the other side of the valley, on the far side of a lively river, sat a large castle. Built from the red stone of the valley, it appeared to have been carved out of the mountainside itself. If Zastra had read her map correctly, this was Lyria, home of their father's friend and ally, Marl Orwin. Behind her stood the Evergreen Forest. A gentle breeze swished through the trees and caused the thin branches to dip and wave in a gesture of farewell. Zastra was not sorry to leave it behind. Although she had become strong from her exertions and her blisters had long since disappeared, the steep, root-entangled slopes had made progress difficult. Then there were the numerous biting insects, angry at being disturbed, that had left red welts all over her arms and ankles. It had taken her several long weeks to battle through the large swathe of forest that separated Gorst Town from the Lyria valley. Thankfully the journey had been uneventful and they had met no one.

Findar seemed excited by the sunlight, reaching out with his chunky hands and crying out in pleasure. The land had been cleared of trees to make way for stepped farmland and houses. A few wagons moved slowly along the floor of the valley below them. Zastra could see only one bridge across the river, linking the red castle to the large, paved track that headed south down the valley towards the coast. According to her map, the border regions lay over the eastern ridge of the valley, beyond the castle. Beyond the borders lay the bleaker terrain of Sendor.

Zastra sighed. In the last few days they had again run out of food and her new found strength was fading. Wearily, she heaved Findar up into his sling and headed down the steep slope towards the bridge. There were a series of half paths and natural steps cut into the mountainside to help her as she scrambled down, but it was hot work, with the late summer sun rising high in the sky. She was parched by the time she reached the bridge. Lyria Castle, which had looked so close from the edge of the forest, now seemed further away, sitting in state at the top of a winding track. The bridge was guarded by four Bractarian soldiers, but Zastra noted with relief the absence of any black robes. She stepped boldly across the bridge, hoping that the plan she had hatched that morning would work. The soldiers seemed more interested in arguing with each other than paying attention to them.

'I tell, you, this is a punishment,' one of the soldiers was saying. 'I asked to be posted in Golmer, where all the action is, or at least in one of the big cities. But a bit of backchat to that flekk of a captain and I end up here, in the middle of nowhere. Nothing ever happens in Lyria.'

'Oh, quit your whining,' said one of the other soldiers. 'We should all be thankful Marl Orwin opened up his gates without a fight. Sensible man, knows when he's beat. Just the sight of the migaradon was enough, never mind that Thorlberd had orchestrated the mindweavers to act on his behalf. That was genius. We get all the glory of conquest without any of the trouble, so stop complaining. You boy!' he gestured to Zastra. 'Where are you bound?'

'To the castle,' mumbled Zastra, 'looking for the healer.'

'The healer? Why?'

'It's my brother,' replied Zastra, prodding Findar into surprised crying. 'I'm worried sick. He's hot as anything and his lips started to go blue just this morning.'

'Blue?' said the man, fear and disgust flicking across his face.

Zastra broke into a hoarse cough, nodding. A fold of material fell away, revealing Findar's face, his lips a bluish-purple against his pale skin.

'On you go,' said the soldier in disgust, backing away and waving them along whilst covering his mouth with his arm. Zastra did as she was told, forcing herself to trudge slowly up the path, despite the urge to run. When they were out of sight of the bridge, she rubbed away the berry juice that she had smeared across Findar's lips. Her plan had worked to perfection.

It was not until they were stood in front of the gates of Lyria Castle that Zastra realised she had not thought of a strategy to get in and see Orwin. She could hardly announce their presence and demand an audience with the Marl. The guards at the gate sent her round to the kitchens, where apparently help was required. Unsure whether she had understood the instructions properly, she entered a small courtyard where a group of boys were playing. Zastra went over to ask them for directions, but they ignored her, intent as they were on their game.

That game was not a pleasant one. Surrounded by several taunting youths was a burly boy with a thick mane of blond hair. He seemed oddly misaligned at first. As he turned towards the ringleader, Zastra could see his left arm was withered and shrivelled; only half the size it should be. He carried his head in a lopsided way, his left eye glassy and unseeing. It was to his left side that the boys attacked, poking him with sticks and throwing pebbles.

'Ho, P-P-Podrik!' mocked the tallest boy, a red haired, freckled youth who appeared to be the ringleader.

The large boy turned ponderously. 'P-please s-stop,' he stuttered, and the surrounding youths rocked with laughter.

'Podrik, the cripple,' they sang. 'Can't even say his own name. Ho, ugly brute.'

Angered, Podrik lumbered towards one of the boys, but he was too slow and his quarry slipped easily away. Another boy threw a clod of earth, striking Podrik in the back of the head. The expression on his face raised a memory in Zastra of a time a travelling circus had visited Golmer Castle. They had brought with them an old plough horse, a mottled grey mare whose protruding ribs and sad eyes spoke of years of mistreatment. Zastra, six years old at the time, had been very upset by the sight. She saw the same helpless expression of fear and hurt on Podrik's face as she had seen on the old plough horse. In response to her pleas, her father had ordered the horse be released into his care and ensured it was looked after; she had been so proud of him that day. Her anger rose and without thinking she strode forward.

'That's it Podrik,' laughed the red-headed boy as Podrik fell to his knees under a sly blow from one of the group. 'Show some respect for your betters.'

'You have to earn respect first,' cried Zastra, stepping into the ring. 'And I don't see anything here to respect. Just a bunch of bullies. It's shameful – five of you with sticks and stones against one boy.' She stood before the red-headed boy, glaring at him.

'Oooh,' cooed one of the other boys, mockingly, 'and who are you?'

'None of your business.'

'Well, what we are doing is none of *your* business,' said the redhead, looking around at his appreciative audience.

'Good one, Terlan,' the other boy said, clapping and hooting.

The boy called Terlan cast his eyes back on Zastra.

'Now clear off, country boy, and let us have our fun.'

'I'm not going anywhere,' said Zastra, 'unless of course you're afraid of a fair fight?'

'Oooh!' hooted the gang, clapping their hands in excitement.

Terlan twirled his stick, eying up his opponent. He looked to be a few years older than Zastra and a good foot taller.

'All right,' he nodded, with a confident grin.

'All right,' returned Zastra with resolute determination, keeping her eye on Terlan as she offered her hand to Podrik.

'Would you look after something very important to me?' she whispered. Podrik nodded and, loosening the sling, Zastra gave over the sleeping Findar to him. She then turned to face Terlan.

'Lyria rules suit you?' the boy said with a sly grin.

'What are Lyria rules?'

'You start with what you've got,' he jeered, holding up his stick to the laughter of his gang. Zastra looked at her empty hands and shrugged. Terlan circled her, brandishing and prodding his stick. Zastra forced her weary bones into fighting stance, expending the minimum of effort as she turned to keep her face towards her circling opponent. Eventually, bored of trying to goad her, Terlan broke forward, swinging the stick hard. Zastra weaved with all the grace of her natural agility and training, and as the stick whipped past her face she used the boy's uncontrolled momentum to trip him and throw him to the ground. He landed in a puddle of wet mud with a satisfying *shlock*. A few of the other boys tittered.

'You stinking…' cried Terlan

'Actually, I think it's you that's stinking,' said Zastra with a grin. 'That mud…'

'That ain't mud,' said one of the youths, wrinkling his nose in disgust.

Enraged, Terlan scrabbled up and attacked her again. This time Zastra stepped towards the challenge, ducking underneath the stick and striking a strong blow to the midriff. Terlan collapsed, winded. As had been the custom at Golmer Castle, Zastra stood back to allow him to catch him breath.

'He's showing Terlan a thing or two,' giggled one of the onlooking gang.

'Good skills,' muttered another, nodding his head in admiration.

'Shut up!' cried Terlan, dropping the stick and running straight at Zastra. He tried to grapple her, no doubt hoping to use his considerable weight advantage. Zastra used the trick she had learnt from Kylen to trip the boy and deposit him on his back with an oomph of exhaled air. She then placed her knee in his chest until he was forced to surrender. As she let him up, he looked at her indecisively. He was saved by a call from the edge of the courtyard. A Bractarian guard marched over. His red hair and features indicated that he was Terlan's father.

'You, boy!' the soldier exclaimed, grabbing a handful of Zastra's shirt. 'Who are you, you filthy thing, to be fighting my boy?'

'No one, sir,' muttered Zastra, suddenly afraid. Would her impetuousness get them caught now, when they were so close to safety?

'No one eh? Well, my captain won't appreciate that kind of answer. Likes everything in order, she does. Do you have any papers?'

'No.'

'Well, perhaps a trip to the mindweaver will jog your memory.'

'It's all right, sergeant. This is one of my new kitchen boys. I'll see he gets punished. But your boy started the trouble, so you may want to do the same.'

A short, round woman, wearing a green apron stained with grease and flour, stepped out of a nearby doorway. Her hair was tied back, with more than a few strands of grey showing through a thick mass of black. Her dark black eyebrows were stitched together in a forbidding frown. Wisely, the soldier chose not to argue.

'All right, Morn,' he said, beckoning Terlan away.

'I'll get you later, country boy,' Terlan spat, as he and his gang headed off. Zastra went to retrieve Findar, who had slept quietly through the whole event.

'Thank you for looking after him,' she said.

'I don't mind,' replied Podrik and a smile as lopsided as the rest of his body lit up his moon-like face.

'Podrik – look at the state of you. Mud everywhere, and I only washed those trousers yesterday,' clucked the woman.

'I'm s-sorry, M-m-ma.'

'Never mind,' she sighed, 'I can guess what happened. Who might you be, young master? I've not seen you before. A stray by the looks and smell of you.'

'Looking for work, sir,' said Zastra, head bowed.

The short woman burst into laughter. 'Goodness me, I don't think anyone has ever called me sir in my whole life! Call me Morn, everyone else does. I'm Podrik's ma and chief cook of the castle. Now, before we talk business, won't you come in and try some of my root vegetable soup? You look half starved.'

Zastra didn't argue. It had been two days since she had run out of food and her stomach was empty and grumbling. 'I've a littlun, too,' she said, as she followed Morn to the kitchen.

'I can see that, duckie. What do you think I am, blind?' exclaimed Morn. 'I'm sure we can find something for the littlun too.'

The kitchens were large. Not quite as big as the ones at Golmer Castle, but still a good size, and hot, especially in the present sunshine. However, Zastra was grateful of a place to sit, as well as the food and water that were given her.

Podrik held out his arms to take Findar, who was grizzling.

'I can look after him,' he said with a confidence that contrasted with his demeanour in front of Terlan's gang.

'Aye, let him duckie. He's good with littluns,' called out Morn from one of the big stoves. Podrik, with exaggerated care, took Findar on his knee, balancing him against his shorter arm, and fed him fruit and milk with the other. Findar was soon content.

'There'll be no hats at table in my kitchen,' Morn ordered, pulling off Zastra's cap and placing it on the table next to her. Zastra was too busy gulping down the soup to complain. It was a long time since she had tasted anything so delicious.

When Zastra had polished off a large bowl of soup and several rolls, Morn, who had been watching her closely the whole time, took her by the hand.

'Come with me, child,' she said, leading her gently into a small pantry and closing the door. Then crouching down so as to be on a level with Zastra, Morn reached out a small, fat hand and softly caressed the girl's cheek, eyes alight with sorrow.

'Oh, my poor dear Anara, I can see you in this child's face. Zastra, you must be. Oh my poor dear child.' And she clasped the girl to her. Zastra, tears unlocked by the unexpected kindness, buried her head in the soft folds of flesh and sobbed without control.

Morn let Zastra empty of tears. She then went back into the

kitchen, issuing a string of orders to the kitchen hands. Then she made some hot chala and brought it in for Zastra.

'I've run you a bath, duckie. I have to see to the castle supper now, but we'll talk properly in the morning.'

Zastra was glad to sink into the large bath, filled with sweet smelling perfumed water. The long forgotten luxuriousness of a hot bath was delightful. Findar too was bathed, slapping the water in his excitement and drenching poor Podrik, who was holding him with great attention. After they had finished their baths Morn gave Zastra and Findar some clean nightclothes and bade Podrik show them to her own bedchamber. Once Findar was settled, Zastra sank into the soft mattress and fell into a deep, thankful sleep.

Chapter
Thirty-four

Zastra woke late in the morning, refreshed but extremely hungry. She looked around for Findar, but he was not in the room with her. Throwing on a robe, she hurried to the kitchens, her rising panic calmed by the sight of Podrik holding her brother. It was hard to say who looked most pleased with himself, the large boy or Findar. The sight made Zastra smile her first real smile for a long time. They were interrupted by Morn, who brought in a large breakfast of porridge and fresh buns, still piping hot, and a large pot of chala. Zastra attacked the food in front of her, while Morn carried on with her work.

'Steady, duckie!' exclaimed Morn. 'You could at least try and taste it. It would be a shame for you to make it this far only to choke to death.'

Zastra nodded but continued eating, occasional grunts of appreciation emerging from her food-filled mouth. When she had eaten her fill and was finishing the last of her chala, Morn stopped doing her chores and came and sat beside her. Podrik, still holding Findar, lowered himself into another nearby chair and forced his features into a serious, concentrated expression.

'It's alright, duckie, my Podrik's no idiot, although some people might take him for one,' said Morn. 'He knows something's up and so I've told him. Otherwise he'd have battered away at me 'til I did tell him. He can be trusted with a secret though, you can rely on him.' Podrik nodded in enthusiastic agreement.

'However, before you say anything, remember to be careful what you tell us. There's several of them black ravens in the castle. They don't usually bother with the likes of us but I'd not wish to give away anything important if my mind was looked into. Same with Podrik. Do you understand?'

Zastra nodded. Morn patted her hand.

'So, what *can* you tell me? All we know is that six or seven weeks ago Orwin opened his doors to these dratted Bractarian soldiers and their mindweavers. Ordered his guard to stand down without a fight. Not that I can blame my Lord really, what with that awful beast screeching above the castle. The mere sight of it made me shiver in horror – thank the stars they've sent it away for the moment. We've heard terrible tales about the likes of the poor Marl of Julan, who refused to surrender. They say the Kyrgs slaughtered everyone in Julan Castle, including the Marl and her family. Worse than that my dear child, we had word last week, that your father and dear Anara are dead. Is it true?'

Zastra sunk her head in her hands, her voice choked with grief. 'Yes, that's what they told me. My father – I was in the room when they came for him, there were so many of them, I don't see how he could have… have survived. He saved us, but wouldn't come with us. He said he was going back for my… my mother. I waited for them to come after us, but they didn't…' Zastra broke off. She could say no more.

'Oh, mercy,' exclaimed Morn, tears flooding her round cheeks. 'Poor, dear, gentle Anara. Betrayed by her own brother-in-law. What a terrible, terrible thing.' Morn was overcome and sat for many minutes, sobbing quietly. Finally, she recovered herself enough to wipe her eyes and blow her nose into a large handkerchief.

'I knew your mother, you see, when she was a child,' explained Morn. 'She is a distant relation of Orwin and spent a lot of time here at Lyria. I was just a lowly kitchen hand at the time, but for some reason she took a liking to me. She and her friend Marta were often in the kitchens. They liked to play at cooking and I would save them titbits of this and that. Anara was so gentle and polite, not full of herself like lots of your rich children. Never had a bad word to say about anyone. She helped me learn to read when she learned that I was trying for advancement. Without her help, I wouldn't be chief cook as I am today. She did me the honour of writing once a year, even when she married the Grand Marl. Only think of that.'

Her reminiscences were interrupted by Findar, reaching towards her face. He appeared fascinated by her thick eyebrows. Morn put out a finger which he grasped stoutly.

'So this is little Findar? You wouldn't imagine anything wrong looking at him. But what about Kastara?'

Zastra coloured, remaining silent. She decided she could say nothing without risking Kastara's safety. Morn appeared to understand this and changed to subject.

'What do you plan to do now, duckie?'

'I don't know. My father said we should come here. He said Orwin would look after us. But I don't see how I can see him without creating suspicion, especially dressed like this.'

'It's a difficult problem, to be sure. We have a whole troop of Bractarian soldiers and a unruly mob of Kyrgs stationed here, so we must be careful. Like I say, I understand why Orwin did what he did, but we may live to regret it in the end. At least we could have died fighting. Instead we suffer this slow strangulation. However, I believe Orwin is a good man at heart and he will help you if he can. His wife I'd not answer for, but I'll get word to him and he shall come and see you. My Lord and Lady are away at the moment. She insisted on going to Gorst Town for some new gowns. How she can be shopping at such a time as this, I don't know. My Lord Orwin always indulges her. He returns tomorrow night and it must be his decision; whether you can stay here in safety, or whether there is somewhere else you can be sent. Until then, best hang around the kitchens with us. I doubt anyone'll question a new kitchen boy.'

Zastra spent the rest of the day with Podrik, who was more than happy to serve his rescuer of the previous day. He showed her every corner of the kitchen and all the store rooms proudly, as if he owned them himself. He insisted on taking care of Findar, showing Zastra a soothing ointment he had used to treat a rash on her brother's legs. Morn told Zastra that he preferred the company of babies to children of his own age and that he was always helping out in the nursery. After seeing how Terlan and the other boys had treated him yesterday, Zastra was not surprised. When he played with Findar, Podrik's stutter vanished completely. It only seemed to come on when he was nervous and afraid. All that morning, he kept plying both of them with food and treats that he made himself. Before long, even Zastra, hungry as she had been for many weeks, could eat no more.

In the afternoon, they lazed about contentedly in the coolest corner of the kitchen. Findar was sleeping and Podrik asked Zastra how she had learnt to be such a good fighter. Zastra explained how she had been taught to fight ever since she could remember. Podrik opened his eyes in astonishment.

'Why?' he asked. 'Why do they teach you all that?'

'So we can become Warriors of Golmeira, I suppose,' said Zastra.

'What's that then?'

Zastra recited some of the stories she had been told of the legendary Warriors of Golmeira. Of Lodara, who had challenged the champion warrior of her enemy to single combat and so won Waldaria for the land of Golmeira. Of Colinar and the beast of Helgarths, and of course, Fostran and the Kyrginites. The stories amazed Podrik as they had Zastra, but he seemed bemused by all the battles and fighting. 'Why can't everyone just get along with each other?' he wondered aloud. Zastra then asked him about himself. He seemed unused to anyone showing any interest in him and, rather hesitantly at first, he told her how his father, a Sendoran called Pintorax, had left when he was only small. He didn't know why his father had left, only that Morn had been distraught and, whenever he asked her about it, she just said "Apparently, Sendorans and Golmeirans aren't supposed to mix," and left it at that. 'Don't really know what she meant,' said Podrik sadly. 'I mean ma and pa mixed all right to make me, didn't they? I don't see why he left. Probably took one look at me, and didn't like to have a crippled son.' Zastra's heart went out to the sad, moonfaced boy.

'I'm sure he'd be very proud of you,' she said. 'Morn is and not everyone could look after Findar as well as you do.' Podrik's eyes lit up at the compliment, and Findar took that opportunity to wake up and tug on a lock of Podrik's straggly hair. His squeal of excitement made the two older children smile.

Morn was as good as her word, and on the evening of Zastra's third day at Lyria, Marl Orwin came to the kitchen to see them. He was a balding man of average height, lines of age and stress beginning to set their marks across his face. He introduced himself to Zastra in a polite manner, but he seemed nervous and tense, his eyes constantly flicking about the room.

'My dear child, how glad I am you have survived the terrible events at Golmer Castle. But you are still in the most awful danger. We all are, whilst you are here.' He nervously massaged his head, causing the remaining strands of hair to poke up, swaying with static.

'What to do now, though? I'm afraid there is no way we can hide you here. They are looking for you. This proclamation was spread all over Gorst Town when we were there. Look, read for yourself.'

He pulled a crumpled parchment from the inside pocket of his jacket and handed it to her, pointing with a thick, trembling finger.

'There, the second paragraph.'

Zastra read the proclamation aloud.

'The traitors to Golmeira, offspring of the deceased Leodra, must be found. It is known that the child, Zastra, left Riverford heading east disguised as a county boy travelling under the name Hedrik. She has with her the baby boy known as Findar. The baby Kastara is believed to have died in Riverford. All young boys or girls with a baby are to be stopped and questioned. Do not worry that you may have the wrong child. It is better to arrest a thousand children than let these traitors escape. A reward of two thousand tocrins to anyone who captures them. Both are wanted alive. A slow and painful death will be afforded to any found harbouring the fugitives.'

Zastra was shocked at the brutal tone. She looked at the signature.

'Brutila, Royal Master at Arms.'

That anyone other than Martek should be master at arms was outrageous and anger rose up within her

'Who is this Brutila?' she asked.

'Ah. That is a story,' sighed Orwin. 'I'm not sure if… no, I suppose you should know. This woman is evil, I have no qualms in saying it. I had thought her dead, but it seems she has been hiding in Waldaria as part of Thorlberd's hidden army. I knew her, many years ago, as did your father and mother.'

'Oh, did you really?' cried Zastra, hungry to hear anything of her parents.

'Yes. You see, Anara is a distant cousin of mine. My father was rich, since he was Marl of Lyria before me, but Anara's parents were much poorer and she was sent here in order to have the best education. It was here she met Leodra, when he was twelve years old and she was nine. Leodra had been sent away to learn about the different parts of the country he was to rule. I was a few years older, but we became good friends. Brutila was one of our schoolfellows, the daughter of Venkar, our teacher. Venkar was an unpleasant tyrant, who had no qualms about beating us, even when we did not deserve it. Leodra and I were largely spared, due to our status, but the others, and Brutila in particular, did not escape his wrath. Indeed, I think she had the worst of it, since in our case his cruelty was limited by school hours. Perhaps due to having such a father, Brutila had a darkness about her. She and a few like-minded fellows were often bullying the younger children. Leodra, always honest and forthright, took issue with her bullying ways and they were often fighting. Leodra was taller and stronger at the time, so he usually triumphed, since Brutila had only just begun her mindweaver training. She had not yet learnt how to use her abilities fully.'

'She's a mindweaver?' Zastra didn't like the sound of that.

'Oh yes. An extremely powerful one, so it is said. One winter's day, a shocking incident occurred. I was in bed with a slight fever, but I heard what happened from the others. Venkar took the class up into the mountains to teach them the art of tracking in the snow. They became spread out and it was a while before Leodra noticed that Anara and her delicate friend Marta were missing. Concerned, he went in search and found them tied to a rock on the mountainside. Brutila and one of her fellow bullies had found the younger girls and tormented them by tying them to a rock and threatening to leave them to freeze. Of course the girls were terrified, particularly Marta, who looked almost dead with cold. Leodra was incensed and after releasing them, he overpowered Brutila and tied her up in the girls' place. "You'll have a taste of your own cruelty," he said, before leaving her there alone. He meant only to shock her, planning to return in a few minutes and set her free. However, Venkar found them and scolded them for wandering off before ordering them back to the castle. Leodra then admitted what he had done, willing to take the punishment, but Venkar insisted he obey. Only Anara, watching silently, realised that Venkar was using his own mindweaving powers to make Leodra bend to his will. Whether Venkar ever meant to go back for Brutila, I know not. It was strange behaviour for any father, even one who showed little love for his child. Eventually, Anara found the opportunity to drag Leodra away, covered by a developing snow storm. She explained to Leodra what had happened, but he had no memory of what had happened. Venkar had stolen that from him. But he trusted Anara, and they went to find Brutila. The snowstorm made it difficult, but at last they found her. She was half frozen and surrounded by a pack of mountain scrittals. Some had begun to crawl over her, no doubt scenting supper.'

Zastra was shocked by the tale. Her parents had taken her to the mountains a few winters ago and she could well remember the vicious chill and the swirling snowstorms. And she had seen some of the scrittals; large carnivorous rodents covered with thick grey fur. She had watched a pack of them chewing on the carcass of a dead horse.

The memory made her shudder. She pictured the child Brutila in her mind, small, shivering, alone with the creatures on the cold mountain. How could Venkar do such a terrible thing to his own child?

'What happened?' she asked.

'Leodra chased off the scrittals and released Brutila, wrapping her in his own fur-lined cloak to try and warm her. He and Anara managed to get her down the mountains and into the kitchens. Morn will remember, no doubt.'

'Yes, indeed,' said Morn, shaking her head. 'Those two girls, grey with cold, and Leodra, the poor boy, distraught with guilt. Anara guided the older girl to the fire, where she thawed slowly. Anara told me some of what had happened, although it would appear that she left out many of the details. I suppose she did not want to get her fellow students into trouble. Brutila just sat staring at the fire, whispering to herself. I remember what she said, because it was so odd, so terrifying. "I could hear their hunger. They were sniffing out the best parts to eat," she kept muttering, over and over. I didn't know what to make of it, but I gave them all hot soup. Anara brought the older girl some chala which she had made herself. Brutila knocked it out of her hands. I don't think that she could bear to be beholden to Anara. Leodra tried to explain and apologise, but Brutila had only hatred in her eyes.'

Orwin took up the story again. 'Leodra and Anara were beaten severely by Venkar for running off, but neither of them minded. Leodra in particular felt he deserved the punishment. A terrible thing it was, but I suppose it was also the beginnings of the love that was to blossom between your parents. But it did not end there. A few days later, my father heard rumours of what had happened. He questioned Leodra, who told him the whole story, including his own part in the sorry affair. My father ordered the arrest of Venkar. However, our teacher had somehow known what was coming and he escaped, taking Brutila with him. With no means of employment, it was rumoured that he was forced to beg for food and shelter, cursing the name of Leodra wherever he went.'

'What happened to Brutila?' asked Zastra.

'I have only seen her once since that day. She was a woman, prematurely grey, with a terrible scar across her face, but her cold, cruel eyes were unmistakably the same. She was being tried for murder in the Royal Court. Your father had transferred responsibilities of judge to Thorlberd, since he believed that even Brutila deserved a fair trial. He would not risk himself being unconsciously biased against her, due to their past history. However, the evidence was overwhelming; it was proved that she had been working as a hired assassin and had killed several people in return for money. Your uncle had no choice but to declare her guilty and had her transferred to Bractaris for her punishment, which was to be death by poison. We all thought her dead, but it would seem that Thorlberd spared her and engaged her services. Her mindweaving abilities alone would make her a powerful ally. To think that we now have to bow down before such a person.'

'And she knows we were headed in this direction,' exclaimed Zastra, fear taking a grip on her.

'Worse, I expect her here within the next few days. When I returned, I found a letter from Brutila addressed to me personally, full of threats. It seems she has a strong belief you would make your way here. And she was right.'

Orwin rubbed his chin nervously.

'You must not be here when she arrives. I will not be able to protect you.'

Zastra sighed. She had started to enjoy the luxuries of Lyria. Even more precious were the feelings of friendship and belonging that she had begun to feel with Morn and Podrik. It seemed that they must be cast out into the loneliness of the open trail once more.

'What's to be done?' asked Morn, frowning.

'Perhaps we can smuggle them out in a log cart and send them down to the port of Castanton. I know a ship's captain who would take them to the Far Isles in return for a hundred tocrins. Surely that will take them outside of Thorlberd's reach. But I must consult my wife.'

'Are you sure that's wise?' asked Morn. 'The fewer people who know, the safer, especially with mindweavers about.'

'She'll find out, she always does! Trust me it's the safest option to tell her. And she is always full of good ideas, she may have a better plan.'

Morn bit her lower lip, but said nothing further. Already she had been dangerously impertinent for a servant but, fortunately for her, Orwin was too full of nervous distraction to have noticed.

Zastra's eyelids were drooping heavily and she was almost asleep in her chair. Morn called Podrik in.

'Take Zastra to my room. She needs rest. You should leave Findar with her. Then come back and find me.'

Chapter Thirty-Five

There had been much for Brutila to organise. The uncomfortable experience at Borsha indicated that she would need a personal guard. Although she had lost some time in returning to Riverford for these reinforcements, it was better to be well prepared. Now that she was certain, or at least almost certain, of Zastra's direction, she could plan a strategy. At Riverford she had found a troop of soldiers waiting for her, sent by Thorlberd. Finton was most obliging, agreeing to release his migaradon with barely a squeak of protest. Messengers were sent ahead to Lyria and the besiegers at Seacastle. A further messenger was sent back to Golmer Castle with the latest news.

When all was set, Brutila set out along the main road with her troop of fifty Bractarian soldiers. The Riverford migaradon was sent out to scour the route ahead, as well as searching a wide area either side of the road for any sign of the fugitives. Brutila forced a fast pace. There were insufficient horses for the whole troop, so two-thirds of the soldiers were forced to run aside the trotting horses. Only at the point of exhaustion were they allowed to swap places with those on horseback. Brutila allowed only one small diversion. The village of Borsha was set on fire. The wails of the peasants pleased her. They deserved such punishment for their insolence. No house was spared, and the pall of smoke followed the troop along the road.

Allowing only a few hours rest a night, they travelled quickly. Seven days out of Riverford they came to large village where there was news. Their quarry had been spotted a week previously, on market day. Indeed there had been quite a commotion, with the Kyrgs all fainting and staying asleep for several hours. Brutila read the mind of one of the villagers to confirm the story. Their prey had received a lift from two cloth merchants and headed east.

Continuing on to Gorst Town, Brutila ordered her soldiers to split up and ask questions at every house and every inn. It didn't take them long to find the inn where the merchants had stayed, along with a young "boy" and a baby. The innkeeper informed the soldiers that the merchants had continued on the main road after spending just one night. Brutila smirked. *Clever boys.* The information confirmed that Zastra was still headed east. Lyria and Seacastle remained possible destinations, but she was becoming more and more certain that it was in Lyria that she would find them. She spurred her troop on remorselessly.

Chapter
Thirty-Six

Marl Orwin intended to help Zastra if he could, in spite of the risks. However, he was keen to consult his wife, Lichinara. During supper, he was fidgety and nervous, a fact that did not go unnoticed by his observant spouse. A lady of noble birth and no small beauty, she was also shrewd and intelligent and after they had eaten she suggested her husband joined her in her chambers. He agreed with alacrity. As soon as the door to her chamber was closed, she turned her questioning eyes on her husband.

'My dear Orwin, whatever is the matter?' she demanded.

'Lichinara, my dear one, you had better sit down.'

'What is it? What's wrong?'

Orwin paced up and down, rubbing his bald head in his characteristically nervous manner.

'Out with it, or by the stars, I'll...'

The words burst from his mouth in a hoarse whisper.

'It's Leodra's children, they are here!'

'Here, in our castle?' Lichinara exclaimed in disbelief.

'My dear, please keep your voice down. Yes, they arrived a few days ago. Leodra sent them, saying I would take care of them.'

'The nerve of the man! To put us in the way of such danger. Of course it is impossible.'

'Yes, yes, dear one, I know they cannot stay. But we must help them, poor dears. I owe this much to Leodra.'

'Orwin, how can you be so stupid?' His wife darted out the words.

'What about the mindweavers? You could never hide the fact you helped them. That awful Brutila woman is on her way here even now. We have no choice, we must turn them in.'

Orwin looked at her in horror.

'But they are just children.'

'Children of an old and now defeated regime. It is very sad of course, but there is no helping them. You do not realise how delicate our predicament is. You are known to be a friend of Leodra. Only my advice not to oppose Thorlberd has saved us thus far. This is an opportunity to demonstrate our loyalty.'

'Loyalty?' cried Orwin. 'What about our loyalty to Leodra? He was a true friend to us in the past. Remember when we were nearly ousted by that liar, who accused us of treason? Leodra had faith in me and stood by us.'

He strode distractedly around the room but Lichinara knew her husband and knew he was wavering. She had saved her best argument for this moment.

'Think of me, Orwin, and what they would do to me. Would you throw me to a pack of wild caralyx? For that is what would happen once that woman comes and reads your mind. Have pity. Have I not been a good wife to you?'

'Oh, yes, my dear one. Of course. But it just seems wrong.'

'All of Golmeira is wrong at present, we are not to blame.'

There was a lengthy pause, while Orwin continued to pace up and down. His wife left him to his thoughts. Only when she judged the time was right did she speak again.

'Where are they now?'

'Asleep, down in the kitchens.'

'I suggest you send a guard immediately and secure them. We can send word to Brutila, and hand them over when she gets here.' *The two thousand tocrins wouldn't go amiss either,* she thought to herself. Seeing her husband still hesitate, she continued.

'It will be better if you do it, Orwin. At least there will be some dignity for them.'

He wished to believe her, but knew too well the consequences of his betrayal.

'At least let them sleep tonight,' he pleaded. 'The gates are locked. They could not escape even if they wanted to. Tomorrow will come soon enough for the poor things.'

Lichinara knew when she had won. 'Of course,' she conceded graciously.

Zastra was in the midst of a nightmare. She was in Lyria Castle, but surrounded by circling migaradons ridden by faceless figures in black cloaks. She found herself roused, not knowing where she was. A strong hand over her mouth caused her to rear back in panic.

'P-please…' a soft voice pleaded.

'Podrik?' she whispered, as the rushing sound in her head subsided.

'C-come. You must leave tonight. Right now.'

Quickly awake, she peered blindly into the dark.

'Findar?'

'H-here, and some clothes too,' the disembodied voice whispered, handing her a soft bundle.

Once she was ready he tugged on her arm and indicated she should follow him.

'What about Orwin?' she asked.

'No good. You're to be handed over t-t-tomorrow. M-ma told me to hide in my Lady's rooms and listen. I h-heard them.'

Podrik led Zastra down a spiral staircase. At the bottom he paused briefly to pick up a length of thick rope and slung it over one shoulder.

'This way,' he whispered, guiding her around unseen obstacles until they arrived at a barred window through which the clear night sky and stars could be seen. A thin sliver of Horval, the larger of the twin moons, was also visible. Below the window was a drop into impenetrable darkness. They were at the rear of the castle, facing the steep mountainside from which it had been carved. Podrik secured the rope against one of the bars and then, using his good arm, he jiggled another bar until it came out of its sockets. The gap between the remaining bars was just wide enough for a child. Zastra could make out the whiteness of his teeth as he grinned and gestured downwards.

'You first. I'll follow.'

Hoisting Findar round in his sling so that she was carrying him on her back, Zastra grabbed the rope and shimmied down quickly. Podrik, being larger, had some trouble squeezing through the gap in the bars. Zastra watched in amazement as he slid expertly down the rope, using only his good arm to slow his descent.

He reached out to take Findar. Zastra flinched and he pulled back his arms as if they had touched a hot pan.

'I'm s-s-strong. C-c-can c-carry, we go f-faster?' he gasped. With some reluctance, Zastra let him take Findar, and Podrik strode off into the dark. He seemed sure of his way, keeping up a good pace. Zastra stayed close behind, using the shadow of his misshapen form as her guide.

They were panting heavily as they reached the summit of the mountain, just as dawn was breaking. Zastra looked back as the warm glow of the rising sun began to spread across the floor of the valley below. Lyria castle was still in shadow, and she wasted no time looking for it.

'Pretty,' said Podrik, smiling with satisfaction, as if he had created the valley and the morning sun himself.

'You've done this before,' said Zastra.

'A good way to escape from Terlan,' he grinned, his stutter gone now that they were safely away from the castle. Findar was awake and crying for food. Podrik led them down to a freshwater spring and dug into the bag he was carrying, bringing out a pot, together with Zastra's fire-ring and some oats. They made porridge and ate a hasty breakfast. A distant sound reached them, carried faintly on the wind from the Lyria valley; a mixture of horns and barking dogs. Podrik and Zastra looked at each other in alarm. No words were needed. They packed up hurriedly and made their way back to the top of the mountain.

Lyria Castle, now bathed in light, was alive and crawling with soldiers and horses.

'I guess they know we're gone,' said Zastra.

'I can come with you,' Podrik suggested, head cocked to one side.

Zastra shook her head, gently taking Findar from him. 'I couldn't wish for a stronger or braver companion,' she said, 'but I cannot ask you to share this with us. You have already risked too much for our sakes.'

Podrik looked as if he might argue, if only he could find the words or the courage.

'Morn needs you, Podrik,' said Zastra, 'and it's good for me to know we have friends who are safe. Friends I can count on if ever I need them.'

A smile burst across Podrik's broad face. 'No one has ever called me a friend before,' he beamed.

'Well, that's because they don't know you like we do,' said Zastra.

Podrik shuffled his feet, clearly unused to compliments. He was unable to look at her as he handed her the bag.

'I packed it myself,' he said. 'I'll run around, throw the dogs off. Be careful. Follow the streams, they'll lead you up the mountains and hide your scent.' He blushed furiously as Zastra gave him hug. She started down the slope into the next valley. Looking back, she saw that he stayed on the mountain ridge for some time, watching them, before running off.

Zastra reckoned they had maybe six hours head start, but with horses and dogs their pursuers would soon gain. Findar had taken this opportunity to start screaming, and Zastra felt sure the noise must carry down to Lyria Castle. She scrambled down the mountain, following the narrow gully of a stream. She was on an open rocky scree, bare and exposed. The entire valley in front of her was dry and sparse, with little cover. Beyond the ridge marking the far side of the valley, she could see a green swathe of forest; somewhere to hide if only they could get to it. She had seen no sign of a migaradon but surely it was only a matter of time. They knew where she was now, thanks to Orwin's betrayal. With despair threatening to choke her heart, she hurried on. She no longer had any destination to aim for, but she vowed to Findar that she would keep running, though her lungs might burst.

Chapter Thirty-Seven

Brutila screamed in frustration at the sight of the rope and the gap between the bars. The mice had slipped the trap. She looked in disgust at the cowering figure of Marl Orwin. His whole body shook with fear. *Well, let him shake. He'd had the traitors within his grasp and had let them get away.* Following her instincts, she had headed to Lyria, arriving at the castle just after dawn to find the place in an uproar. Orwin's mind had revealed everything. The entire castle had been searched and it was clear that the children, asleep and innocent not twelve hours before, had escaped. She cast a frosty glance towards the top of the mountain. At least the horses and dogs were already prepared. If only the migaradon were here. They had left it at Gorst Town, needing rest and food, but she had ordered it to follow them as soon as it was able.

She called forward the soldier who was responsible for carrying her personal belongings. This was the end game, and she needed to be at the height of her powers. After drinking down a large dose of cintara bark, she called for a horse and rode out at the front of her troop. She could not see the fugitives, but the dogs had picked up the scent and were racing up the mountainside. She spurred on her horse, following the dogs as keenly as if she herself had scented their quarry.

Shortly before noon they arrived at the top of valley of Lyria. Here, the scent seemed confused, the dogs pausing and sniffing around in circles.

'What's occurring?' demanded Brutila.

'Nothing to worry about,' replied the dog handler nervously. 'They must have stopped here, or tried to put the dogs off. We'll soon pick up the trail.'

As if on cue, the dogs formed an arrowhead and raced off northwards along the top of the ridge. The troop followed, struggling to keep up with the excited dogs as they pounded along the sloping ridge.

'We must be close now,' puffed the handler as the baying of the dogs increased in volume. Sure enough, the dogs paused at the foot of a small outcrop of rock and raised themselves on their hind legs, scrabbling upwards against the steep rock face in a frenzy of excitement.

'Look!' exclaimed one of the guards, pointing upwards. A leather strap was visible, jutting out over the top of the overhang. There was no easy way up to the top of the cliff.

If only the migaradon were here, thought Brutila, staring at the sky in frustration. She sent up two of her most agile soldiers. The smooth rock made the ascent treacherous, and the heavier of the soldiers lost his grip, falling to the ground with a sickening thump. Brutila paid no attention to his screams of agony, tapping her grey-gloved hand against her thigh with impatience. The first soldier reached the top.

'There's no one here,' she called down, holding up the bag. Reaching inside, she brought out a large chunk of sausage. The baying of the dogs doubled.

'You fool,' cried Brutila, glaring at the handler.

'I'm sure they'll find the trail again,' he spluttered, tugging desperately at something in his backpack; a sheet they had taken from the bed Leodra's children had slept in. He gave the scent to the dogs. However, the dogs appeared confused and unsure. Many seemed eager to return down the valley. Brutila closed her eyes, opening her mind to communicate with the lead dog. The scent leading back down the valley was not the same as the one on the bedsheet.

'It would seem they doubled back,' said the handler.

'That would make no sense,' barked Brutila, annoyed that her concentration had been broken. 'Think, man. Clearly the traitors had help to escape. Their helper thought to fool us and it looks as if he, or she, succeeded. No, we go back to the summit of the valley, where the trail was uncertain. I'll lay any odds that Leodra's brats continued east.'

Retracing their steps, the dogs eventually found a scent leading eastward, down into the next valley.

'Ride,' ordered Brutila in triumph, gesturing her troops forward. They had wasted considerable time on the detour, but now there was no doubt of the trail.

Zastra's lungs were burning and her thighs and arms shaking with exertion. She had reached what she had thought to be the top of the mountain on the far side of the valley, only to see another steep ridge rising to the sky above her. Sighing in dismay, she allowed herself the smallest of rests, using the time to give Findar some food and water. Her baby brother, whose generally docile temperament had been a boon during their long journey from Golmer Castle, was wailing raucously. Zastra could not afford the time to soothe him. Casting a nervous eye back across the valley, she made out a string of tiny figures on the brow, dark outlines against the pale sky. They must be her pursuers. From the south, grey clouds scudded towards them, driven by an ever strengthening wind.

She heaved Findar back into his sling and continued onwards. As she reached the true summit of the valley, she pulled up short, almost overbalancing. Below her, dislodged stones plunged down a sheer cliff, crashing into the floor of the valley far beneath. Another step and they would have been over! She took a deep breath, trying to quell the tremor of her startled heart. Scanning left and right, it seemed the way north might be passable, although there was no cover for several leagues. There was no time for indecision and, glancing anxiously behind her, she headed in that direction. It was difficult terrain, requiring a good deal of scrambling and climbing, with treacherous loose stones threatening to overbalance her. Zastra recalled a clambering expedition she had enjoyed with her friends, up one of the small outcrops of rock in Highcastle Forest. Then, she had relished the challenge, but that feeling now seemed distant and unreal. Besides, the rocks in Highcastle Forest didn't compare to the scale of what she was currently facing. Several times, Zastra was forced to traverse the narrowest of ledges, clinging tightly to the rock face, trying to ignore the dizzying drop below her. She could only hope that her pursuers would have similar difficulties.

Heavy grey clouds hurried the onset of darkening night. Zastra continued as far as she could in the gloom but at last she was forced to halt. Further progress in the dark was impossibly dangerous. In any case, she was worn out, her legs and arms trembling from the efforts of carrying her brother over the difficult terrain.

She found them some kind of shelter on a relatively flat piece of rock beneath an overhanging ledge. Rummaging in the bag, she discovered that Podrik had packed a change of underwear for Findar, which was sorely needed, along with a thin blanket, and some food supplies. After a small supper, Zastra encased her brother in her arms, covering herself as best she could with the blanket to protect them from the gathering chill. Exhausted, they slept.

The soldiers murmured in disapproval, but were too frightened to argue. They were to carry on the chase, even as dark descended on the valley. Torches were lit, and the progress continued in the gloom, albeit at a slower pace. The dogs had been put on leashes to prevent them becoming lost in the darkness. They had almost reached the top of the valley when a driving rainstorm extinguished the torches. Brutila gave the command to continue, but the captain refused, claiming the danger made it impossible to continue. Brutila pondered whether to use mindweaving to urge them on, but she could not control the entire troop, and even the dogs were lying down, panting in exhaustion. They would have to halt until the rain stopped, or dawn came. Growling in frustration, Brutila called for a second fur cloak; she did not like the chill that had begun to seep into her bones. An image of another cold mountainside broke out in front of her, and for an instant its white paleness seemed real. She could hear the scratchy sound of a multitude of little claws scrabbling against rock. Quaking, she banished the vision from her mind and waited impatiently for the rain to stop.

Zastra awoke, shivering. Rain was biting into them and Findar was wailing with strident intensity. It was still utterly dark. She set her back to the rain, protecting her brother by enveloping him in the thin blanket, and tried with little success to go back to sleep. As soon as the first hint of light crept into the sky she rose, stiff and cold, and they continued their journey along the mountainside. The first few hours were the most perilous, the rocks made treacherous and slippery by the rain. Zastra's cold, cold hands seemed impossibly clumsy, and would not obey her will. At least the rain may have washed away the scent, she thought. It was their only hope.

The Bractarian troops were underway as soon as dawn broke. The dogs had lost the scent in the rain, but Brutila was confident of their path: upwards and eastwards. The rain continued, fog steaming from the rocks as they reached the summit. An unwary dog bounded over the top and plunged to its death over the vertical cliff that dropped into the valley below. The captain of the troops was still peering cautiously down into the depths as Brutila loomed like a ghoul beside him, her grey uniform camouflaging her against the rock and enveloping mist.

'We cannot see where they went,' he said, water dripping from his nose. Brutila reached out with her mind but could not find what she was searching for. She called for a draught of cintara and drank it greedily. She felt her strength increase almost instantly. Probing into the mist, she detected a mind more than a league away. She thought she could pick up a glimmer of fear and cold, but the feeling was too faint to locate and receded even as she sensed it.

'We'll rest and eat,' she said. A small delay wouldn't matter now. The children had nowhere to go and no one to help them.

After a short delay the rain began to lift and a faint glow of pale sunlight seeped through the grey of the clouds. Slowly the valley began to clear. Using a telescope, Brutila scoured the valley in all directions. Finally she found a small scrambling figure moving with painstaking slowness around the northern rim of the valley.

'Move off,' she ordered, snapping the telescope shut in satisfaction.

Chapter
Thirty-Eight

Zastra reached the head of the valley. Looking back she could see no pursuers, yet the distant baying of dogs carried to her on the wind. They were closing. Wearily, she turned and looked ahead. She had reached the apex of three valleys. The one she had traversed, one to the northeast and a third valley to the southeast. The lower slopes of the southeast valley were covered in dense woodland and she made for the distant patch of green at the fastest pace she could manage.

'At last!' exulted Brutila. A dark speck was visible high in the western sky, becoming larger as it closed on them, wings beating with an appearance of laziness. It charted a varied and indirect course, appearing to be searching for something. Brutila sent out a call with her mind. The beast ceased its meandering path and headed straight towards them. The troop had made only slow progress along the valley ridge. They had been forced to leave the horses behind, and the dogs and humans had struggled equally with the treacherous rocks and narrow ledges. Now that the migaradon was here they would have the advantage. The troop cowered in fear as the creature landed next to them, emitting its harsh, high-pitched cry. A black robed, helmeted figure rode on its back, straining hard at the chains that served as reins. The figure made no attempt to dismount.

'You took your time,' Brutila snapped.

'I had to feed and rest the beast at Lyria, else we would not have had the range. It is always hungry,' said the faceless rider.

'Waste no more time,' ordered Brutila. 'Zastra and the baby. I saw them to the north not two hours ago. They are likely to have reached the head of the valley by now. Find them and bring them back. I want them both alive, but I don't mind if you have to damage them a little.' A cruel smirk broke across her scar-ridden face. The helmeted rider nodded and kicked at the dark scales that covered the body of the migaradon. A heavy gust of air was driven down by the powerful wings as the beast rose into the air. Its flight was graceless and laboured, yet it made rapid progress. Reaching the head of the valley, it circled. Not finding what they were searching for, the creature made a wider circle, and then, with a shriek of triumph, it powered off towards the southeast.

Zastra heard the shrill cry and looked back in horror. A distant speck appeared in the sky behind them, looking like a small bird, but she knew it was no bird. At such a distance, a mere bird would not be visible. She broke into a run. The patch of forest was close now, if only she could reach it in time. Findar began to cry as she jolted him awake in her haste, but she took no notice. She fought the overwhelming desire to look back at the onrushing creature. To do so would slow them down. All too soon, she felt the harsh beating of heavy membranous wings, like the breath of a living thing. Then, as she had been expecting, a searching probe tried to invade her mind. They would never make the trees in time. As the beast swooped, its shadow blotting out the sun, Zastra flung herself behind a large rock, crouching down in its shade. The migaradon's claws scraped against the rock, only just missing the cowering children. As it wheeled up and round for another attack, Zastra glanced upward at the faceless helmet of the rider. Recalling what Gil had told her, she walled up her conscious thoughts and as she felt the mindweaver's probe deepen she let loose all her suppressed hurt and sorrow. The loss of her parents, leaving Kastara, the death of Teona and Martek – all of it flooded out.

A terrible cry of pain rent the air and the winged beast veered away. Zastra felt the mindweaver's probe snap away, and without hesitating she dashed towards the safety of the trees, expecting a further attack at any moment. None came.

They reached the tree line, ducking under its cover. Zastra tripped over a heavy tree root and pitched to the ground. Looking up through the gap in the trees she could make out the migaradon, bucking and screaming in the air. She turned and ran deeper into the forest. As the trees became more densely packed around her, her progress slowed, but at least the canopy of leaves masked the sky. She took a sharp left turn, seeking to throw off her pursuers. Alas, the rider had brought the creature under control and back on their tail. A huge three-fingered claw reached down, raking through the trees to try and grab them, but the canopy was too high and thick to allow it easy entrance, and the claw grasped only leaves and branches. After several futile attempts the migaradon gave up trying to reach them, letting out a cry of anger and frustration. Nevertheless, it continued to follow. The mindweaver made no further attempts to dig into Zastra's mind. Zastra attempted to dodge and weave but the creature held fast to their tail. Through the thick web of trees she stumbled, half sobbing with weariness. Behind her, the barking of the dogs grew louder. They must have picked up the scent. Zastra's paced slowed. She was almost spent, unable to move at more than a desperate crawl. To her dismay, she sensed the trees were beginning to thin out, indicating her cover would soon run out. A steep slope reached up in front of her and she attempted to stagger up it.

'I'm sorry Findar,' she sobbed in utter despair. An answering cry of woe echoed through the forest, somewhere to their left. Zastra moved towards it, drawn by the sympathetic emotion. She almost fell into the hole, weary as she was, scrabbling back just in time. She looked down. At the base of a deep pit stood a fellgryff, bellowing with misery. It looked young, not quite full grown, with a striking circle of darker hair around its neck. Zastra caught its eye, holding its gaze until the proud animal bowed, yielding. She sized up the situation. The fellgryff had been caught in a trap; a sheet covered in soil and leaves, no doubt originally concealing the pit, had been pulled down with it. The animal appeared unhurt, but was making frantic leaps in increasingly desperate attempts to jump out. Zastra looked down with pity. She had no time to stop, but couldn't bear to leave the creature in such distress. Then a thought struck her. Perhaps if she could free the fellgryff, she could ride it and they might be able to outrun the dogs.

'I'll be right back,' she said to the fellgryff. Its sentient eyes looked at her, and it lifted its chin as if it was trying to understand. Scattered around the pit were rocks of various sizes. Laying Findar on the ground alongside her bag, Zastra began to hoist up the largest stones she could lift and cast them into the pit, trying not to hit the fellgryff as it shied away.

'I'm trying to help,' she explained, attempting to soothe the creature. It took many minutes and arm aching exertion before a small pile of rocks had built up. Eagerly, the fellgryff danced onto the pile and made a leap for safety. In spite of a prodigious jump, it fell short and slipped back down into the pit.

'Wait, I'll find more,' Zastra cried, scouring around breathlessly. There were only a few more stones, which she threw on top of the existing pile. In despair, she realised it was still not high enough for the fellgryff to escape. The peaty ground gave a little beneath her, giving her an idea. Kicking away the edge of the hole, she was able to dig a small channel at an angle, a small ramp leading down into the pit. A fragment of flat rock helped her dig with increasing frenzy. The baying of the dogs was now so close that they had but a few moments. The channel in the side of the pit was a few feet deep and she pulled back, gesturing at the fellgryff.   Understanding her wordless intent, it crouched down and sprang onto the pile of rocks and then up towards Zastra. Its front legs landed in the channel and, with Zastra tugging as hard as she could at the matted hair on its neck, it scrabbled out of the trap. It pranced sideways, shaking off the dirt.

'Please wait,' cried Zastra, picking up Findar and looking anxiously back down the slope. The first dog raced into view, followed by another, and then the whole pack. Zastra looked at the fellgryff. It bowed its two-pronged head. Using her very last reserves of strength, Zastra sprang onto its back, some kind of muscle memory holding her in place as the creature bucked and sprang into the air.

'There they are!' The yell came from below. A crossbow bolt ripped through the air. The fellgryff needed no urging to spring away up the hill. Another bolt whipped by them, barely missing Zastra's ducking head.

The strong, bucking gait of the fellgryff soon drew them away from the soldiers. Before long the dogs also fell back. Findar howled in distress, the jerking of the fellgryff jolting him most severely but Zastra cried out with relief and exhilaration. However, her joy at their escape was short-lived. The tree canopy began to thin out alarmingly and the migaradon closed in again, sensing that its prey would soon be unprotected. Zastra steered left, trying to stay under the cover of the trees, but could only delay the inevitable. As they shot out of the trees and sprang up the slope towards the top of the mountainside, the migaradon dived down. It reached out with a triumphant yell. The fellgryff sprang sideways, almost throwing Zastra off with the suddenness and force of its movement. The migaradon howled in pain as its claw clashed empty-handed against the rocky mountainside. Ponderously it flapped its huge wings, circling up and round for another run. Again and again it dived down, and each time the fellgryff, with perfect timing and agility, sprang out of its ravening grasp. With a cry of wrath, the migaradon began to lift up large rocks and drop them down at the escapees. One rock shattered on the ground and a wild splinter drew blood from Zastra's cheek. The fellgryff continued on undaunted, zig-zagging up the steep slope towards the top of the mountain.

Brutila reached the edge of the tree line and took in the scene: the giant beast chasing a small figure hunched on the back of a strange, ungainly animal. She called with her mind. Obediently the rider directed her mount to wheel back and land next to the grey figure.

'I'll do it myself,' Brutila said, a wet gleam of impatience filling her pale eyes.

'But you are not a rider,' the mindweaver protested.

'I am fully qualified,' snapped Brutila. Laying her hand on the bridle, she merged her mind with the beast, quietening its madness. The rider relinquished control with some reluctance.

'It is almost exhausted and will soon need rest and food,' she warned, but Brutila had already kicked the beast into the air. Minutes later, the migaradon and its new rider had reached the brow of the ridge, just as Zastra and the fellgryff arrived.

Zastra felt a spear of pain in her head, so harsh as to block out all senses. It had broken through the firm mental wall that had become a constant part of her. She gasped, doubling over in agony. Her training and practice lent her just enough resistance to understand what was happening and prevent her losing consciousness completely, but the massive strength and weight of the attack was much more than any she had felt previously. Using all the mental blocking techniques she could muster, she worked to push back against the silent heaviness that oppressed her. A small window of sight came back to her, a pinprick through a cloud of darkness, but the pain did not diminish. She made out a blurred shadow descending towards her, but she was frozen and the fellgryff, obedient to her will, was stilled likewise. She heard, as if a great distance, the thin wail of a baby crying. 'Findar,' she gasped in sluggish recognition. The desire to help her brother broke through her fear and she found her vision clearing a little. The pain in her head dulled slightly, no longer quite crippling, although still debilitating. Everything seemed to be moving much more slowly than normal, and the sounds of the world were dulled, as if shrouded in soft, thick cushions. With painful slowness, she flicked her foot, the movement as difficult as swimming through thick syrup. The fellgryff, released from the thrall that had held it, leapt forward, but it was all an instant too late. A slashing pain ripped into Zastra's back as one of the migaradon's claws caught her with a vicious blow.

'Now I have you!' an alien voice echoed inside her mind. Striving to raise her head against the seeming weight of the whole sky, Zastra forced her eyes upwards. Seated astride the migaradon, she saw a grey-haired woman, a scar on her face giving her mouth the appearance of a terrible, lopsided grin.

Brutila, thought Zastra, and the image of the cold, snowy mountain and a stranded child attacked by scrittals formed in her head, mixed with powerful feelings of pity and fear, just as the grey woman dug deeper into her mind. The effect was shocking and instantaneous. The grey woman folded over, as if cracked, and the huge migaradon collapsed downwards, spinning like a corkscrew as it was drawn towards the ground. It crashed into the mountainside with a shocking impact, bounced once, and then plunged down the steep slope, rolling over and over, gathering an avalanche of rocks as its despairing wail carried back up the valley. Zastra looked in horror as the beast gained speed before crashing deep into the bank of trees. It was several moments before she realised that the agonising grip on her mind had lifted. She lost no more time in urging the fellgryff onwards, and they disappeared over the mountain ridge. A rainstorm came, torrents of water soaking through Zastra's clothes. It would wash away their scent – the dogs and soldiers would never catch them now.

Chapter
Thirty-Nine

Etta, a farmer who made her living in the border mountains, looked anxiously out of her window. Her son, Dalbric, was late returning from checking his traps. She hoped he had found something this time; they would need a good stock of dried meat to see them through the harsh winter that was rapidly approaching.

At last, his wiry figure emerged from the forest. He was running and carrying something with great care. As he burst through the door, Etta was shocked to hear a pitiful cry coming from the dirty bundle.

'A baby!' cried Dalbric. 'And there's a girl. I think she may be dead. Back in the forest. A creature – a fellgryff, I think, was with them, but it ran off. What shall we do, Ma?'

'Calm down, Dalbric,' said Etta, taking hold of the bundle. 'Go and fetch this girl while I deal with the baby.'

'Right,' said Dalbric, crashing into the doorpost in his haste to depart.

Etta plucked at the bundle, rocking back at the smell. It seemed the baby had not been attended to in several days. Tutting, she cleaned away the mess and tended to a nasty rash on the baby's bottom. Blue eyes stared out from a pale face, meeting her eyes in an unspoken plea. Etta shook her head, battling a long forgotten emotion that threatened to rise up within her.

Dalbric returned carrying a lifeless girl. As they removed her damp clothes, Etta gasped. The back of the child was disfigured by a large, bloody wound, a slash of two parallel lines that ran across from the left shoulder almost down to the waist. Some cloth was stuck to the skin around the gash. Etta disengaged it gently and washed the injured area. The still form barely moved in response to these gentle ministrations, and Etta clucked in sorrow and amazement that such a thing had been allowed to happen. She worried for the girl.

Within a day, as Etta had feared, a fever set in, the child alternating between icy shivering and a burning fever. Etta looked on, sensing the girl lay astride that thin line that separated the living from the dead. There was little she could do, other than to keep her warm and clean. It was a matter of whether the girl had the will to battle the fever and live.

The baby boy, however, was thriving. Etta found herself drawn to the quiet stoicism of the little fellow. She knew she could not become attached to the children. They had precious little food, barely enough even for herself and Dalbric – the last thing they needed was more mouths to feed. As she watched, the little baby, crawled with great determination across the floor towards his young companion, who lay unconscious on the hearthrug. He attempted to rouse his sister with the touch of his chubby little hands. When she didn't wake, he laid his head on her stomach and fell asleep. Etta was moved in spite of herself, and she stared at them for a long time before finally rousing herself to perform the chores that had been too long delayed.

The days grew shorter, heralding the long mountain winter. Still the older child hovered between life and death. The fever had lessened somewhat, but her sleep was troubled, her frail body jerking with hidden nightmares. Etta watched in concern, shivering as she contemplated what the poor girl might be suffering.

Late one evening, as the wind whistled around the mountain, Etta and Dalbric were startled by a rap at the door. Visitors were extremely rare, especially at such a late hour, since their dwelling was several leagues from the nearest village. Etta glanced at their guests, sleeping together in front of the fire, and jerked her head in the direction of the kitchen. Dalbric nodded in understanding and disappeared into the kitchen, reappearing shortly afterwards with a sharp knife and a mallet. His face was filled with grim resolve. He gave the knife to Etta. Only then did she go over to the door and open it.

A tall figure, cloaked in black, stood silently before her. The wind whipped at a hood that obscured the face so that she was unable to distinguish any features. A chill ran through her frame and she tried to slam the door shut, but the figure reached out and held the door open. Inexplicably, a fog descended across her vision and confusion raged in her mind. Looking down, she saw a snake writhing in her hand. Horrified, she threw it away. The fog cleared. To her dismay she realised she stood before the visitor unarmed and defenceless. Dalbric too had dropped his mallet and stood empty handed and equally bewildered.

The black-cloaked figure raised his hands and pulled down his hood, revealing an elderly man with an ugly face. His eyes lit upon the children by the fire and he made as if to step towards them. Dalbric held out an arm to block his way. The intruder held up his hands.

'Please – I apologise for my intrusion,' he said. 'I assure you I mean no harm. I have long been searching for the children you have here. I would know that they are safe and have not been harmed.'

'They are safe enough,' exclaimed Etta, 'but someone has tried to harm them. How do we know you are not one of their tormentors? What was that trick you played on us just now?'

The stranger stepped backwards. 'I'm sorry,' he said. 'As you can see, I carry no weapon, so I used a gift I have in order to resolve things safely. I would not have entered your minds, except for the danger of the situation.'

'I don't know who you are, or what you want, but these children are under my protection,' Etta said.

'Your sentiments do you great credit,' said the old man, bowing his head. 'My heart is glad to see that they have been taken in by such kindness. But I assure you I mean no harm. It is a sad time when suspicion is in everyone's hearts.'

'A sad time when such things can happen to children,' retorted Etta.

The stranger's face crumpled and there was a catch in his voice as he asked, 'Why? What has happened? Is Zastra hurt? Or the little one? Tell me I am not too late.'

His anguish was clear and Etta relented slightly.

'The girl is gravely ill. The fever has lessened now, thank the stars. If it weren't for the nightmares that disturb her rest, I think she might recover.'

As if on cue, Zastra began to writhe and thrash beneath the blanket, her face scrumpled in fear, although she was still asleep.

'I can help her, if you will allow me to try,' said the man.

'I don't trust him, Ma,' Dalbric said, folding his arms. Etta's eyes flicked from her son to the stranger. With a sigh, she made a slight motion of her head toward the fire. The visitor needed no further encouragement. Kneeling by the girl, he laid a hand gently on her head and closed his eyes.

Zastra was trapped in a swirling vortex of migaradons, burning castles, black-cloaked mindweavers and scar-faced assassins. She was trying to pull Findar and Kastara out of the vortex, but they were too heavy. Their tiny hands slipped from her sweaty grasp and they were sucked into the depths. She was drawn in after them, with no power to resist. Then, miraculously, she felt a presence; a strong, quiet calmness, and somehow she was lifted out of the vortex and deposited on a grassy, sunlit hillside. Blissfully, she drifted into a deep and peaceful sleep.

Etta and Dalbric saw only that the child had calmed under the gentle touch of the old man.

'Such things should not have been witnessed by one so young,' said the man, sadly. 'My poor, dear Zastra.'

They sat for a while, watching over the sleeping children. The night drew in, and the wind grew into a gale. Rain clattered against the shutters. Etta looked around the small cabin. Normal hospitality would have her invite the stranger to stay, but they had not much room and even less food. With the two children to tend, they would struggle to feed another mouth. The man stood up.

'I will trespass on your hospitality no longer,' he said. 'Will you allow me to return in a few days to see to the health of the children?'

Etta nodded. 'If the girl asks, who shall I say you are?'

'Tell Zastra that Master Dobery called,' said the man, raising his hood and departing into the tempest.

Zastra tried to open her eyes, but they seemed locked shut, sticky and heavy. A dim, unremembered nightmare dragged at her. As she moved, a sharp pain jagged across her back, prodding her in to semi-consciousness. Her blurred vision made out a small figure with hair the colour of hay. It was nursing a baby. Zastra felt a nagging sense of urgency. She strove to wake, fixing onto the baby like a drunk who must hold onto a stationary object to stop the whole world spinning. Seeing her move, the baby pointed and clapped his hands in delight.

Findar... She sank back into the depths.

The next day, Zastra woke fully. An unknown hand gave her a cup of water, which she swallowed gratefully, her throat as raw as sand. The same gentle hand then supported her as she was fed some hot soup. She couldn't really taste it but the sensation of warm liquid was pleasant and soothing. Even in the dimness of the hut the light seemed unnaturally bright. Findar crawled toward her and Zastra recognised her brother, weeping tears of joy as she clasped him to her.

She looked up to see a tall, thin boy and his mother. The family resemblance was clear in the straw-coloured hair, green-blue eyes and the slightly hooked nose.

'You are safe here, Zastra,' said the boy. 'Both of you are safe.'

'Dalbric found you,' said the woman, smiling encouragingly. 'You were both in a bit of a state, but the littlun is fine. You've had quite an adventure, by the look of you.'

'Yes,' whispered Zastra.

'Where are you from?' asked Etta. 'Do you have family? Your parents will be worried.'

There was a long silence.

'Our parents are dead,' Zastra managed to utter at length, and turning her back lay and stared long into the depths of the fire.

Chapter
Forty

Zastra recovered slowly. The mixture of malnutrition and long illness had made her extremely weak, but the kindness of her rescuers slowly brought her back to health. After a few days she was able to sit up for short periods. When Etta told her about the visit of Dobery, Zastra's eyes lit up and she looked out impatiently for his return. It was several days before he reappeared, laden with a large sack of food. Zastra tried to rush over to him but her legs were too weak. Dobery dropped his parcel and grasped her in a firm embrace.

When Zastra and Dobery had recovered themselves, everyone sat down to a hearty meal of roasted meat and vegetables, cooked using the supplies Dobery had brought. Findar was then put to bed and Etta asked Zastra to tell them her story. Zastra hesitated, looking to Dobery for advice.

'These are good people, Zastra,' he said. 'We owe them the truth.'

Haltingly at first she related her tale, from the terrible events at Golmer Castle through to her escape from Brutila. Etta and Dalbric listened in amazement.

'We knew nothing of this,' said Etta. 'We seldom go down into the valley, and even then we rarely see soldiers. We pay tax once a year when we sell our goods down in the valley – which I resent, since I don't see what we get back for all the money we pay.'

'You really don't know what's happening in the rest of Golmeira?' asked Zastra.

'Don't know and don't care,' exclaimed Etta. 'We keep to ourselves up here. Of course, every once in a while, one of the village children has an impulse to go and live in the valleys. Most come back. Poor and tough our life may be, but it's ours and it keeps us free from bother most of the time. But I don't understand how you escaped from that horrible woman with the grey hair.'

'Me neither,' Zastra said. 'One moment I was trapped on the ledge, expecting her to swoop down and kill me. Then the migaradon just crashed into the mountain.'

'Tell me,' said Dobery, 'what were you thinking at the time?'

'I was remembering what Orwin had told me about Brutila – about when she was a girl and they left her on that snowy mountain with the scrittals.'

'That may explain it,' said Dobery. 'When a mindweaver enters your mind, they can see what you see. That picture must have been terribly traumatic for Brutila. I suspect that she was taking cintara bark, which can make visions seem like reality. She would have been transported back to that time when she was a helpless child, alone and abandoned. Her mental control over the migaradon would have been broken, with terrible consequences. It was your compassion for the child Brutila that saved you, as nothing else could have.'

'What do you mean, mental control?' asked Dalbric, who had listened to the tale with fascination.

'Ah, that is a long story, young man,' said Dobery, 'and it is getting late. I should be on my way.'

'No, stay,' said Etta, reaching out towards him. 'You brought food, so you've earned the right to stay. We'll find room for you somewhere.'

'Thank you. Your kindness...'

'No need to thank me,' she said brusquely. 'Now, I'll make us some hot chala. I can see these two won't get any sleep anyway until they hear your story, Master Dobery.' Dalbric and Zastra fidgeted impatiently while the chala was made, until at last Dobery could tell his tale.

Chapter Forty-One

Dobery began with his trip to Waldaria with Morel and her company of soldiers, organised in response to the murder of one of the council of mindweavers.

'When we arrived,' he said, 'it was clear that something was very wrong. The locals were frightened but no one would talk to us. There was a region of the Waldarian Forest that seemed to hold particular dread, so Morel decided we should investigate. We were ambushed by a large force of Kyrgs, allied with black-cloaked mindweavers. Thorlberd had laid his trap well and we were heavily outnumbered. Morel saw the hopelessness of our position and gave the order to flee.'

'What about Morel?' asked Zastra, anxiously. Dobery shook his head, his brow knitted in sorrow.

'She fought bravely, forcing a gap in the line of Kyrgs so that many of our men and women could escape, but in so doing she was overpowered. At that point, I too turned and fled deep into the forest, leaving the ambush and its terrible toll far behind. After wandering aimlessly for some time I came upon a clearing in which gangs of soldiers were tugging on huge chains against something deep within a vast cave. It was a migaradon; without doubt the most fearful sight I have ever seen. A black-cloaked mindweaver mounted the beast. I saw how the rider made mental contact with the insane monster to calm and control it. That night, silhouetted against the moons, I saw a flight of the evil beasts leaving the forest, their terrible cries renting the air. With despair in my soul, I saw that they headed in the direction of Golmer Castle.

Seeking to understand what I had seen, I probed all the minds I could reach. I found some answers within the mind of an old man called Algin. He had been a servant in the household of the Lady Migara, Zastra's grandmother. You never knew her Zastra and be grateful for it. She was a ruthless, ambitious mindweaver. Perhaps because he sensed her lust for power, her father, Fostran the Third, decreed that his grandson Leodra should succeed him, rather than Migara, as would usually occur. Migara was incensed at being passed over. She began experiments within the Forest of Waldaria, crossbreeding bats, otters, vizzals and many other varieties of beast. Her aim was to breed a giant flying beast to conquer anyone that stood in her way.

This man, Algin, had a mindweaving ability so rare that I have never heard it described before; a special power of healing. Migara discovered his ability and forced him to assist her experiments. He was able to repair defects in these crossbred animals that would otherwise be fatal even before they were born. With Algin's help, many survived in spite of their deformities. The first successful pups were derived from otters, but covered in scales and with stubs on their back, like stunted wings.'

'I don't understand,' said Dalbric. 'What was she doing?'

'The migaradons...' whispered Zastra in horrified realisation. Dobery nodded.

'That's right, Zastra. Over the course of many years, the migaradon began to emerge until it begame large enough to carry a person. However, they could not control the wild nature of the brute. Born as it was from an unnatural mix of identities, its mind was filled with conflicting instincts, leaving it on the verge of madness. When Fostran died and Leodra became Grand Marl, Migara was already suffering from the illness that was to kill her, and so she persuaded Thorlberd, her favourite son, to continue her work.

'Why?' exclaimed Zastra. 'Why would he plot against his own brother?'

'It seems he shared her desire to make Golmeira a military power. He also resented being ruled by a non-mindweaver, even if that person were his brother. Migara died, but Thorlberd carried on with the experiments, eventually discovering that crossbreeding with fellgryffs instilled enough intelligence into the beast so that they could be controlled by those mindweavers with the art of communicating with animals.'

'Communicating with animals?' cried Dalbric. 'Is that possible?'

'Indeed it is – a rare, but not unknown ability,' replied Dobery.

'Like Colinar,' said Zastra.

'Exactly so, my dear.'

'But to use fellgryffs,' exclaimed Zastra, her brow furrowing as she recalled the quiet intelligence and courage of the fellgryff that had saved them in the mountains. 'Oh, it's just too horrid!'

'What will Thorlberd do next?' asked Dalbric.

'Do you think he might attack Sendor?' interjected Zastra, her thoughts turning to Kylen and Zax.

'I fear so. I have been prying into any mind I could access and I have learnt much that our council should have seen. Even as Thorlberd was plotting the downfall of your father, he was also thinking of Sendor. He sent spies to stir up trouble in the borders and he had messengers from the Sendorans killed in order to prevent the peace talks with your father. When Mendoraz came in person, Thorlberd arranged for the caralyx to be smuggled into the castle. It was supposed to kill Kylen or Zax, which might have been enough for war to be declared. In the end, pinning the blame on the Sendorans worked just as well. The chance of peace was lost and when your father sent more soldiers to the Sendoran border, the defences at Golmer Castle were weakened. It was a very clever plan. I've no doubt your uncle will invade Sendor as soon as he has Golmeira under his control.'

'That's sad news indeed,' said Etta. 'They still tell awful tales of the last war down in the village. It set families against each other, here in the Borders. I'd hate to see such times come again.'

'How did you find us, Dobery?' asked Zastra.

'After seeing the migaradons in the Forest of Waldaria, I headed back to Golmer Castle as fast I could. Alas, I was too late.'

Dobery paused, placing his hand on Zastra's shoulder.

'I do have some news which I hope will comfort you, my dear. On my way to Golmer I passed through the village of Hurlbridge. I was sneaking along the back of the houses to avoid the soldiers, but as I did so a door opened and I found myself face-to face with Bodel. It would appear that sneaking is not one of my better skills. Bodel said I made more noise than a herd of fat goats frolicking in a field of dry twigs. A rather harsh judgement, in my opinion, but I cannot deny she had heard me.'

'Bodel!' exclaimed Zastra, her body stiffening in excitement.

'Yes. She told me what had happened with you and the twins at Highcastle village. A few days after you had gone, she heard from your friend Heldrid that Bedrun was missing. Bodel was filled with joy and wondered if Bedrun might have gone to Hurlbridge, her sister's village. She took Dalka and Kastara there. It turned out to be a most fortunate decision, since Brutila and her guards broke into Bodel's house just a few days later, looking for you and the twins.'

'What about Kastara? Is she all right? And Bedrun? Did they find her?' The questions tumbled from Zastra in her impatience.

'Bodel found a note from Bedrun, pushed under the door of Dalka's house. She had been with the acrobats when the fighting started and they all escaped together, climbing down from the outer ramparts.'

'Jofie!' exclaimed Zastra. 'Bedrun really liked him; she must have gone back down to talk to him again. Their acrobatic skills would have made it easy for them to escape over the walls. But why didn't she go to Highcastle?'

'Bedrun overheard the Bractarian troops saying they had orders to hunt and kill any friends of Leodra and his family. This terrified her, since she was known to be a friend of yours, Zastra. Understanding her danger, the troupe offered to take her with them. They were heading north for the Aridian mountains, planning to cross the border into Aliterra. When they passed through Hurlbridge, Bedrun was able to leave her letter.'

Zastra was heartily glad that Bedrun had escaped from the horrors of the castle, although saddened that her friend's life was in such danger because of her. Dobery continued.

'As for Kastara, Bodel passed her off as little Joril without difficulty. Her sister Dalka's illness had been a lengthy one and she accepted the baby as Joril, grown a little bigger and a little different while she had been ill. The blue fever can cause some memory loss and confusion, which helped us in this case. Dalka suspects nothing and has been spared the grief she must otherwise have felt at the loss of her daughter.'

'So Kastara is safe,' said Zastra. A warm sense of relief and joy washed over her.

'Yes, my dear,' said Dobery, patting her hand affectionately.

'What did you do then?' asked Dalbric.

'I headed after Zastra and Findar as fast as I could. First to Highcastle village where I discovered that Thorlberd had set Brutila the task of finding you. Hers was an easily trail to follow,' he said grimly. 'At Riverford, she was wasting time searching all quarters of the city, so I went on ahead of her. Bodel had told me that you were headed to Lyria. I almost caught up with you at the market.'

'You were there?' gasped Zastra in surprise.

'I was indeed. You hid your mind well, Zastra. It was only when the Kyrgs were questioning you that I realised I had found you. Only for those cloth merchants to snatch you away from under my nose. I tried to chase after you but my old bones are not meant for running. I did what I could, using my abilities to keep the Kyrgs asleep until you were long gone. Gil's sleep suggestion would have worn off after a few minutes.'

Zastra recalled the black-cloaked figure that had pursued the trap. To think that it had been Dobery.

'I hurried after you on foot, but Brutila and her troops soon overtook me and I could not keep pace with them. I arrived at Lyria in time to see the troops returning in disarray, carrying a body on a stretcher – alive or dead I could not tell, and for a terrible instant I thought it was you, Zastra, until I was able to scan the mind of a stray soldier and find out what had happened. Since then, I have been searching the mountains. A chance sighting of the fellgryff by some villagers several leagues away helped me narrow the search. The unusual marking on its neck identified it as the one you had escaped on. And so, at last, I found you.'

'Amazing,' said Dalbric. 'Mindweavers and migaradons. It's like the poems, or something they tell to children. Tell me again, Dobery, about the Lady Migara. And Zastra, what about—'

'Dalbric, leave the poor souls alone,' said Etta. 'Right now, it's time for bed. We've chores to catch up on the morning, and I for one need my sleep.'

Chapter
Forty-Two

The next day, whilst Etta and Dalbric were occupied in rearranging one of their storerooms, Dobery came and sat by the fire with Zastra and Findar. The little boy was full of energy, delighting in his new ability to stand and stagger a few steps before collapsing back down to the ground. He was amazed by everything in the small house, reaching out to grab every fascinating object with wide-eyed glee.

'I've been thinking about Kastara,' said Zastra. 'I should go back for her. Father said I must take care of them both.'

'Hush, dear child,' said Dobery. 'I know it is difficult, but decisions such as that, once made, must be adhered to. To go now back would put both yourself and Kastara in terrible danger. Findar too, if they caught you. Your sister is in good hands, and we must trust that Bodel and fate will keep Kastara safe. Brutila believed that Kastara died of the blue fever, so no one will have reason to suspect little Joril. She is safe in her new identity, safer even than you and Findar. I believe you made the right choice.'

'Really?'

'Yes. My dear Zastra, you have achieved something remarkable. You succeeded in escaping across the breadth of Golmeira, in spite the full power of Thorlberd. You have kept your brother and sister safe. All that, without being a mindweaver. I'm very proud, and your mother and father would be too.'

'But what about Golmeira? What about Thorlberd? We can't just let him get away with what he has done.'

'No, indeed. The time will come when we will fight back. But for now you must rest and heal. I will seek out those that defy Thorlberd. Seacastle is not yet taken and Sendor will not fall without a fight, if history be our guide. All is not yet lost.'

There was comfort in Dobery's words and Zastra's recovery continued until she was able to walk and even venture outside. Etta's sturdy wooden house was set in a clearing on the mountainside, close to a small stream that supplied it with water. The air was pure and clear, although increasingly cold as winter approached. They were enclosed in a protective shield of green-forested mountains that extended away from them in all directions, yielding only to the mighty, snow-topped peaks of the unnamed mountains in the distant north. Enclosed, but not imprisoned. As the wind whipped through her hair, Zastra pulled her fur-lined cloak, a gift from Etta, closer round her body. She felt a strange contentment in their isolation. It was as if Golmeira and the rest of the world no longer existed.

Her thoughts were disturbed by Dobery and Dalbric returning from a hunting expedition.

'Shouldn't you be resting?' said Dalbric, with concern.

'I've been resting for quite long enough. I don't want you to think I'm some useless rich girl, expecting to be waited on all the time,' replied Zastra with a small smile.

'Well, I was beginning to wonder,' Dalbric returned with a wink. 'Come on, we've caught a vizzal – it'll make a good supper.'

Zastra insisted on helping Etta with the meal, preparing the vegetables with great zeal.

'You are taking off too much skin,' said Etta. 'We can't afford for you to throw away half the good stuff. We're not all daughters of Grand Marls, you know.'

'Sorry,' said Zastra, concentrating on making her peelings as thin as possible.

'When you've done, they need cooking,' said Etta.

Zastra hesitated.

'I only know how to make porridge,' she admitted.

'There's nothing wrong with porridge,' said Etta. She then explained to Zastra what had to be done with the vegetables and watched over her whilst she attempted to make gravy. At last the meal was brought to table.

'What took so long?' said Dalbric, despite a stern look from Etta. He looked in trepidation as Zastra poured some rather lumpy gravy on his plate, but then took up his fork with a show of enthusiasm.

'Um, it looks lovely,' he said.

'Yes, indeed,' said Dobery, bravely crunching on some severely undercooked yellow-root.

Etta glanced across at her son.

'Dalbric, I was thinking of asking Zastra and Findar to live with us. What do you say?'

'Great idea,' he said, grinning. 'It'll be nice to have the company.'

Etta turned towards Zastra.

'I doubt anyone will come looking for you here,' she said. 'We're several leagues from the nearest village and only go down the valley a few times a year. The soldiers don't tend to venture into the mountains – they like their valley comforts too much. I can say you are a distant cousin. No one would question that. However, we can't have passengers. Everyone here must work, and it's hard work at that.'

Zastra felt deeply the generousness of the offer – Etta and Dalbric had so little, yet were willing to share it with them, although they were strangers.

'That's a very kind of you,' she said, 'especially as you've seen how terrible I am at cooking.'

'Awful,' agreed Dalbric, pushing away a half eaten plate of food.

Findar took that opportunity to fling some of his mashed vegetables across the table with a squeal of discontent.

'Even Findar hates it,' sighed Zastra.

'I'm sure you'll learn,' said Etta. 'You have shown that at least you are willing to try. Now, suppose I rescue the vegetables and make some gravy that deserves the name?'

Findar clapped his hands with delight, almost as if he understood.

Zastra looked at Dobery.

'Will you stay too?' she said.

'I'm afraid not, Zastra. I would bring too much attention. My face, as you know, is rather distinctive and I have been listed as an enemy of Golmeira with a reward for my capture. You will be safer if I am not here. Besides, I have things to do, as you know my dear, which cannot wait.'

'Please say you'll stay, Zastra,' said Dalbric. 'You'll be safe with us.'

Zastra nodded. 'Yes,' she said. 'I believe we will.'

Zastra's adventures continue in...

Murthen Island

Zastra is eager for revenge against her Uncle Thorlberd but has been forced into hiding with her young brother. Only a small band of Sendoran rebels stand against the usurper. An act of sacrifice results in Zastra's conscription into her uncle's fleet, where she is forced to serve a brutal captain. When Zastra's crewmates mutiny, she discovers a horrifying scheme of Thorlberd's to ensure his grip on power becomes absolute. If she is to thwart her uncle, she must join forces with the Sendoran rebels and find the mythical Murthen Island, defended by Thorlberd's most powerful mindweavers and an invincible migaradon.

Acknowledgements

I would like to express my deepest thanks to Wendy Tomlinson, Michele Hutchison, Amanda Benjamin, Sylvia Ratcliffe, Richard Ratcliffe and Sharon Gubby for reviewing the manuscript and for their many insightful comments and helpful suggestions.

.